SHOOTING
AT
HEAVEN'S GATE

PRAISE FOR *Shooting at Heaven's Gate*

"Kaye Hinckley has more than earned her keep as a significant contender vying for a living Catholic literature."

~ JOSHUA HREN,
author of *How to Read (and Write) Like a Catholic* and co-founder of the MFA program at the University of St. Thomas, Houston

"With a brisk narrative pace, *Shooting at Heaven's Gate* by Kaye Park Hinckley invites readers to explore the complicated lives of characters suffering with loss, illness, addiction, and deception. The plot twists make this novel both entertaining and thought-provoking with the reassurance that good does win."

~ JOHNNIE BERNHARD,
award-winning author of *Sisters of the Undertow*
and *Hannah and Ariela*

"Faith and faithlessness do battle in Kaye Park Hinckley's thought-provoking, unsparing new novel. She reveals the hellish torments…and heavenly convictions…of everyday people in a small Alabama town in an age of mass shootings. Bring faith as you enter Heaven's Gate."

~ CHARLES McNAIR,
author of *The Epicureans*

"Family relations and lifelong secrets, human brokenness and the grace of transformation, mass shootings, deception, sin and forgiveness. These fundamental themes of the human search for meaning, of the challenge of faith, reconciliation and conversion, are woven throughout this story of a small town in rural Alabama. The complexities of each character, from university professors to farm hands, become the stage for an exploration of the human condition, in the style of C.S. Lewis, with echoes of T.S. Eliot, Geoffrey Chaucer, *Macbeth* and many others. The novel is followed by a list of themes, questions for book discussions and selected quotes, making it all the easier for study groups of any kind.

~ FR. CHRISTOPHER VISCARDI, SJ,
Chair and Professor of Theology, Spring Hill College

SHOOTING
AT
HEAVEN'S
GATE

KAYE PARK
HINCKLEY

CHRISM
PRESS

SHOOTING AT HEAVEN'S GATE

Copyright © 2022, Kaye Park Hinckley
Adapted from a short story by the same title, published by Wiseblood Books in 2014.

Chrism Press, a division of WhiteFire Publishing
13607 Bedford Rd NE
Cumberland, MD 21502

ISBN: 978-1-941720-91-2 (print)
        978-1-941720-92-9 (digital)

*Man cannot commit a sin so great
as to exhaust the infinite love of God.*
—Fyodor Dostoevsky

*A university is just a group of buildings
gathered around a library.*
—Shelby Foote

BETHEL UNIVERSITY

There are some places in this world that are sacred. Upon entering them, one mentally, if not physically, bows with respect because there is something intangible and hallowed inside, something with the capacity to complete and make whole. Of course, this respect is prevalent in churches, but Bethel University is not a church.

In the 1830s, Bethel University was the pride of South Alabama, constructed by order of the state legislature who did not want South Alabama to lag behind the rest of the growing state. Its crown of glory was an enviable library of over six thousand rare European books that were said to glow in the minds of some like blessed candles in the dark. The beloved books were brought to America a decade before by a learned young Prussian gentleman, the illegitimate son of a prominent but ill-favored duke who had not sided with Napoleon. When the duke was assassinated, the son feared for his life. Gathering as many possessions as he could, the young man escaped to America, into the port of Mobile, Alabama. There he bought a horse and wagon and traveled to Bethel, where he offered his rare books to the new university under construction.

In a span of three years, the grateful town of Bethel built a wooden rotunda for the books, after which former Scottish stonemasons, who had long before settled the area, created an arched entrance that read: *This is a haven for those who first wonder and then strive to know.* Among the books that the young gentleman donated was a centuries-old Bible—one of the first Bibles transcribed into Old English. The young man insisted that it be displayed on a stone pedestal, always open to the same verse, Isaiah 1:1.

> *Your land is desolate,*
> *Your cities are burned with fire,*
> *Your fields—strangers are devouring them in your presence;*
> *It is desolation, as overthrown by strangers.*

At the dedication of the rotunda at Bethel University, the young gentleman said to the people of Bethel, "The Bible, the verse, and its placement on the pedestal are to remind you that the wars happening in my cherished homeland can easily happen to yours."

Near the end of the American Civil War, on the third and fourth of April 1865, the young man's words were proven true. The treasured University of Bethel, its library, four dormitories, classrooms, and public buildings, along with much of the town, were indeed burned to the ground by strangers—Federal troops ordered to destroy the South. All the rare books were obliterated by fire, including the ancient Bible. The Prussian gentleman, an old man by then, was crushed by the burning rotunda when he tried to save the sacred book. Only the stone pedestal that held the Bible remained standing, and in its shadow lay the old gentleman's blackened corpse consecrated by the ashes of charred pages.

The university lay gutted, and the town shattered. Bodies littered the streets. "Like hell on earth," the suffering people of Bethel cried as they assessed the damage. Yet those remaining soon found hope and a conviction to rebuild. The stone pedestal was cleaned and buffed for a rebirth, and a new Bible, opened to the same verse, was set upon it as if to dare the repeat of destruction.

Today, Bethel University sits proudly among towering oaks, its white Greek Revival architecture surrounded in the spring by clusters of pink azaleas. It is a smaller university than most, but its courage and once-renowned reputation still allow an endowment for select humanities and social science doctoral programs.

In the shade of a high hill, the rebuilt, square-shaped town of Bethel touches the university on three sides. On its fourth is the Chattahoochee River, dividing Alabama and Georgia. Most of the small businesses of Bethel are located in one large brick building that partially survived the Federal burning. It had been erected as a hotel in 1820 when the town was founded as a port-of-call for steamboats on the Chattahoochee. Back then, Bethel bustled with success. "Heaven's Gate," the old riverboat captains called it, as though heaven's portal had come down to earth—until the railroads came, and then the flames of the Federals. After that, the name Heaven's Gate did not seem appropriate, and the town became Bethel again.

*Envy is a littleness of soul, which cannot see beyond a certain point,
and if it does not occupy the whole space, feels itself excluded.*
—William Hazlitt

PROLOGUE

Mal

D r. Malcom J. Hawkins III, Professor of Psychology at Bethel University, sits at home in his favorite chair with a pompous grin on his face. His hands move ritually up and down the chair's arms, endlessly soiling the upholstered pattern of apples and bananas. Day by day, as he rubs the arms of the chair, the smell of rot increases. Day by day, he eyes the table beside the chair and the drawer where he keeps the gun he plans to show the fool. Day by day, he patiently assesses the progress of the despicable Ginnie Gillan, wife of the fool. *Why is she so admired by everyone at Bethel? How is she even a tenured professor?* He read her many publications—too many, in his opinion. Nothing but drivel about spiritual warfare going on beneath the surface of all the earthly things one does. She contends that great literature portrays a battle between personified love and hate, good and evil in the flesh. In one of her silly articles, she even challenges the reader to choose a side. "Whom do you follow?"

Ha! Mal follows *Me*, not *Thee*. He is interested in a more powerful deity, one who will not allow himself to be crucified but will live and destroy all loftiness, all goodness and love, leaving only the reality of down-to-earth hatred behind.

Ginnie Gillan and all her kind must be destroyed. Not by him, though. Mal will keep his own hands clean. Instead, he has chosen the perfect pawn.

The one who does most to avoid suffering is, in the end,
the one who suffers most.
—Thomas Merton

CHAPTER ONE

Edmund

Some people in this world go unnoticed—quiet people who never win first place in any contest because they never ask to play the game. They make no argument when they are pushed to the back of the line and raise no protest when something is taken from them. They are the backdrop against which more self-assured people act, the timid shadows that give definition to the bold. And yet, on occasion, one of them will satisfy the hauntings of a confused nature, darting back and forth between good and evil because he cannot determine which to pursue. Edmund K. Gillan is one of these.

Edmund—born in the middle of the month of August on the hottest day on record in 200 years for Montgomery, Alabama—arrived prematurely, not quite five pounds, and nearly died at birth. He came feet first, without crying, the last of six children, the only boy, and the only blue-eyed child of brown-eyed parents. Because the house he was born into was very large and busy, with ruling voices louder than his, by the time he was five years old he had learned to burrow himself into a corner of his mind that blocked all sound, a hiding place from those voices who blamed and condemned him for being himself. In that hiding place, he needed only to *be*, not to *do*.

In his daily life, he did not want to be noticed. Yet there was a silent, agitated voice that continuously pricked his thoughts: *Affirm yourself*, it said. But he did not. He did not make waves, did not create a problem for any one of his tall, beautiful sisters, yet each of them seemed to relish creating problems for him. Because of his smallness, they thought him inconsequential and denounced him as the runt. Soon his handsome, successful father called him the same. Not his pretty mother, though; she called him Eddie, and sometimes, "my big boy." He loved the nickname—but of course, he wasn't a big boy, so he sometimes wondered if his mother was making a joke.

He created walls for his hiding place made of thick, impenetrable stones, through which only he could see. He believed himself to be invisible to anyone who crossed the path beyond his walls, yet those who crossed were not invisible to Edmund; he noticed each one, imagining what it would be like to walk beside them, to be like them—the bigger-than-life people, the handsome, the beautiful, the brave. But he made no effort to join them.

When he was six, Edmund saw death for the first time and was, of course, blamed for it. Not a human death; only the death of a kitten belonging to his curly-haired sister, the one closest to him in age.

"Princess has gotten out!" his sister screamed from the kitchen. "Princess is gone!"

"Who left this open?" his pretty mother asked, coming in to shut the kitchen door.

"It wasn't me! Edmund did it," shrieked the eight-year-old. "Edmund left the door open, and now Princess is gone!"

"Edmund!" His mother stood with her hands on her hips. "Go find that kitten right now!"

Edmund had not left the door open, but he didn't say so. He could see that his mother knew the truth, too, yet she gave him a look of disappointment and let him take the blame. Was she hoping he would learn to stand up and fight for himself? Well, he did not. He went to look for the kitten, first on their property and then beyond it, where he found a bully instead. The boy pushed him down in the dirt alongside his sister's dead kitten, now mangled by the bully's dog.

"What you get!" the bully shouted, stomping Edmund's hand with his shoe.

What I get for what? he wanted to ask. But he did not. He hid behind his walls, hid his face in the dirt until the bully left. Then he picked up the dead kitten and ran home, carrying the bully's sin. It was not his sin, not this time, but he was the one who paid for it.

His sister kicked him. "Edmund left the door open," she continued to whine to his mother. "It would not have happened if he hadn't left the door open!"

Outwardly, Edmund simply took it and walked away from her. Only behind the fortification he'd built in his mind did he stand up for himself. "I did not leave it open! I would never leave it open!" But in his head, a voice shouted back, "You might as well have done it. Always, you'll be accused."

Apart from the singular conversations Edmund had with himself—and he had many over the years—he rarely conversed with anyone. When his father, a tall, handsome man with black hair, stood towering over him and asked what he wanted from his life, Edmund shrugged his shoulders. His father scowled then, the way he often scowled at the one thousand and one employees who worked under him in Montgomery's only soft drink bottling plant. "I might have known you had no ambition." Then his father walked away.

In truth, Edmund had an ambition. He wanted to be a teacher like his mother, ever since he left his own second-grade classroom on the first day—no one noticed he'd left—and sneaked into hers. At first, he watched her from the hall until he saw her turn to the chalkboard, then he crept into a shadowed back corner. When his mother faced her class again, she did not see Edmund, but he saw her, smiling at her class. He could see how much she loved her students, and he wanted to be one of them.

He ought to have told his father he wanted to be a teacher, but he worried that the dream would disappoint him. His father expected his only son to be courageous and possess other virtues Edmund did not have and didn't imagine he ever would have.

Because he was afraid of being himself, Edmund lacked authenticity, leaving him as some sort of counterfeit brand, like a pair of cheap shoes tied together by their laces and tossed into a box of bargains in the back of a Dollar Mart.

Still, he had affection for his pretty mother. At times, he simply stood in front of her until she noticed him. Sometimes she held him close while her sweet perfume attached itself to his clothes. He saved those clothes and did not put them in the laundry basket to be washed as his bossy oldest sister instructed. He put them under his bed. During the night, when the house was silent, he tucked them beneath his sheets to breathe in the sweet smell of his mother, as if she were holding him again—only him, not the others. His pretty mother, his only flesh and blood harbor in the march of his young life, was the only person he loved. But he never imagined telling her so.

His mother spoke to him in gentle ways, even when she corrected him, and she was a wonderful baker of all kinds of pies. He would watch as she made the fillings, waiting for her to finish and then hand him the spoon to lick. She always did that for him—no one else. "Here's the spoon, Edmund. It's all yours." Those times, he thought of shouting so she could hear, "I love you, Mama!" Yet he could not release the words. He could not take the risk of making himself even more vulnerable. Oh, how he wished he had!

They were—all eight of them—in the station wagon when the accident happened; the accident that took the life of every family member except Edmund. He emerged outwardly unscathed except for a head injury he caused himself by beating his forehead against a piece of twisted steel—all that was left of the station wagon's front seat where the distorted, dead bodies of his mother and father were entrapped, then pried out and taken away before his eyes, along with the battered bodies of his sisters.

Just before her death, his pretty mother moved her brown eyes toward him as if there was something she urgently wanted to say to him, and right then, he tried with all his might to tell her he loved her. But he was unpracticed and could not make his voice heard. The moment was forever missed, and he still hates himself for that.

One day after the tragedy, he turned ten years old, but his distraught grandparents on his father's side, who took him two hours south to Bethel, Alabama to raise as their own, didn't even remember his birthday.

Soon after the accident, he began having violent headaches, as if the walls he had built in his mind were crumbling in a war against a much stronger entity than he. As he wept, his grandmother wrung her hands in front of her heart. "Oh, look how he suffers!"

His grandfather, Bethel's shrillest preacher, raised his arms upward. "The world is full of suffering, boy. Overcome it or live under

Satan's foot!" The first of many warnings he would fasten in Edmund's head.

Edmund is in his late thirties now and an adjunct professor of sociology at Bethel University, where he began as a freshman years ago. When he met his wife, Ginnie, he'd just begun working on his master's, and Ginnie, a few years older, was already a tenure-track professor. Edmund likes the freedom of being an adjunct and does not mind the lesser salary. Ginnie makes enough for both of them. His agonizing headaches persist, but he supposes he's overcome suffering. He's told no one about the pain except Ginnie, who dismisses it; and Dr. Mal Hawkins, Professor of Psychology, who provides Edmund with a special type of relief.

Imagination is more important than knowledge.
For knowledge is limited to all we now know and understand,
while imagination embraces the entire world,
and all there ever will be to know and understand.
—Albert Einstein

CHAPTER TWO

Alma

S ome people in this world are born to love and be loved in return. Sixteen-year-old Alma Broussard is one of these. People are drawn to her because the door to her heart is open. She moves through life like the butterflies who flit through the fields, bringing a glimpse of beauty to a sometimes ugly world.

Alma's mother, Moline, has no idea who Alma's daddy is, but she and her sister—Alma's Aunt Pauline—deeply love Alma. When Alma thinks of her mother's finger softly stroking her cheek, the brush of her mother's lips across her forehead, the converging of her mother's arms around her, she is content with the family she has. How blessed she was to have had her loving, departed grandparents be part of raising her on their farm. She remembers the window by her crib that opened to a green pasture, a vast blue sky, and the white curtains rustling at the touch of a gentle wind.

Still, there are days when Alma creates pieces of her unknown father in her mind—a loving, handsome face, and a strong, healthy body with caring arms. She imagines his voice, low and smooth and compassionate. She imagines his words to her: *You are good. You are kind. You are mine.* A whisper of her own virtues.

Goodness binds Alma to others, especially her friend Angelina. She is certain she remembers Angelina as a toddler standing beside her crib, with Angelina's father, Jose, in the background. Only him; Angelina's mother plays no part in her daughter's life. She is invisible too, like Alma's father. That they each have only one parent drew them together.

Alma smiles and sighs as she thinks of Angelina's delicate hands, always reaching for her, and the loving smile she casts her on a whim. For years, they have been inseparable, imagining themselves as blood sisters.

Today, because Alma turned sixteen years old, that dream has come true, but not quite as they dreamed so long ago.

Alma has donated the blood Angelina must have to survive leukemia.

While the rest of Angelina's high school class have been at their graduation ceremony, she and Alma have been at Bethel Hospital. When the transfusion process is over, Alma says, "We're real sisters now. I'm part of you."

"The part that makes me whole." Angelina opens her palm to Alma, who places her hand inside. Their fingers entwine, and at once, Alma thinks of Mrs. Baker.

Mrs. Baker was Alma's homeroom teacher in ninth grade. She arrived at Bethel High from a previous position at a high school in Georgia to teach English literature. Alma—and everyone else— noticed she had only one arm. No one knew what happened to her other arm, and no one dared to ask. On her first day, the new teacher wore a suit with a white silk blouse beneath it. As she passed down the rows of desks, the empty sleeve of her suit fluttered. Naturally, there were looks and whispers about her missing arm, so when Mrs. Baker returned to the front of the class, she stood there smiling, caressing her empty sleeve as if it needed something more than their full attention. "All of you can see that my arm is missing." Another pause while everyone stared, quiet as spiders spinning webs. "Do you think its absence makes me less of a person or a teacher?" All heads moved fast in the negative, side to side—after all, Mrs. Baker would be handing out their grades. "Then should it make me more of a person or a teacher?" Some heads nodded yes.

Alma only listened, reflecting on the question.

Mrs. Baker paused for their thoughts and then continued. "In this literature class, I hope you will learn that the whole is not always equal to the sum of its parts. The whole is much, much more than that."

On that first day, no one honestly understood what Mrs. Baker meant, including Alma. But her words remained stuck like a bur in Alma's mind. Every day afterwards, the lack of Mrs. Baker's arm was disregarded by the class, except for her. Off and on for the rest of the school year, Alma considered the absence of Mrs. Baker's arm. There were so many absent things, Alma thought, to compare it to. First, there was Angelina who had a debilitating disease. Was she less than a whole person because of it? A tree absent its leaves in the fall was not less than a tree, and one could imagine its tender green growth in the spring. A dark moonless night did not make the sky itself less because everyone trusts that the moon will soon shine again. A flower clipped from the bush did not make the bush less than it was, nor did it make the flower, set in a vase, less beautiful. And a child absent a father or a mother did not make the child less deserving of love. Even in her class's latest reading assignment, *David Copperfield* by Charles Dickens, a fatherless boy finally found the love and kindness that had long been absent in his life. After she read the novel,

Alma counted herself fortunate to have the life she had. So, was the whole equal to the sum of its parts? The world she knew, the people she loved, and Mrs. Baker were living proof that it was not.

As the semester drew to a close, Mrs. Baker repeated the statement, as she had done many times during the year. "The whole is not always equal to the sum of its parts. The whole is much, much more than that." She paused, as she always did after she asked the class a question, because she wanted them to think a while. Critical thinking, she had taught them, helped make a reasoned judgment. After she decided that enough thinking had been done, she asked the class, "So, how do you see the world, and how would you like the world to see you?"

Many hands shot up, but with her one hand, Mrs. Baker let them know that this was a thinking question too, not to be answered on the spot. There was another pause. And then she said, "Your last assignment in English literature is to begin an original project. It can be a poem, an essay, or even a drawing, as long as it answers the questions I presented. You may start it today in class, but you will have the final few weeks of this semester to work on it at home, then you'll turn it in, first thing, on the last day of school. I will grade it that day, and you may take it home. And remember, do not be lukewarm about your project," Mrs. Baker said with emphasis. "Life itself demands passion."

Grunting and groaning rose from some of the students, but not from Alma. She began at once with a drawing, inspired by the bur-like thought she'd kept in her mind the entire school year, about the whole and the sum of its parts. She drew pieces of a man she'd never known, seen, or touched. She drew her own father, believing she could grasp the mysterious whole of him, even in his absence. She knew it could be done, like drawing God in her mind when she prayed. She felt the breath of both God and her father, the warm arms of both, the steady beat of both hearts in hers. God's gift of her own imagination could do that. She sketched throughout the class, sketched her father's imagined handsome face, his broad shoulders, long arms and legs. Then she took the drawing home to begin all the other pieces of him, picturing him in a suit and tie, maybe with a book in his hands. Or maybe he should be casually dressed, in a rocker, with Alma as a baby in his lap. Or even a drawing of the two of them walking together, smiling and happy—the best drawing of all because it was at least possible she might meet him someday.

Her daydreams evoked the way she wanted to see the world—as good and kind as she wanted the world to see her. She entitled it *The Whole Is Greater than the Sum of Its Parts.* Oh, how it excited her! She'd envisioned it all, created something from nothing, something whole to fill what was missing in her. A father that she could see not only in her mind, but now, on paper. An image she could cling to.

On the last day of school, Mrs. Baker gave her the highest grade in the class and a tight hug with her only arm. At home, Alma did not show the drawing to her mother, but put it into a drawer beneath her night clothes.

Daily, she pulls out the picture and imagines meeting him, making herself entirely complete.

Sickness, insanity, and death were the angels that surrounded
my cradle, and they have followed me throughout my life.
—Edvard Munch, Norwegian painter

Chapter Three

Edmund

S atan is crouching at your door! You ain't seen him coming, boy. Nobody seen him coming but the Lord Jesus Christ. Now, he's after you. Don't wait for his spear. Conquer him!
On the last day of the spring term at Bethel University, Edmund K. Gillan is standing in front of his class when his mind goes blank, and he can't remember the point he was making because his grandfather's fanatical voice won't stop badgering him. Edmund mumbles an apology. His voice begins to tremble. He lifts the sheet of notes he'd made as a reminder, but the notes seem to will themselves into a crumpled ball then fly from his hand toward the back of the room. His students look stunned. Several dodge the paper ball, and the rest turn their eyes downward, as if they are embarrassed for him, as if he doesn't measure up to their expectations and never will.

He feels nauseous, mumbles an excuse, and leaves the classroom, heading down the hall to the men's room just as the squatty shadow of Dr. Mal Hawkins emerges from its fluorescent glare. Edmund's grandfather's voice rises in his brain. *And therein lies your ruin, Edmund. I've told you to nip him in the bud. But will you listen? No!*

"You alright?" Mal asks, holding open the door for Edmund to enter.

"Fine!" he snaps, something he's never done to Mal before, while in his mind his grandfather goes on about the fact that Edmund is not fine. Not fine at all.

"See you tonight then," Mal says. "We'll talk—get you feeling better. That is, if your wife will let you out."

Edmund usually finds himself in the middle between his wife and Mal, trying to please them both. "Oh, she'll let me out alright. She doesn't tell me what to do," he says as if he is in charge of himself and his marriage, which he is not. Mal grins as he leaves, and the door to the men's room swings closed behind him.

Are you afraid change will be painful? Let me tell you, Edmund, it will be painful. It will hurt like fiery hell, but it sure beats going there!

Edmund looks at his face in the bathroom mirror, deep into his eyes for signs of inherited lunacy. The face of his grandfather looks back at him, a wild face with lips set tight. He can't escape that face because it resembles his own, with the same name as his: Edmund. Whether through nature or nurture, his grandfather is not only embedded on his face but inside him too. "Pulled right out of my pocket," the old man once said, setting Edmund, the boy, on his knee.

His grandmother giggled. "Oh yes, he's just like you. It's possible he could be a preacher as well." And then his grandmother added, "Or even a priest," because Edmund's mother had become a devout Catholic after she married his father. "After all, he would still be following the same God."

"No!" Edmund says to the face in the mirror as he remembers those long-ago words. He is not a preacher. He will never, ever be a preacher or a priest! Follow God? He will not follow any God that let his mother die, the only person besides Ginnie he's ever loved in this world. A God like that is to be avoided at all costs—which is exactly why he needs help from Mal, the godless psychologist who never fails to offer it.

When Edmund arrives home after his classes, he tells Ginnie, "I'm going for a run." She is standing by the stove, stirring gravy. Her dark hair hangs loose rather than being piled on the top of her head as it is when she is in her classroom, but she is still in her teacher clothes—a pink silk blouse and gray skirt that looks good on her. He is overcome with love for her, but just like with his mother, he is hesitant to say so because he does not deserve her. She is so much better than he is in every way. He should keep a certain distance, but at that moment, desire for her fills his thoughts. Why had he berated her to Mal? Yes, sometimes she's hard to love; over-bearing, so sure of herself, while he is mostly indecisive. And yet, he adores her. Some of the things he does and says don't make sense, as if he has no mind of his own, as if he only does what he is told by two opposite voices: his grandfather's and now Mal's, goading him into contrary actions that suit each of them, not Edmund. Where is the confidence that he should have in himself? The self-assurance Ginnie says he needs to develop? He feels like an actor playing two divergent roles in his own splintered life. He isn't a whole person, and it sickens him.

"Dinner's almost ready," Ginnie says, turning to him with a smile. "Come give me a kiss. I've made your favorite, steak and gravy."

He wants to do more than kiss her, yet he says, "I'll eat when I get back from my run." Then he proceeds to the bedroom to change his clothes, proud he's being assertive.

"Why can't you run after dinner? It won't be as good when you get back. And I've put a lot of effort into it because I thought you'd like it."

When he says nothing, she proceeds into the bedroom where he is changing into his running clothes. He glances up at her as he puts on his shoes. He can tell she's upset by the way she's looking at him—with pity, like he's some underfed pet she needs to pick up and cuddle.

Her voice doesn't show disturbance, only control. "Edmund, I don't believe you are going to run," she says softly, almost like his mother might have said it. "I believe you're going to Mal's house, aren't you?" She comes close, puts a hand on his arm. "Please don't."

Of course, he is going to Mal's house. He doesn't want to be manipulated by his grandfather's voice, but he does not want Mal to think he's manipulated by Ginnie's voice either. He is a grown man. And hopefully soon, he will be a tenured professor too. After all, he's slowly working on his doctorate, and he has a few publications. *I can do whatever I want, and I mean to,* he tells himself. But even in his head, the words sound false. After the embarrassing day in his sociology class, he needs the help Mal offers in getting rid of his awful headaches and the old man's demanding voice.

But he knows that more than he wants confidence, he wants cocaine.

Ginnie frowns as if she can see the craving inside him. "You don't need the drugs."

He removes her hand from his arm. "I'm going to run! I'll eat when I get back." He pushes past her to the hall and into the living room, crossing the blood-red carpet she chose when they moved in—the carpet he hates because whenever he steps on it, the color reminds him how angry he was on that night, about a year after their marriage, when she realized Mal offered him more than a listening ear.

Mal greets Edmund with a smile, offers him a seat on the chair upholstered with bananas and apples, and then listens patiently while Edmund tells him about his disastrous day in class.

"It's not good for a teacher to be frightened, Edmund. A teacher must be courageous. I can take away your fear." Mal dangles a bag of white powder near Edmund's eyes.

At once, Edmund hears his grandfather's reprimanding voice. *That's the bothering work of the devil! Walk away!*

How can he walk away from the possibility of being a courageous person when that is what he's always wanted? What is wrong with a little cocaine if it gives him courage—and silences the voice of the old man?

Mal taunts him. "Do I have something you want?"

Edmund wants to get up, walk away. But doing so would require courage, and his courage is in that little plastic bag. So instead, he only nods.

As soon as he enters his house that night, he sees Ginnie surrounded by the color red. Though he tries hard to be himself, her expression says she is aware of his abnormal talkativeness, his shakiness. She twists around and heads for their bedroom, slamming the door behind her.

The first time he saw Ginnie, Edmund only glimpsed her in the hall, but he saw she was beautiful, with dark hair and blue eyes like his. He noticed her fast smile when she stopped to speak to one of her students. "Oh, don't worry about the quiz, sweetie, you'll do fine. You're a smart girl." He looked back to see her give the girl a quick hug.

He didn't think he'd have a chance with her, so he only watched her from a hidden corner and never tried. But Ginnie was different. Anything that attracted her, she went after full force—with courage, not fear. For some reason Edmund hadn't been able to figure out, she came after him.

He met her during a play production at the university, which must have been fate because he'd never before been in a play.

The play was produced by the English Department. Henry Patton, Dean of Social Sciences, who always took part in the productions, encouraged Edmund to take a small role. Of course, Edmund said no, he wasn't really interested in theater and had no experience acting, but Dr. Patton eyed him with an intensity that clearly stated he'd seen Edmund socially stumbling. "Experience doesn't matter. Acting will be a good way for you to feel more comfortable in front of a classroom."

So, Edmund agreed to a small role, the role of the undertaker in the production of *Our Town* by Thornton Wilder. He had only a few lines and had not known that Ginnie would even be there—certainly not that she would be playing the lead. But perhaps he should have sensed it by the way she entered the auditorium that day, head held high, her eyes scanning the stage, the actors, the director, to find—what? How she'd take control of it all?

Of course, in the play, she could not take control of death. It was he, as the undertaker, who appeared in Act III to literally dig Ginnie's grave. His cue was when he heard the stage manager in the play say, "Everybody in their bones knows that something is eternal." Naturally, he'd paid attention to the line; he didn't want to embarrass himself by coming on late. For days before the first practice, he said the sentence over and over in his mind, until he actually heard it shouted in the long-ago voice of his preacher grandfather, promising an eternity of fire and brimstone to those who turned their backs to God. *Everybody in their bones knows that something is eternal.* But the words made him think about his dead mother too.

At the first practice, Edmund came forward at just the right time and found Ginnie, to whom he'd never before spoken a word, looking at him with eagerness, as if she perceived the hidden holes of self-doubt within him and had at once committed herself to filling them. And fill them, she had. For a while. Act III of *Our Town* was the beginning of Act I for Edmund and Ginnie. She was the one who asked him out after their first practice, the one who continued to ask him out, sometimes for a movie, sometimes only for a walk. He loosened up a bit, and then grew used to her. Soon, he was certain he loved her, but he didn't seem able to tell her that, afraid she might not return his feelings and leave him looking foolish.

Then one day, as if she was tired of waiting, Ginnie put her arms around him and pulled him close. "I love you, Edmund."

Her words alarmed him. They stopped his breath, constricted his heart as if she had roped it, pulling him closer, squeezing him harder and harder for a response. "Well?" she questioned, her lips brushing his ear.

In a breathless whisper, he said, "I feel the same," expecting she would push him for more than that. But she only drew back a little, gave him a perceptive smile as if, by now, she understood everything about him.

She whispered back, "I know you do."

Of course, Ginnie assumed marriage would follow. He wanted to marry her, too. But he couldn't find the courage to ask. So, again, Ginnie took over. "We'll have a small wedding, only the people who matter most to us." Then immediately she began to talk about where they would live. "Somewhere near the university," she decided. She called the priest at Sacred Heart Church to schedule a date, then made up a guest list and ordered invitations. "Mostly people from the university," she told him before he asked. No mention of their families then. Not hers. Not his. He had heard her parents were deceased and almost asked her about that, but he did not, unready to trigger any conversation about himself, the accident, or his instability because of it.

But when the invitations came, she asked for his parents' address. "Don't bother," he said, rubbing his forehead to get rid of the pain. "They won't be able to come." She looked at him oddly, as if she perceived some deception, but let it go.

After their marriage, their life and love seemed immaculate and new. Ginnie had no hidden holes inside her, nothing she tried to hide. She told him stories about her childhood, about growing up as an only child and how she'd missed having brothers and sisters, that both her parents were brilliant lawyers, but her mother was a sickly woman. Ginnie and her father ended up taking care of her like she was a baby.

"My father loved her tremendously," Ginnie said, stroking Edmund's hair as he lay beside her in bed. "Daddy was crushed when she died. Afterwards, his health failed, too. He passed away just after I graduated from high school, so I was on my own." She paused as if expecting some response. When Edmund did not respond—he did not know what to say—she sighed and went on. "All that made me stronger, I think. I miss them, but I can still hear their voices telling me how beautiful, how smart, how kind and generous they thought I was. I was lucky to have them. I hold onto that." She turned her face to his. "Now, tell me about your family."

His relationship with Ginnie gave him a closeness Edmund had never had before. He wanted so badly to reveal himself, as she had done. And he started to. "I had five sisters, and…"

When he paused, Ginnie stroked his arm and gazed at him. "Edmund? Go on, tell me about your sisters. Were you close?"

"No."

"No, you weren't close? Or no, you won't tell me?"

He was going to tell her about the accident that killed them, but that was as far as he got before the walls in his mind began to thicken, making his head feel heavy. But back then, Ginnie was his balm, a prescription tablet for his shortcomings. He gently took her in his arms. "I'd rather be close to you."

So, she smiled and kissed him, clearing his mind and breathing freshness into him.

Nevertheless, Ginnie persisted. Slowly, methodically, she pulled bits of his history from him, but he never discussed his family. Then one night after their lovemaking, after he'd turned over, his face away from hers, she shook his shoulder. "Edmund, I want to know more about your sisters and the rest of your family. Where are they?"

"Dead and buried," he murmured, half asleep.

"What? How did they die?"

And then, he had to tell her the rest. "They were all killed in a car accident. I'm the only one who survived."

"Oh, Edmund, I'm so sorry! No wonder you didn't want to talk about something so sad." She snuggled up to him, moving her fingers up and down on his back.

The next morning, she couldn't keep her hands off him, like she was trying to wipe away all his dejection, stroking his face, rubbing his shoulder, until he honestly could take no more.

"Stop it," he said a little too harshly, and she stepped back, her eyes filling with tears.

"I was only trying to… It's just so tragic about your family."

"Yeah, I'm a walking tragedy," he snapped. "And maybe I don't want to be treated like one. Look, it happened, and it's over with. I don't have to deal with any of them anymore. I don't want to talk about it again." He thought he sounded very much in control then, until she looked at him like some sort of psychologist, almost like Mal, as if she saw right through him. He knew then that she saw a seriously damaged human being, something she hadn't reckoned on.

The memory flares through Edmund as he stares at the bedroom door that Ginnie just slammed in his face after he returned from Mal's. A deep sense of regret sets in. So many times, he doesn't really listen to Ginnie—he just nods, pretending he's heard what she said. He tries to recall what Ginnie told him about her own family. He believes he listened then, but he cannot recall it now; his mind is still racing from the cocaine. *The drugs.* They're affecting his memory and tearing him away from Ginnie. He knows something must be done—that *he* must do something—and yet, he can't imagine giving up the respite they bring, that fleeting feeling of wholeness. He needs them—and needs Mal, who provides them.

We all got holes in our lives.
Nobody dies in a perfect garment.
—Louise Erdrich

Chapter Four

Moline

Alma's mother, Moline Broussard, holds no degree; she never went to college. She is almost always blond unless she decides her persona needs a change. She is tall and, unlike her twin, indiscriminately tolerant of most anything that passes before her. Moline says she learned her open-mindedness from her favorite rock star, Chancee Wile. She's been a fan of the aging rocker since fifth grade, even dressed like the bleached blond woman and received first place at a Halloween costume party. She still has the award-winning costume folded neatly in her bureau drawer alongside the lacy lingerie and nylon hose she wears beneath one of the two boring pink polyester uniforms she uses for her job as a receptionist in a dental office. Moline puts it there so she can see it every morning and remember the chorus of Chancee's "Have to Be Me," to remind her that life is more than making appointments. When she pulls her expensive lingerie from the drawer—*I have to be me, whatever you fools saaay, this is my day!*—she doesn't consider the danger of having the pointy, metal bustier from the old costume rip into the delicate lace. Moline takes the gamble.

Every Saturday, Moline and Pauline allow themselves $4.99 each to buy their choice of an on-demand cable movie, which the other agrees to watch no matter how much she does or does not like it. When the bill arrives, they split it in half, as they split everything, even Alma, who used to call them her "interchangeable mothers." The tables are turning a bit, though. Sometimes, Moline thinks Alma sees herself as the mother, and she and Pauline are the two cantankerous children.

Pauline likes movies about long ago, "when man was becoming man." However, the dinosaur movie that she has picked does not go over well with Moline, who thinks of herself as being more progressive than her twin. "I like cutting-edge movies," Moline says as the ending credits roll. She runs her fingers through her blond hair. "Old albatrosses are impediments to our future."

"Well, Sister, the old albatrosses were here first."

Moline looks as if she'd never considered that, so Pauline repeats it. "Yes, first! Right here in Alabama, long before human beings disturbed Alabama's forests and streams, our landscape was once reshaped, Sister. It was bent, broken, and changed because powerful forces took over. Everything convulsed and shifted. Everything! Mountains were moved until the Alabama coastline lay just south of Birmingham. That was hundreds of millions of years ago. Thirty-foot-long dinosaurs were swimming everywhere, so I think they deserve every bit of our respect."

Moline sighs. Her sister likes to show how smart she is. "Then you give them your respect. Just let me know when it's all used up. My turn is next, and I've picked a movie starring Chancee Wile."

As Moline walks out of the living room, Pauline hollers after her.

"You need to grow up, Sister. She's the albatross, a teenager's idol, and a has-been at that."

"I'm…not…listening," Moline sings from the kitchen. She turns the water faucet on high. "I'm washing the dishes."

"I'll come help," Pauline calls back.

Moline and her twin clean the Saturday morning breakfast dishes in their usual manner. Moline pours out the leftover coffee and washes and dries the three matching fat mugs, blue as robin eggs, though one of them is beginning to chip around the edges of its brim. She hands the mugs to Pauline to set in the top kitchen cabinet. The fourth mug in the set remains far in the back of the cabinet now, hidden because it is old and seriously cracked, too cracked to hold coffee, but Moline continues to hold onto that useless mug, the same as she holds onto her veneration of Chancee.

Pauline scrapes the yellow-crusted remains off the blue plates while Moline wipes the whitening bacon grease off the stove and countertops. They work in silence until Moline can stand the quiet no longer. "Here's the thing, Pauline. Chancee's not timid on stage or off. That woman enjoys life and never shies from risk."

"But Sister, Sister, are they worthy risks?" Pauline, much shorter, rather plump, and by Moline's standards, stiff as a new broom, points a finger. "You'd do much better to imitate the mother that raised you than try to behave like some Hollywood-crafted caricature who always looks like she's performing a sex act on stage."

"Pauline!"

"Well, it's true. Your standards are getting as far from what they ought to be as hell is from eternal life."

"Put yourself in Chancee's shoes. She can't worry about things like that when she has to worry about—"

"What, her wardrobe? Reviews?"

"Oh, come on, you're too harsh on her. Surely, you're not jealous?"

Pauline purses her lips as if in deep thought. "Well, I agree with you, Sister. Many actresses and rock stars do indeed take risks. Come on, we'll watch your movie. A deal's a deal."

Despite Pauline's caution, Moline knows that there are risks worth taking—and how hard it is to watch the people she loves take them.

As soon as Alma turned the required sixteen years old, her blood was tested to see if she could donate to Angelina. All that was supposed to match up, did, and Alma was delighted she would finally be able to give a part of herself to her friend. The first time she went through the process, Moline and Pauline, who were not familiar with blood transfusions, worried about someone in charge doing the wrong thing, maybe even drawing too much of her blood and hurting Alma. So, Moline drove her to the hospital and stayed in the room while it was going on, and Pauline went to Mass at Sacred Heart to pray for both girls. Moline did not say a word during the transfusion; she only stared ahead, occasionally biting her lower lip, a habit she had if she was worrying.

After nearly two hours of anxiousness, Moline noticed the nurse smiling, first at Angelina, and then at Alma. "Okay, we're done. And Alma, you can go, sweetie." So, Alma kissed Angelina goodbye and left with Moline to go to the hospital parking lot. Neither said a word until they got into the car. Then Moline turned to Alma, reached for her hand, and squeezed it.

"Oh, sugar! I was so afraid something would happen to you. I mean I was praying for Angelina, too, but you're the one who's my baby."

"I'm fine, Mama. It really wasn't that bad. And the nurse said it would help Angelina."

"Well, all I could think of was the night you were born and how I looked into your little face and was amazed that I—Moline, the worthless—had brought you into this world."

"Why do you say you're worthless? You're not! I love you, Mama, and I wouldn't love someone worthless."

Moline thought Alma was much too naïve, but then again, Alma didn't know about all the things Moline had done. Still, her daughter's words struck something inside her. She took a tissue out of her purse and wiped her eyes. "I love you, too, Alma. But it's true that I'm not worthy of you. I've never been worthy of you. You've grown into a real person, a whole person. There's nothing missing in you, like there is in me. I've always been full of holes, and you know it."

"I like your holes. Sometimes they're lots of fun."

Moline gave a cynical laugh. "Oh, like the time I got us both arrested?"

"You know that policeman did not arrest us. He just thought you'd been drinking when you hadn't been."

"That's true. I hadn't been drinking. I'd just forgotten to put a color on my lips, and was fingering around for the lipstick that had fallen out of my purse onto the floor and…"

"And you ran off the road. But the policeman ended up being very nice."

"Yes, he went to Sacred Heart and was a friend of Pauline's. Except he did give me one of those breathalyzer tests."

"Which you easily passed. And later, you told Aunt Pauline all about it." At once, they both burst into laughter.

"Telling Pauline was almost worth the incident," Moline said between giggles. "What did she say? I can't remember. Was it something about Heaven's Gate?"

Alma answered in a voice meant to sound like Aunt Pauline's. "Moline, Moline! Don't you know, Sister, that when you pass St.

Peter at Heaven's Gate, he is not going to say, 'Stop Moline! You can't come in. You don't have on your lipstick!'"

"Oh yes!" Moline laughed. "There is nothing more enjoyable than listening to the tutorials of a reformed sinner. Pauline can be so comical, and she doesn't even realize it! One day, we'll have to tell her, kiddo, about how very amusing she is." Then Moline became serious. "I'm so proud of you, Alma, for giving your blood to Angelina. If that's not a risk, I don't know what is. So, come over here and give your worthless mama a big hug."

Commit your way to the Lord;
trust in him, and he will act.
—Psalm 37:5, ESV

CHAPTER FIVE

Jose

Angelina's father, Jose Alvarez (not his real name) was born in Mexico of well-known and prosperous parents, but he actually came to America from Cuba, a secret he never revealed even to Angelina. At thirty-seven years old, he is a tall man—much taller than any of his four older brothers—because he took after his mother who came from the Iberian Peninsula and was of French descent. His brothers are all dead now, along with his beautiful mother, always praying the rosary, and his very wealthy and political father whom Jose had never seen pray. Jose has always been strong in body, like his father, and abundant in spirit, like his mother. But he might have been dead, too, if he had not been exiled from his home—and by his father, of all people.

The youngest of five boys, Jose was serious, intelligent, and sensitive, while his older brothers were fond of the nightlife, expensive cars, and willing girls. Jose was fifteen years younger than his eldest brother, so he became an amusing family pet, especially when he began writing music and playing his songs on the guitar his mother gave him for his tenth birthday.

"Play and sing for us, baby brother!" his eldest brother bellowed, calling in their siblings. Then he poked at Jose as if he was the organ-grinder and Jose his monkey. Jose wrote and sang lots of songs for his brothers, but the song they liked best was Jose's take on a poem his mother read to him as a young child, "The Spider and the Fly." When he sang it for them in two voices—one for the spider, one for the fly—they beat their feet on the floor and howled, egging him on.

> *Said the spider to the fly,*
> *As soon as she came flitting by,*
> *What pretty wings you have, my dear!*
> *Don't run away; glide over here,*
> *And trust me.*
> *You've got a line that sounds so fine*
> *I'd like to know what's on your mind*
> *But by tomorrow I might find,*
> *You'd change it.*
> *Tomorrow's far away, the spider said,*
> *And I have such a pretty bed.*
> *I'll show you what love's all about.*
> *Just trust me.*

Laughing and hollering, his brothers shouted, "Grind it out, baby brother!" And so, he kept going. With made-up words just for them, he put all he had into it, as if he were their rock star, on their stage.

> *Trust is just a word you use.*
> *You only say it to confuse.*

How am I to know for sure
You will not harm me?
My dear, you seem to have some doubt.
Come over here. We'll work it out.
Don't flee from opportunity,
For I'm as good as I can be.
No, spider, I can't overstay.
I don't live just for today.
Your web of lies is not in play.
Bye, bye, said the fly, and she flew away.

His mother heard her sons' hooting laughter and stood in the doorway to listen. "Sing it again."

And so he sang and played it again. Only for her. His brothers left to find other distractions.

"You have a gift, Jose." His mother pointed out his long, slim fingers—fingers like hers—and whispered, "Your brothers have stout fingers, like your father's, that curl to make fists. I pray that your fingers will always make beautiful music." No doubt, he was her favorite son.

Jose grew up in the midst of corruption in Mexico. His father, who was in the upper echelon of the government, was part of that corruption, overseeing bribes paid with kickbacks to finance his favored political party. Jose's older brothers were not bothered by the dishonesty and went along with their father. They had plenty of money and lots of "things," while Jose, even in his youngest years, rejected their consumerist lifestyle. There was something in him that he knew was holy, something in all human beings that attached them to an entity much greater than themselves. He knew before he was taught that the entity was God. His mother must have sensed this on the day she fell to her knees, pulling Jose down beside her, to pray that his father and his older brothers would come to their senses. But they never did.

Though he had great love for his father, as a teenager, Jose could see the pain his father's wrongdoing caused his mother, so he felt called to stand up to him. "Father, I beg you to give up your corrupt ways and be an example for your sons."

His father slapped him for his insolence.

His mother saw it and was appalled. She rose up against her husband, knowing it was dangerous to do so, and stood before his father. "Why did you slap him? Because he is not like the others? Because he is not like you?"

His father grabbed her by the wrist and tightly held her hand in the air. Jose knew it would cause a bruise. He'd seen bruises on her before. "Jose should be grateful to me. I have given him many privileges—this fine home, the clothes on his back, a good education. All I ask is that he follow my lead and learn to be a strong man."

His mother knew where his father would lead him, and she would have none of it. After Jose's father left the room, she whispered, "You are already strong, Jose. And a better man than your father or your brothers. I love them all, but your brothers are in danger because they have chosen to pursue your father's criminal ways." Tears streamed down her face. "You must call your father out to the authorities, Jose, or he will get himself and your brothers killed!"

Jose was stunned. "But what will happen to them if I do such a thing? I don't want to send them to prison. And what will happen to you and me? We will lose all that we have now!"

She took his face in her hands. "Jose, you are good, but you are young. As yet, you haven't seen much of life. I know you love your father and brothers. I do too. But do we love them enough to help them save their souls? We do not speak of the terrible things your father, with the help of your brothers, have imposed upon helpless people, but you know them. You know they have killed for our corrupt government. You know that they have stolen so much from the poor that many have died from starvation while we live in luxury. You know this is sinfulness, and what we have now, what we've grown used to, comes from that sinfulness."

"Yes, but—"

"We can no longer be complicit in sin, Jose!" His mother raised her voice. "We cannot share in the immorality of your father and brothers by hiding it any longer. It is a secret that must be revealed to the police. You must inform the authorities."

Because he trusted his mother, Jose did so.

But his mother was naïve; she assumed the National Revolutionary Police were trustworthy. Instead, they were, of course, cronies of his father, and immediately informed him of Jose's accusations. His father was livid. Still, he loved his son, perhaps even admired him. He knew that the Mexican government would take revenge on Jose, and that even killing his son was not out of the question. So his father sent him to the Mexican embassy in Havana. At least that was what his father intended, but Jose finagled his way out of the tumultuous life of political intrigue that being his father's son required and into the lives and generosity of the Cuban people. Then, at twenty years old, on a boat filled with fleeing Cubans praying the rosary as his mother had done, he headed for Miami.

At that time, Cubans caught at sea trying to make their way to Miami were allowed into the United States and were able to become legal residents. But Jose never applied for legal residency because he had no papers to say he was Jose Alvarez—and of course, he wasn't. Still, a Cuban man and his wife, Mr. and Mrs. Lopez, already in Miami, took him in. He gave them his false name when they asked. They gave him a tiny room with one chair, a cot to sleep on, and a job as a landscaper. For two years, he kept in the shadows of Little

Havana in the city of Miami. And when Angelina came along, he kept her in the shadows, too.

That was long ago.

But today, he remembers it all, sitting beside Angelina's bed as she sleeps in Bethel Hospital. Angelina does not look like him, has none of his Mexican coloring. Her mother was Irish, with fair skin and blond hair. She may not resemble him, and she isn't a baby anymore, but she is still his beloved little girl. "*Mi niña*," he says, lightly touching Angelina's shoulder.

Then the door opens, and Fr. O'Hara of Sacred Heart Church comes into the room. "How is she?"

"She is better, in remission again, and can soon go home. Maybe even tomorrow."

"That's wonderful, Jose. God has answered our prayers for this beautiful girl."

Jose's eyes turn to his daughter. She is beautiful, he thinks, in every way. That Angelina is kind never goes unnoticed by Jose or any of the Broussard family he works for. All of them seem to love her as if she were their own. She might even pass for a Broussard. She is as fair and blond as Alma, with whom Angelina is very close. Close as sisters, both of them claim. Since Fr. O'Hara introduced him to Miss Pauline and she brought him to Bethel to help with her chicken farm, Jose has felt part of the family as well. He is grateful that God answered his prayers for a job, a place to live, and a family to love.

I look inside myself and see my heart is black.
—Keith Richards, Mick Jagger, Abkco, Inc.

CHAPTER SIX

Edmund

Ginnie brings in the mail one evening, pulls open an envelope, and grins at the card. "An end-of-summer party for social science and humanities professors," she reads, "at the home of Dr. Malcolm Hawkins." She immediately writes the Friday night date on their calendar.

Edmund looks up from the book he's reading. "You mean you're actually going to a party at Mal's?"

"Wouldn't miss it for the world!"

He sees sarcasm in her expression, but he knows she's serious. He wonders why but doesn't ask.

A few days later, Ginnie goes to Dillard's and buys herself a new black dress. When she returns, she seems unusually excited as she pulls it out of the department store box to show it to him.

"Nice," he says. "But why the change of heart toward Mal?"

She smiles broadly. "Oh, I haven't changed anything, my darling." Her eyes are as ravenous as those of a fox crouching in front of a henhouse. "He's an absolute devil."

"Then why do you want to go? Is it because Eleanor Burke from the English Department will probably be there with her husband?"

She gives him an odd stare as if, again, she's read his mind. "You mean my dermatologist, Dr. Burke? Of course not!" She places a hand on his cheek and looks into his eyes. "There's no reason to be jealous of him, Edmund. He's a fine man, a former marine who lost a leg in Iraq. You will like him. And you'll understand why I want to go to the party after we get there. It will be a nice surprise, one I think you'll be happy with."

Nice or not, Edmund is not fond of surprises.

On the night of the party, when she puts on the dress, it's a little too tight and low-cut for Edmund's approval around other men. She's also had an outbreak of acne, which means she'll need another visit to her dermatologist, Dr. Burke. She had a small basal cell skin cancer on the side of her face that the doctor treated, which required her to return several times a year to check for more suspicious spots. So far, there had been none, only some acne, mostly when she became emotionally upset—a rarity, but Dr. Burke treated that too. Still, even though she's gained at least ten pounds over the summer, she looks confident. She looks good, and Edmund, somewhat out of character, tells her so.

As they approach Mal's house, she takes in a breath and lets it out. "This is an important night for me."

"Why?"

She gives him a quick kiss. "I told you, it's a surprise, Edmund. I don't want to ruin the surprise."

Edmund pushes open the door and they step inside. Immediately his eyes turn to the table where Mal usually lays out his drugs. With Ginnie by his side, his guilt is overwhelming, until he's distracted by a rush of loud music. A barely-known group Mal is infatuated with called Snakes with Stripes plays loudly. Blanketed beneath the music is the sway of conversing voices, faculty members attempting to be heard. Several people notice the Gillans and wave a hand. Fine wines and whiskey line the buffet in the dining room along with several platters of hors d'oeuvres, including caviar. A gracious Mal, impeccably dressed in a dark-colored suit and bright red tie, comes toward them. "Help yourselves," he says, gesturing in the direction of the buffet.

Ginnie says nothing and heads toward the food as the music booms. *Don't believe them when they say I have a tongue that's forked.*

Edmund shakes Mal's hand. "Interesting music."

Mal shrugs. "I like The Snakes."

Edmund follows his wife to the buffet as the lead singer of Snakes with Stripes whines above his raucous band. *I feed on a diversity of prey. Big and small. I devour them all.*

Eleanor Burke, an attractive brunette, notices Edmund and comes over with her husband, Dr. Burke. He hobbles behind her, using a cane to balance his missing left leg. "Hello, Edmund. Have you met my husband, Adam?"

"Not in person." Edmund shakes Burke's free hand. Then the doctor steadies himself, putting a hand on Eleanor's shoulder.

"Nothing like the support of a good woman." Dr. Burke smiles.

"So true," Edmund agrees. The man who looks after Ginnie's skin isn't at all how Edmund pictured him. Maybe it's true what Ginnie said—he's her doctor and that's all. He decides he'll try to enjoy himself. *I'd crawl on the ground for you. Yeah, yeah.*

Eleanor Burke puts her hands over her ears. "I'm going to ask Mal to either put on another album or turn down the music. It's just playing over and over again, and it's hard to hear a conversation."

She and her one-legged husband head off to look for Mal. A few minutes later, The Snakes are silent.

Ginnie is across the room, talking to Dr. Patton. Mal is across the room, too, behind Ginnie. Each time she speaks, or laughs, or tugs at her too-tight dress, Mal's dark eyes flit toward her. Is he attracted to her? No, Edmund shouldn't worry. Ginnie doesn't seem at all aware of Mal's interest, and even if she was, it's her habit never to pay him any attention. Besides, Edmund has reason to believe Mal's interest tends toward a different type.

Mal tugs at his sleeves, looking agitated, and then disappears for a moment. When he returns, Snakes with Stripes return as well. *Now I see you've guessed my name, but not my game.*

Ginnie is conversing with board member Anne Evans. Edmund hears Anne say something like, "Do it, Ginnie. Do it now."

He can tell Ginnie has had more than one glass of wine when she raises her voice over the music and says, "Ladies and gentleman, I want to make an announcement." This must be the surprise she told him about. "Everyone, gather round. I want to tell you all about my good fortune, and I hope the good fortune of the entire university."

Mal's guests stop talking and turn their attention to Ginnie. Edmund notices Mal's face go hostile, but the music continues. *Yeah, I'm an ancient mime, been round a long time. Messed with Adam, 'course Eve was fine.*

Eleanor insists again, "Mal, please lower the music so we can hear what Ginnie has to say!"

Mal doesn't budge.

Ginnie smiles slyly. "It's alright, Eleanor. I have a forceful voice." For the first time, she looks pointedly at Mal. "I've developed a new course for my fall semester English classes. It's called The Voice of God in Literature. It's going to be a pilot for the future possibility of a religious studies degree at Bethel. The provost thinks we really need a program like this to balance out some of our more secular psychology courses. If it generates enough interest among the students, I'll become the program director and begin writing the new curriculum for next fall."

Mal's once-covetous eyes immediately cease to flutter. To Edmund, it looks as if he's angry—which, considering Ginnie just attacked his department, he probably is. But Ginnie's criticism is correct. Edmund knows that Mal does not believe in God. He's heard him say so many times, strongly encouraging his students to embrace his non-belief. A degree program in religious studies would certainly bring in more opposition to Mal's theories. So, while other members of the faculty flock around Ginnie, chirping cheerfully, Mal sets his drink down hard on the glass table and abruptly leaves the room—his usual sign that a visit, or even a party, is over.

If ever you've got a problem, don't linger at my door. Just ring the bell and come on in. No one else will give you more.

Ginnie doesn't appear the least concerned by his exit. In fact, she seems delighted that she disturbed him. No one else seems to notice his absence either, as Ginnie goes into the specifics of her pilot literature course with God as the main character, the one who will run the show. "We'll start with Shakespeare and the religious elements in *Macbeth*. Shakespeare consistently keeps before his audience the consciousness of choice. Man is never forced to choose evil. I believe we should implant that important message in our students."

Most of the faculty applaud her and give their congratulations.

"I think it's wonderful, Ginnie."

"Yes, we do need a change."

"And a degree in religious studies? That would be terrific, especially if you were in charge!"

Ginnie grins from ear to ear.

Have a little understanding. Use a little taste. Show all your mama's manners, or I'll lay you to waste, mmm yeah.

Anne Evans calls out, "Mal! Where are you? Come turn off the Snakes. I think we've heard enough."

Mal doesn't answer or appear.

"What's wrong with him?"

"I hope he's not unwell."

"Do you think we should leave?"

"With all that food and drink? No way."

So, the party goes on without its host. The Snakes go on too. *For many a year, I've been around to steal your worthless faith.*

When the wine bottles are near to empty and the buffet has become sparse, the party goers begin to depart with goodbye hugs and kisses, multiples of, "See you soon," and still no Mal.

On the way home, Ginnie asks Edmund, "What did you think about my surprise?"

"A good idea, just not sure that was the place to do it."

Ginnie gives a broad smile, reminding him of the Cheshire cat. "Oh, it was the perfect place to do it!"

Early the next morning, Edmund answers a phone call on their land line. It's for Ginnie from her cousin Sam, the provost. "Yes, she's awake," Edmund says, and hands her the receiver.

She becomes more and more upset as she listens to what her cousin has to say; then she slams down the phone and turns to Edmund. "Mal called Sam at home to point out that many of our donors might withhold their contributions if Bethel starts teaching religion. Sam sloughed him off, so Mal took it to Richard, the Dean of Humanities—that spineless worm. I think Mal has him hooked on drugs too. This is Alabama! There aren't even enough atheists on our donor list to make a dent! He just doesn't want to lose his free cocaine, so he's going to cancel my course—and the new degree!" Her face reddens in anger. "I will not let Mal Hawkins crucify my program!"

Edmund follows behind her, picking up the pillows and clothes she throws all around the bedroom. "You're resourceful. You'll come up with something."

And of course, she does. Ginnie makes another phone call, applying her forte, a razor-sharp ability to uncover a person's defects—an ability she comes by naturally. Before they died, her parents were legal malpractice lawyers. Unafraid to probe and unveil disreputable lawyers, they won many lucrative cases all over the state of Alabama and beyond. The highly respected law firm they founded in Huntsville still exists and is run by an associate who worked closely with them, Chris Gray. Ginnie stays on the phone with Chris for at least an hour listening to his advice, then puts down the phone and sits quietly on the end of the bed, her eyes gazing at nothing as she makes her plan.

"What are you thinking?" Edmund asks.

"I'm going to pay a visit to Richard," she says calmly. "After all, it's Saturday and I've got all day. I'm going to point out a few of his seamy flaws I've just learned about from Chris, and then make it clear those imperfections will be extremely interesting to my cousin Sam, the provost."

"Are you sure about that?" Edmund wonders if she'll tell her cousin about Mal and the cocaine. If she reports that, will she mention him? Or get him cut off from the drugs too? "It's pretty cold-blooded."

"Not nearly as cold-blooded as Mal."

She dresses and leaves the house, not returning until late in the afternoon. Edmund is putting a frozen pizza in the oven when she comes into the kitchen, smiling. She slaps her car keys onto the counter. "Okay! My course and the degree program are back on track," she says as if she's reclaimed her territory and never doubted that she would.

Edmund hugs her. "That's great." But his spine tingles as he wonders whether his own secrets are still safe.

His cell phone rings—Mal, whose ears are everywhere, must have learned about the reinstatement.

"Answer it," Ginnie commands.

Mal starts talking at once. His voice is loud enough for Ginnie to hear, and he's angry. "Why didn't you stop her? Whose side are you on?"

"I'm not taking sides." Despite his misgivings, Edmund is impressed by Ginnie's vigor.

"Lukewarm, huh?" Mal scoffs. "Look, let me tell you one thing. I happen to know that even your grandfather's so-called god doesn't tolerate *lukewarms*. Better hope he doesn't spit you out of his mouth!" He says it like it will be a while before the door of his house will be open to Edmund.

He glances at Ginnie.

Her face hardens. "You don't need him." She pronounces each word emphatically. Lukewarm, she is not!

Edmund doesn't disagree. To do so now would not be in his best interest; but in his mind, he perceives this new conflict as a threat to his ongoing "therapy" with Mal.

Love the animals, love the plants, love everything.
If you love everything, you will perceive the divine mystery in things.
—Fyodor Dostoevsky

CHAPTER SEVEN

Alma

Though Aunt Pauline and Alma's mother, Moline, are twins, they are surely not identical in appearance or mindset. Aunt Pauline is well-educated with a degree in philosophy, which she never fails to use in what she deems her "daily study of the mysteries of life." She is good at making promises too, but not so good at keeping them. Three times promising "until death we do part" is just one example.

Aunt Pauline is rather short, with graying, fox-colored hair, bright crystal-blue eyes, and is generally intolerant of certain people—the people she calls "sinners." But sometimes, when she says the word, Aunt Pauline gives a tender side-glance to Alma's mother, a fleeting look of disappointment, even grief, for a woman who's never promised "until death we do part." It's as if Aunt Pauline has seen trouble in Alma's mother's soul and weeps for her.

Aunt Pauline should have been a nun, except a nun has to keep promises—which isn't her forte, considering she dumped the first husband for the second, and the second for the third, and the third for a life with her then pregnant and unmarried sister Moline. She loves her sister better than she had any of her husbands, she often tells Alma.

"On the day I learned you were on your way into the world, my fickle past came to an end," Aunt Pauline said years ago. Then she pinched Alma's cheek.

This morning, Alma's mother is engrossed in the final scene of Chancee's twenty-year-old movie when Jose comes in to tell Aunt Pauline that he will soon take down the dilapidated barbed wire fence and replace it with something less hazardous. "I know a new barbed wire fence is cheaper and that the chickens don't wander out very far," Jose says, "but barbed wire is dangerous for wildlife."

Aunt Pauline raises a hand to her heart. At once, there are tears in her eyes. "Oh, Jose, I remember the owl you once found trapped in it. The poor thing was so badly hurt!"

Alma's mother has left the room but is within hearing distance as she surveys herself in the hall mirror, checking out the hot-pink highlights she recently put in her hair to match Chancee's. She says without turning, "Goodness, Pauline, don't be so utterly dramatic. It was only an owl!"

The owl was near death by the time Jose cut it free and gently carried it to the farm in a blanket. Like a baby, Alma thought. She and Angelina helped him nurse it back to health in a homemade cage. The owl had only been about a foot tall, with dark eyes and a white, heart-shaped, almost human-looking face. On its underside were reddish brown speckles, and it had a wingspan of about three feet. Jose said it was a female barn owl and that as a boy in Mexico he saw many owls like it. Then he relayed to the girls what his grandmother once told him. "Don't keep secrets, Jose. Owls will not tolerate secrets. If you ever have any skeletons in your closet, reveal them right away because an owl will find them out and be sure they come to light."

"Do you have any secrets, Papa?" Angelina asked, teasing him with a smile.

Jose was feeding the owl one of the small rats Alma and Angelina had found in the field for it to eat. He shrugged his shoulders as the owl swallowed the rat whole. "If I do, I don't think about them, mi niña." Then he left quickly to go tend the chickens.

When the owl was well enough to let go, Alma and Angelina watched it fly away. "I wasn't sure the owl would live. It was so badly injured," Angelina said, looking up at the sky. "But just look at her now. I think it's a miracle, don't you?"

"Yes, I do."

"I'm waiting for a miracle like that," Angelina said softly.

Alma hugged her. "You will have it. One day, your disease will be gone, and you'll be as well and free as that owl."

Alma thought miracles happened every day, especially when people helped them along. Once, Alma was alone in the pasture and saw a baby deer caught in the dinosaur-like fence. It still had its spots and must have tried to jump over the barbed wire. Even then, the old fence had only three of the five strands left, but it was still too high for a fawn. The little deer's back legs were entangled on the two lower strands, and it cried pitifully, a high-pitched cry like a human baby. Alma had to do something to help it. So, she responded as Jose or Aunt Pauline would have. Stretching the strands with one bare hand and lifting the fawn's legs with the other, she freed the young animal. How bloody her palms and fingers were as she watched him scamper away!

Well, she thought, the letting of one's own blood to save lives can produce a miracle. That's why, as soon as she turned sixteen, she donated blood to Angelina, and afterwards, Angelina went into remission. For miracles like that, she'd give her blood to Angelina whenever she needed it.

The devil would be powerless
if he couldn't entice people to do his work.
—Idowu Koyenikan

CHAPTER EIGHT

Mal

M al shifts in his armchair and stares at the drawer where the gun sits, waiting to do its duty.

When Edmund first announced his engagement to Ginnie, Mal wasn't affected. He didn't know anything about her then except that she was new in the English Department. He pictured her as someone on the same wavelength as Edmund—a fool. But on the day of her marriage to Edmund, his opinion of her drastically changed.

Ginnie immediately seemed familiar, like someone he'd come across before, someone who tried to alter him in the minds of others. Someone like his silly sister, Charity, who fell to her knees before her non-existent God and ridiculously prayed for him, though he knew that prayers were not what he'd get from Ginnie.

He remembers the look of superiority she gave him when Edmund introduced him as his best man—as if she already knew Mal and felt nothing but disdain for him. He recalls her stinging aloofness when she said, "Thank you for serving Edmund as his best man." Serving Edmund! And without addressing him by name, as if he was a nobody instead of an important professor. Oh, he remembers that for certain!

He goes over it, again and again, page by page in his mind—her lackluster gratitude for him at the wedding reception and how she turned her back on him while greeting the other guests with hugs and kisses and laughter.

He sits in his chair and nurses his hatred, letting it grow larger and larger.

He remembers walking over to the group of professors to whom she was talking, thinking he could win her over, but she saw him coming. Her smile turned to a threatening frown as if to say, "I know who you really are." Then she deliberately turned away.

He would not stand for such disregard! He tried again, striding across the room to her while she was in the middle of a conversation. She twisted around, her white wedding gown swishing as she looked at him like he was a bothersome bug she wanted to swat. Her eyes, he recalls, questioned him—what do you want? But she didn't say a word even when the crowd around her became quiet, waiting for one of them to speak.

He forced himself to break the silence so that he would not lose face. "I've heard good things about you," he lied, insinuating the good things came from Edmund, though he'd never asked Edmund about Ginnie. She gave him a half-smile but said nothing. Not one word. He couldn't think of anything else to say, at least in front of his colleagues, so the lie smoldered in his mouth. Truthfully, there was nothing good about her, nothing equal to his own capabilities.

But his colleagues did not share that opinion.

He cringes as he remembers Henry Patton breaking the silence. "You're right, Mal. Ginnie is very well-liked by her students. I knew her parents, and I've known Ginnie since she was a girl. She came highly recommended."

Anne Evans joined in. "Yes, she's very intelligent. Plus, she's pretty as a picture."

And then Jim Brackin, Assistant Professor of Mathematics. "She ought to be chosen for department head next term. She's as smart as they come!"

Oh, how jealousy, despise, and anger erupted inside him!

Even now, he bristles at Ginnie's replies. "Thanks so much," and, "Oh my goodness, you are sweet to say so." He clenches his fists around the arms of his chair. Though he did not like the Dean of Social Sciences—Mal wanted the job for himself—he followed Henry Patton across the room when the crowd of Ginnie-worshipers began to disperse, and then stopped him in the parking lot to learn more about Edmund's new wife.

He grits his teeth as he recalls his words to Henry. "I suppose they'll make a great couple. You seem to know a lot about her."

"Oh yes," Dr. Patton answered, "you won't find a better person than Ginnie. She comes from a great Catholic family."

Even now, Mal stiffens in his chair just as he stiffened at that moment when Patton continued, "Her parents were both malpractice lawyers from Huntsville. They're deceased now, but her daddy used to say that he could smell a devil from four blocks away, trip him up, and get him convicted the same day. I don't think Ginnie's any different. Fights for what she believes in, you know."

He ignored that Patton was his boss as well as Edmund's and poked him with a final question. "Just what does she believe in?"

Patton gave him a glare. "Probably everything you don't."

Mal remembers that exchange—it was the moment he perceived Ginnie as his greatest adversary, one he must take down. Of course, he immediately saw Edmund as the tool. No matter how long it took, he knew the time would come when Edmund would be ripe enough to do his bidding.

Mal sighs and stretches back in his chair. He enjoys watching the disintegration of Edmund bit by bit. But now that Ginnie has embarrassed him in his own house, the time has come to make the final move. It's time for Edmund, the fool, to take down his own wife.

There are two ways to live: as if nothing is a miracle,
or as if everything is a miracle.
—Albert Einstein

CHAPTER NINE

Alma

Alma slips out of bed and dresses to walk alone in the pasture, a daily routine she began when the school year ended a few weeks earlier. The cool morning air cuts through the thinning material of her favorite pajamas—faded red flannel Christmas pajamas imprinted with snowmen. They are noticeably too small and marred by a hole in one knee from where she snagged it on a wire in the chicken house when she was helping Jose throw out some feed. She pressed a patch on it, but it has come off and the hole is widening. Aunt Pauline promised to sew it up, but of course she hasn't.

Alma stops to watch the squirrels contort themselves on the fence rails like tiny, static statues of Buddha, their tails curling around them like crossed knees.

The Broussards' house is ten miles from Bethel, the twins' beloved hometown, on fifty acres of old family land that was once a profitable peanut farm run by the twins' stoic, hard-faced but soft-hearted father. The old man was a fierce opponent of the Catholic Church, but that never kept Alma from loving him. When Alma was seven years old, Aunt Pauline—who believed in telling the truth to anyone who'd reached the age of reason, which Alma had, according to her and the Catholic Church—sat her niece down and told her that she didn't have to like everything about a person in order to love them because nobody was perfect, not even Alma. "So, Alma," she said, "be aware of the things you do in life because they can cause some people to break. You should know that your mother and I have been guilty of that kind of breaking. My beloved father, your grandfather, had his first heart attack over my conversion to the Catholic Church—a conversion for which I've never been sorry, even though it was to please the third man I married. Then, your grandfather had his last one, the heart attack that nearly killed him, when your mother gave birth to you without being married at all."

Alma stared at her aunt, taking in a bigger picture of her family. She had never heard that Aunt Pauline had been married three times, or that her mother was never married to her father. Yet, she hadn't been bothered by any of it, or loved her mother and aunt less. If anything, she loved them more, and tried to use that love to heal the brokenness she saw inside them.

From the pasture, Alma notices her aunt heading down the red dirt road in her yellow bathrobe printed with daisies. She's heading to unlock the gate that seals off the paved county road from the red dirt road leading up to the house.

They used to leave it unlocked, only closing it to keep predators away from the chickens. Then, one morning, Pauline discovered footprints in the red dirt too large to be any of theirs, and she was certain some vagrant or crook was milling around on the property. At once, she went to the hardware store and bought a new padlock with a key. Now, every night before dark, Aunt Pauline leaves the house, walks down the red dirt road, and locks the gate. And every morning, she goes back to unlock it for easy daytime exit and any expected delivery men.

Alma can't imagine feeling compelled to lock out the world that way, to hide from other human souls. If there were vagrants, shouldn't they feed them, give them shelter? At least pray for them? She asked Aunt Pauline those questions a few days after she bought the padlock.

"Well, yes, we should pray for them." Aunt Pauline pointed a stiff index finger in Alma's direction. "But remember, praying for someone who is homeless does not mean they won't try to take *your* home and harm you in the trying. A homeless person can be just as evil as a man who lives in a mansion. One more of life's mysteries."

Alma heads toward the gate as her aunt unlocks it. The six-by-three-foot rectangular sign Jose built to advertise the chicken business still stands next to it. The girls painted the sign together years earlier—purple on white—when Alma was three and Angelina was five. Angelina's misspelled words are still readable: Chickin Eggs. Hole Sale. Or Jist You. Angelina painted three perfect white ovals to advertise the eggs—the last thing she drew for a long time. Only weeks afterward, she was diagnosed with leukemia and grew too sick to draw anymore.

"Aunt Pauline," Alma says as she and her aunt return up the dirt road toward the house, "Why would God allow Angelina to be so sick?"

Aunt Pauline hugs her. "We can't know the mind of God any more than a grasshopper can know the mind of a human being. All we can do is trust that what He allows will somehow turn out to be good."

Today is good, Alma thinks. *Today, Angelina is in remission, out of the hospital, and at home. Because of me.*

She and Aunt Pauline reach the house and go inside. "Have to be Me" is playing upstairs in Moline's room. Alma puts bread in the toaster while Aunt Pauline hangs the key to the gate on a hook under the kitchen counter. "Are you going to visit Angelina today?"

"Yes, I can't wait to see her."

Abruptly, the music stops, and Moline hurries downstairs in her pink polyester uniform. "Good morning, my darling girl." She kisses Alma on the top of her head, leaving behind the strong scent of *Crazy in the Head* perfume. It's from Chancee's latest beauty line, immediately purchased by Moline. On sale for seventy-five dollars an ounce.

Aunt Pauline fans her face. "That stuff gives me a headache."

Moline ignores her. "I hope you've unlocked the gate, Sister. I'm running a little late, and don't need any roadblocks in my way."

"She always unlocks it," Alma says, defending Pauline.

Moline grabs a piece of toast. "Good. But your aunt is too suspicious, you know. It's hard to enjoy your life if you're suspicious of everyone in it."

"I am not suspicious of everyone, Sister. Only those who deserve it."

"Ah, Pauline, while you're locking and unlocking gates, you're missing the best of life. I'd like to tell you all about why, but I'd better run." She opens the kitchen door to go to her car then turns and grins. "And by the way, most anybody can pick a lock."

After her mother drives off, Alma heads to the stairs. "I'm going to get dressed and then go visit Angelina."

"I made a squash casserole for her and Jose." Pauline opens the refrigerator and places the casserole on the counter. "Will you take it when you go?"

"Sure."

When Alma arrives at Jose's house, he has already left to tend to the chickens, so Alma puts the casserole in their refrigerator then goes into Angelina's room and finds her sitting on the side of the bed, looking pale but relieved. "Did you hear I'm in remission again?"

"Yes. It's wonderful. But you need some sunlight. Let's take a walk."

They walk until they see Jose in the distance, working on the old, barbed wire fence. He waves them forward.

Despite Alma's young age at the time, she still remembers how badly Jose cut his hands when he put up that fence, even with his gloves on, and how she and Angelina cried when they saw him bleeding. Now the fence is old and weak, surrounding the pasture like the ragged bones of a dinosaur in the movie her mother and Aunt Pauline watched on Saturday.

"It's a wonderful day, isn't it?" Alma says when they reach Jose. "The air itself smells like kindness."

Jose comes over to hug his daughter and then Alma. "Remission can do that. But the honeysuckle vines are responsible for that sweet smell." Jose is a natural teacher and shows them the blossoms on the fence. "See how some of the honeysuckle blooms are snowy white while others have yellowed? The yellow blooms are the older ones, those already pollinated by bees and butterflies, or brushed against by animals. The white blooms are the newborns, the untouched innocents, same as the baby chicks that peck around the legs of their mothers, never wandering too far away. We have some eggs that should be hatching about now. Let's go see if they are."

The farm is mostly egg-producing hens, with only a few roosters around to produce baby chicks. Jose shoos one of the roosters away and leads them inside the 500-square-foot coop to the hatching area. Sure enough, several fledglings are breaking from their eggs, one of them working harder than the others to peck its way out. Jose puts a gentle finger on the cracking shell to ease the breaking, and the tiny chick emerges from the pieces, its feathers wet and its tiny breast throbbing. "No matter how many times I see this," he says, "I think it's a miracle."

In spite of Angelina's illness, Alma believes Jose sees the world in the same positive light that she does—a world where miracles often come out of fractured things and bring new life with them. After a while, Jose ushers them out of the coop and goes back to working on the fences.

Alma and Angelina walk back to the house and sit in the front porch swing. Angelina's face is rosy and her movements much less strained than usual. "I'm so happy you're in remission," Alma says. "You look much better than you did in the hospital."

Angelina touches her arm. "Could it be your good blood?"

"I'm glad I'm old enough now. I always wanted to donate."

"Papa told me you'd asked. And when you were finally able to, I think he was as worried about you as he was about me. I was a little worried too. I still don't think you weigh a hundred and ten pounds," Angelina teases.

"Jose was worried about me?" Alma recalls the paper father she drew. The drawing looked a little like Jose, though Jose is taller and darker than the father in a suit that she imagined, and she's never seen Jose in a coat and tie. "I wish Jose was my father too."

"You couldn't have a better one."

"I've always thought of you as my sister, Angelina."

"You are my sister, my blood sister, now that I have your blood in my veins."

"A lot of people say we look alike too. Your mother must have had blond hair and blue eyes like ours."

"I don't remember her at all. Papa said she died when I was a baby, but I think I saw a picture of her once, when I was looking for something in Papa's bureau. The picture was underneath his clothes. I don't know if it was of my mother, but I think it was."

"I'll bet she was as beautiful as you are."

"Well, she did look like me. I haven't asked Papa much about her though. I don't want to make him sad. He has enough to worry about." She turns to Alma. "So now that you're sixteen, are you going to learn to drive?"

"Of course I am. I've been talking about it with Mama and Aunt Pauline. And when I get my license, I'll drive you wherever you want to go."

As soon as she gets home, Alma brings up driving lessons, but only with Aunt Pauline, who seems the safer bet. "Yes. I should be the one to do it," Aunt Pauline agrees. "Your mother—you know I love her—but she understands nothing about a vehicle except the foot peddle that allows her to go as fast as she can and the brake that allows her to come to a neck-popping stop. Moline has no conception that she can control her own car. Instead, she lets it control her, as if something inanimate made of metal and rubber has any sort of brain!" Then Pauline insists on using her own car for the lessons. "My car is less used to dangerous mistakes. Besides, my car is visited by a cardinal. It comes every day to look at itself in the side view mirror. Some say it's a blessing, but I don't know if that's true." Pauline gives a quick laugh. "It may be the bird is plainly vain like your mother."

Alma has seen the bird herself—a beautiful red cardinal clinging to the window casing of Pauline's car, pecking at its reflection in the side mirror.

"I asked Jose about it once," Alma says. "He told me that his mother used to say that when cardinals are here, angels are near. And he said he'd read that a cardinal mates for life and the two are inseparable. Maybe he thinks he's found a mate in your car mirror."

The next morning at breakfast, as if she's been thinking about it all night, Aunt Pauline says, "I believe something must have happened to the bird's mate. The cardinal thinks he sees her again in his own image in the side mirror of my car. That's why he's always there pecking."

"That's the silliest thing I've ever heard, Sister," Moline replies as she butters her piece of toast then piles strawberry preserves on top. "Anyway, female cardinals are brown, not red, so he can't see a female in his own image."

"I don't care if she's brown or red. My car is blessed. That bird sees a lifelong love in his own image, like God sees us. And that is a blessing!"

"Sister, I don't think your degree in philosophy was about the mindset of birds, was it? And lifelong love? You of all people should rethink that one."

Aunt Pauline scowls and leaves the room.

For Alma, the idea of lifelong love, even from a bird, thrills her. She doesn't mean to take Pauline's side over her mother's, but she researches the cardinal on the computer in the chicken business office and finds an article entitled, "When a Red Cardinal Visits You, It's a Visitor from Heaven." Just as Pauline said—a blessing. She prints a copy, and that afternoon, before her mother gets home from work, she gives it to Aunt Pauline to read.

The next morning, Aunt Pauline sits across the table from her twin. Her blue eyes sparkle as if she has something to talk about and can't wait to get to it. "It is not silly to say the cardinal is blessed, Moline. It's symbolic, and here is the proof." She slaps the article down on the table in front of Moline. "The cardinal's red color signifies the Blood of Christ. It is a sign that God is present, urging us to let go of all our hurtful problems from the past and trust him with the problems we have today. Read it and see."

Moline tightens her lips and fingers the article, leaving a sticky handprint of bright red strawberry preserves on the back of the paper. She reads it quickly. When she finishes, she wipes her hands with a napkin for quite a while. Then, as if a sense of resentfulness has set in, she says to Pauline, "Alright. Maybe your car is blessed. But what I don't understand is why God sent that cardinal to your car instead of mine? I park it right next to yours. It doesn't seem fair God wouldn't pick mine. After all, I have a lot more problems than you."

"It's not about the number of problems you have. It's about whether you get through them by trusting in God. But first, you have to listen to Him—another reason why you should start RCIA and become Catholic."

Alma cringes. She knows her mother's reaction will be the same as it always is when Aunt Pauline challenges her to join the Church.

Moline shoves her chair back from the table so hard her neck pops backward. The legs of the chair passing over the tile floor emit a screeching sound exactly like a car braking at top speed. "Oh, you people!" She snatches up her cellphone and heads for the back door while hitting number one on her playlist. Then she turns the volume as high as it will go. "Chancee Wile is Live!" a voice shouts. At once, Chancee belts out her ten-million dollar song from ten years before, "I Don't Listen to Nobody but Me!" And the sound of a crowd from the past screams her praise.

Even Satan disguises himself as an angel of light.
So it is no surprise if his servants also disguise themselves
as servants of righteousness. Their end will correspond to their needs.
—2 Corinthians 11:14-15 ESV

CHAPTER TEN

Edmund

After the debacle over Ginnie's new degree program, Mal bans Edmund from coming to his house. But it doesn't worry him much. With Mal, bans and the lifting of bans is business as usual.

About a week later, just after the start of the fall term, Mal calls him. "I have to say, I miss our conversations, Edmund. I don't think we ought to let your overly assertive wife push either one of us around, do you? So why don't you come over tomorrow evening?"

Give it up, Edmund! Get rid of it! The old preacher shouts inside his head once more, just as he did on the first night Mal gave him cocaine shortly after his engagement to Ginnie. Afterwards—after his night in the motel room with the woman in red patent leather boots—self-reproach devoured him, and he swore he'd never take the drug again. For a while after their marriage, he did not. He stayed away from Mal and concentrated only on Ginnie, his degree, and research for another publishable article. He was happier then, even a little proud of himself. But he knew he was weak, certainly weaker than Ginnie. Though he loved her strength and convictions, he began to resent those qualities because he lacked them.

Little by little, as the headaches and the voices grew worse, his craving for Mal and his drugs returned.

As Edmund prepares to leave for his usual "run" to Mal's, he opens the front door, and for a split second, feels cool air on the back of his neck. Is it Ginnie's breath? Is she waiting behind him? He considers turning around to kiss her, to lead her to the bedroom and make passionate love to her. He could say he's sorry, that he won't go to Mal's tonight or any other night. But he doesn't. With a bang, he shuts the door and heads off, imagining the lines of cocaine the professor will set out for him.

Once there, he's disappointed. Mal offers him marijuana instead, setting a plate full of joints on the glass coffee table between them as Ginnie might set out a snack. Mal doesn't take a joint; he never takes his own drugs. But that makes sense; he is the doctor, and Edmund is the patient.

Edmund smokes two or three joints while unburdening himself with a recitation of his grandfather's rants while Mal sits across from him in a plush velvet chair sniffing, or frowning, or raising his chin disapprovingly. Then, looking bored, the psychologist gets up, goes to his desk, and opens a drawer. Edmund stops talking and watches, hoping to see Mal take out the cocaine he never buys himself.

When Mal turns to face him with a gun in his hand, Edmund gasps and jerks backward.

Mal's clay-colored skin hangs on the sharp bones of his face, creased by his wry smile and narrowed eyes. He tosses the gun into Edmund's lap and sits across from him again. "Now, you're in control, just like the old man says you should be."

Edmund sits motionless, wondering what he's expected to do.

"Take the gun! Hold it!" Mal orders. "Be in charge!"

Take it! Hold it! Be in charge! More words from his past—words his grandfather yelled at him on the day he first took Edmund hunting. *To make a man out of you,* his grandfather said as he pulled a gun out of its holster and shoved it into Edmund's boyish hands while two wild hogs bolted out of the woods and rushed toward them. Edmund stood petrified with the gun dangling at his side. *Don't dither! Do something, Edmund! Be decisive!*

Then, seeing that Edmund would not take charge, the old man snatched the gun from him and shot both hogs dead.

Edmund shakes his head to get rid of the memory and studies Mal's gun in his lap, almost a replica of the old man's gun from all those years ago. Mal is supposed to be helping him adjust to his past, but this is unnerving, not helpful at all. Still, Edmund lifts the revolver as if he has no power to do otherwise. At once, the weight of it in his hand invigorates him. His grandfather taught him about guns. This one is a Bersa Thunder .380 with an exposed hammer, steel slide, and an aluminum alloy frame. Surprisingly, the gun feels good in his hand, a salve to the uselessness he feels about himself. He looks over at Mal and sees the professor smiling triumphantly.

"Your grandfather is dead," Mal says, "and—I should hardly have to say this, because we both know it well—the god he holds over you was never alive. It's you who invented both their rants, so it's you who must get rid of their voices." He laughs, then, and throws up his hands as if it is all a joke. "Of course, the gun is only a symbol to remind you of that." He taps his fingers on the arm of the chair, waiting for Edmund's response.

Edmund supposes what Mal said is simple. Even reasonable. The gun is merely a symbol of death—and the voices inside him need to die as surely his grandfather did. His body has lain for years under the ground in Heaven's Gate Cemetery.

"Maybe he is dead," Edmund agrees, not sure if he means God or his grandfather.

Mal stands quickly. "*Maybe* is not the correct answer." He grabs the gun from Edmund's hand and tosses it back into the drawer as if he is tired of bothering with someone mindless. He nods toward the six joints still on the table, the booby prize for Edmund in a game he's lost. "Take a few of those home with you. I'm not sure I can help you tonight." And tilting his head to meet Edmund's gaze, he says sharply, "Maybe next time." Mal gives a knowing smile. "That is, if your wife will let you out next time."

When he is halfway down the steps, Mal calls to him. "I am a noble man, Edmund. I said I would help you with your problems, and I will. But on my terms."

Edmund turns to look at him, wondering if he's supposed to thank him. He says nothing.

On his way home, his thoughts about Mal and then Ginnie jumble together in his head. Will there be a next time with Mal? If Ginnie had anything to do with it, there wouldn't be. Will he have to choose between them? Who is right? Mal, who says he is noble yet puts drugs and even a gun into his hand? Or Ginnie, who is always questioning him, challenging him, pushing him in ways he thinks himself too inadequate to go?

Edmund first met Mal in the student union building. He was days away from beginning his master's degree, and he did not know Ginnie at the time—though by then, she was at the university, too, teaching and living with her cousin, Dr. Sam Williams, who happened to be provost, and his wife, Betty.

Impeccably dressed in a suit and tie, Mal was sitting at the head of a table like a king surrounded by his surrogates, several male students who were listening to him, seeming to hang on his every word. As Edmund passed by the table, Mal called out, "Mr. Gillan," and then motioned. "Come and sit."

Edmund stared at him, wondering who he was and how he knew his name.

Mal stood and introduced himself as a professor in the Psychology Department.

"Dr. Hawkins is a great professor." One of the students gave a devious laugh. "Private sessions, you know, to take away our worries and keep us all mentally fit."

"Sure," Mal said a little too quickly. "Any time, Mr. Gillan. We can talk about all your problems. I'm a very good listener."

That's when it started, the nights at Mal's; innocently at first, when Edmund believed this great professor might help him calm his headaches and send his grandfather and his sermons back to the cemetery where they belonged. Edmund had not yet come undone—at least, not in the sight of others.

The first time he showed up at Mal's door, he hesitated and then forced himself to knock. After waiting a full minute, he turned around to leave, but then, the door opened and there stood Mal, smiling. "Come in, Mr. Gillan." He ushered him into his living room with an open palm. "Have a seat over there by the fireplace."

Mal was charming and complimentary, almost as if he were grooming Edmund for something grand like a real father might groom his son. "Oh, I can see it now, Edmund," he said on that first night when Edmund mentioned his strong ties to his preacher grandfather. "With the right guidance, you're going to be a great teacher. We just have to get rid of a few of the useless voices in your head, the ones that try to control you. We'll replace them with something else, something stronger than they are."

Mal made no mention of what that something would be. There was no offer of drugs then. But as the headaches got worse, Mal had done what any good doctor would; he provided relief, until at last, it was only the cocaine that kept Edmund coming back.

But never before had there been a visit like the one tonight. Never anything like the gun in his lap.

When he returns home after his alarming meeting with Mal, Edmund finds a clean kitchen, so typical of Ginnie, who likes everything neat and in its place. Naturally, she has put away dinner because he wouldn't eat it when and where she wanted. Mal would say it is her way of dominating him.

Through the open bedroom door, he sees Ginnie in bed, probably pretending to be asleep.

He isn't hungry anyway, he tells himself, despite the gnawing in his stomach caused by the marijuana. He takes out one of the joints Mal gave him to take home and sits in a rocking chair on the small back porch to smoke. The chair is an old one he bought when Ginnie thought she might be pregnant. She wasn't, of course. Another of his malfunctions. She began praying the rosary for a baby, prayed it nightly for quite a long time. He couldn't say how long, and he couldn't say he was sorry that she hadn't gotten pregnant, though she might have been a good mother. But what would he, Edmund, do with a child except ruin him or her?

He gets ready for bed and slips in beside Ginnie, taking a deep breath and feeling relaxed from the marijuana. Again, he thinks about the gun, and as if to excuse it in some way, he says aloud, "Mal is a noble man."

Ginnie sits up at once. He can almost smell her rage. "Falsely noble. You're not thinking straight. He is using you, Edmund. He'll do nothing for you unless it's good for him too. He's poison!"

He tenses. Her maligning of Mal, and Edmund's defense of him, has become all too frequent.

"Mal recommended me to the provost. I wouldn't have my position without him."

"He did not!" She slides off the bed and stands to point a finger, angling it toward him like a yellow jacket ready to sting. "That's the garbage he's putting in your head. I'm the one who recommended you to Sam. Remember?"

He frowns, remembering correctly now. She recommended him when she heard the sociology position was open. After all, Sam Williams, the provost, was her cousin. Had Mal tried to rewrite the past while Edmund was high?

"Well, Mal helps me cope with my headaches."

"Helping you cope through drugs? Is that noble?"

"He says the drugs are for my greater good."

"Making you an addict? Is that your greater good? The man is a pure narcissist. He's the one who needs help. Why can't you see that?"

Edmund fills with fury. Ginnie sounds like his lunatic grandfather. "I don't have to please you. You don't tell me what to do!"

She stares at him for a moment, her blue eyes wide with ire. But she does not say a word, only turns toward the edge of the bed, moving as far away from him as she can get.

She is still enraged the next morning. She slams down the coffee carafe so hard, it's a wonder it doesn't break. "You don't see him for what he is, Edmund. He's a predator. Don't trust him. Run from him! The man is godless, and somebody needs to stop him!"

"Stop him?"

"Yes! If you knew what he's really after, you wouldn't give him the time of day."

"What do you mean by that?"

She glares at him for a moment then snatches up a stack of papers from the counter. "I don't have time to go into it. I don't want to be late for my meeting with Sam." She shakes her head at him and slams the door as she leaves.

A short while later, Edmund stands at his teacher podium, repeating one of his many memorized lessons on social ethics. "It was Aristotle who first described human beings as social animals because our human world is a social world. Ethics is between our self and the other." The well-practiced jargon simply rolls off his tongue, but his mind does not connect his words to his own actions. Vacantly, he continues. "Ethical conflicts and dilemmas are a part of the human condition. We live with the 'other,' and our sense of empathy for the other plays a major part in whether our humanity, or our inhumanity, comes forward."

Of course, his thoughts are not concerned with any part empathy might play in his own life. His thoughts return to Ginnie and Mal and their aversion to each other. He thinks about the significance of Mal tossing a gun in his lap, and that he hasn't told Ginnie about it. He knows what she will say: "Do not go over there again! Stay away from Mal." The thought of not seeing Mal anymore disturbs him so much that he goes blank in front of the class. He cannot remember the rest of his memorized lesson. Instead, he raises a fiery voice. "This lecture is over for now. You may go!"

He watches his students depart. They look happy to be leaving. Leaving him? Is he good enough to ever be hired for a tenure-track position? Not if his students don't like him. Will they say they don't like him to his boss, Henry Patton? Now he questions his own value, even as an adjunct professor. But he appreciates his students, and he knows that on better days than this one, they appreciate him, too.

Just before the summer, in the Student Union cafeteria, three or four girls from his morning class sat down at his table to eat lunch with him and said, "We just love you, Professor Gillan."

"Yes, we enjoy your classes." It meant a lot to him that they felt comfortable enough around him to chatter about themselves, about their parents, even a problem or two. He listened when they talked and found himself opening up to them as if he'd known them for a long time.

When one of them asked where he was from, he told them about the historic house in Montgomery where he'd lived, and a little about his childhood—only happy things. "The house was big and beautiful, and there was a graveyard behind it where I used to play. Revolutionary War and Civil War soldiers were buried there."

"Wow! Were they related to you?"

"Yes, on my mother's side." He swelled with pride. "Some had actually lived in the house before they went to war and were killed."

"They were heroes, I'm sure," another girl said. "You lived in a house of heroes, Professor Gillan! Not many can say that."

He knew he had not inherited any hero genes, but he accepted the compliment with a smile.

Why didn't he finish his lecture on human beings as social animals? How had he reached this point? Was it the drugs—or the lack of them? He sits in his classroom a while, thinking about all he could have said about humans longing for approval. Approval is what he wants to see in Ginnie's eyes. He doesn't want Ginnie to think him weak when she has no weakness at all.

"Be honest, Edmund," she shouted the night before when he returned from Mal's. "If he can't ruin you himself, he'll see that someone else does! That's the kind of person he is."

Edmund doesn't agree with her, but he should have told her about the gun. Mal called it a symbol, yet it still seemed menacing. Maybe Ginnie could help him figure out what Mal meant by it. She would certainly have an opinion on the sudden appearance of a gun—but she also teaches English literature. Symbols are supposed to be her expertise.

He decides to send her a text. "Would you like to go out for dinner tonight? Someplace quiet, so we can talk without arguing?"

She answers at once. "That would be lovely, if you'll be honest about yourself."

"I'll be honest." Though he wasn't sure about that. "Mangiamo's at six?"

She texts him a red heart. Edmund smiles, but his smile disappears quickly when he realizes that he can't be honest. He hasn't been honest in all the years of their marriage, packing away his pain and fears, reinforcing the shell he's built around himself. He can't tell her how lost he is, how alienated he often feels, so overly cautious and indecisive in his life, his marriage, his career. Why would a woman like Ginnie—a rising star, soon to be the head of her own degree program—want someone like him? She might throw up her hands and leave him, maybe even find someone who suits her better. Maybe she would seek out her dermatologist. In Edmund's opinion, she visits him too regularly as it is.

After her last appointment, he looked up the address for the dermatology clinic, wrote it down on a torn-off edge of paper, and put it into his wallet just in case he—what?—wanted to spy on her? No, he only wanted to see the place where she spent her time away from him.

He decided to drive by the place. What a surprise! A kind of startling yet rotten joke. He hadn't realized the dermatology clinic was in the building that had once been his grandfather's holiness church. Of course, the cross on the rooftop was removed, but the building had the same peaked roof and arched windows he remembered from childhood. He pulled into the parking lot and sat in his car, befuddled, for quite a long while. Was it some sort of malicious sign to accompany the old preacher's voice in his head, some sort of omen? Or was it just coincidence? Ginnie certainly wouldn't know; she wasn't even in Bethel when the building was a church.

Maybe tonight at dinner he should mention the building's reconstruction, from saving human souls to saving human skin. He could use it as a way to mention his problematic headaches, which would be a good lead-in to the voice of the old preacher in his head. Yes, he decides, that's what he will do, so that Ginnie will understand why he needs Mal's help—and maybe even a few drugs.

When he arrives at Mangiamo's Italian Restaurant, Ginnie has already chosen a table in a dimly lit corner, perfect for quiet talk. He walks over to her, bends to kiss her cheek, and then takes the seat across from her with his arms crossed around him as usual.

Ginnie frowns. "Edmund, uncross your arms. You don't need protection from me."

He grits his teeth as he uncrosses them. "I hope not."

After the waiter takes their order, Ginnie looks at him with the lopsided grin that he loves. "Okay, I'm ready for honesty. You first."

He shudders as the timeworn pain of his shrouded wounds reopens. He knows there is much he should tell Ginnie about himself, so much he's kept secret and left to fester since his boyhood, like a young lion dragging a slaughtered carcass to a hiding place and covering it over with branches for later consumption. But even a lion will not leave its catch for long because dead flesh decomposes and will slowly be eaten by maggots, not lions. He wants to tell Ginnie that when his parents and sisters were killed, he was left to spoil, to be devoured inside by his own apprehensions, and that is why he needs Mal.

In his mind he expects her to say, "You don't need him!" but she remains silent.

"You know that my family was killed in an automobile crash—it's how I ended up in Bethel with my grandparents."

She reaches across and touches his fingers, which he has splayed on the white tablecloth. "Yes, you told me. So sad."

"I didn't tell you that I never recovered from the accident. I still have terrible headaches that come and go." He looks into her eyes. She seems to be listening intently. "But even before that, I had a painful childhood." He always feels guilty when he calls his childhood painful because of his affection for his mother. "I loved my mother most and knew that she—only she—loved me. But she didn't protect me."

"Protect you from what?"

"From myself, I think. And maybe my father and sisters. I had a hiding place in the yard to get away from them. My mother would ask, 'Edmund, where are you going?' But when I answered, 'Where I can't be seen,' she didn't wonder why I did not want to be seen, or why I might need a hiding place. She just kept making her pies, and said, 'Well when you come back, you can lick the spoon. I'll save it for you.' I never understood why she did not protect me, when I loved her so. A weak person like me needs protection. It's the reason why I visit Mal. He helps me protect myself."

Ginnie's steady eyes haven't left his face, but at the mention of Mal, they fill with fire. "Edmund, you are not weak! It's Mal who makes you think so. Mal will do anything he can to keep you from acknowledging that fact. He is godless. Honestly, I think he's Satan in disguise, a monster. Mark my words, he will try to make you a monster too."

The waiter returns with their order. The steam rises from the lasagna, making Edmund think of incense and purification. In his mind, he sees Ginnie as an altar girl swinging a censor.

"The last time I saw Mal, he tossed a gun in my lap."

Ginnie gasps. "What for?"

"He said it was only a symbol to...to take control and get rid of the memories of my grandfather."

"That sweet old preacher that raised you?"

"Well, he wasn't exactly what I'd call sweet, and Mal thinks he was a bad influence."

Ginnie forcefully sticks her fork into her lasagna. "I will snatch that man off his pedestal even if I have to die doing it!"

Edmund falters. This isn't going as he planned. He decides not to mention the dermatology clinic and its reconstruction from his grandfather's old church. He takes a deep breath and forces a smile. "How will you do that, my sweet, intelligent wife?" He leaves out "spiteful," though it is certainly first in his mind.

Still, she smiles back. "Turnabout is fair play, my love, when it comes to someone like Mal. His undeserved seat at the table of nobility is about to come to an end."

Let the morning bring me word of your unfailing love,
for I have put my trust in you.
Show me the way I should go, for to you I entrust my life.
—Psalm 143:8 NIV

CHAPTER ELEVEN

Jose

A dozen years have passed since Jose learned of Angelina's leukemia.

The first indication that there was anything wrong came one night when Jose and Angelina were on the screened-in side porch of the Broussard house with Alma, Pauline, and Moline. Pauline was sitting in the porch swing with five-year-old Angelina while Moline rocked Alma, who was three. Jose sat on the steps making up music on the old Gibson guitar his mother had given him long ago, which he'd brought with him from Mexico to Cuba and finally to the United States. Although it was winter, the night was warm.

Pauline put a hand on Angelina's forehead. "Jose, I believe Angelina has a fever. It's probably nothing, but you should take her to see Dr. Roberts in the morning."

So, he took her. He was there all day long with Angelina, and after many days of tests, the doctor came in with his diagnosis. Childhood leukemia. Right then, Jose felt as if his heart were bleeding into his chest, and for a while he hadn't been able to breathe.

Again, they took their places on the side porch, this time with the awful diagnosis strangling their thoughts. "At least it's a lovely night," Pauline said, stroking Angelina's head as she slept beside her in the swing. Jose knew she was trying to lift his spirit, and it truly was a nice evening. There was a half-dollar moon and a gentle, fresh wind that brushed across his face as if he was being consoled by the tender touch of a woman he could not see, a woman like his mother.

"Yes, a lovely night. If only…"

"We have to trust, Jose," Pauline said quickly. "And we will. All of us."

Holding back tears, he nodded yes.

Moline said, "Jose, Angelina will be okay. All she needs is a real good wind to make everything better."

"Yes, only a real good wind," Pauline agreed.

Moline nodded. "Make up a song about that, Jose. Play something to lift us up. A song like Chancee might sing."

Always, Moline deferred to Chancee when it came to the creation of music. And always, Jose heard and ignored it, knowing that any music he created would suit her.

"Alright." He picked up his guitar and went to sit on the top step. Pocketing his melancholy for a while, he struck a few slow, un-Chancee-like chords and began to compose, gathering together his broken thoughts and spinning them into hope. At times, his voice faltered, but he swallowed his tears, cleared his throat, and continued on. The song came from the depths of his heart, swirled around his mind like the fluttering dress of a little girl dancing. A little girl loving her dance, and loving herself, not knowing how or when the dance would end.

All we need is a real good wind
To lift us up to fly again.
Wait a little longer, stay until the end.
All we need is a real good wind.
We'll take this trouble in our stride
On that wind we're gonna ride.
Our broken wings are sure to mend.
All we need is a real good wind.

If only for a few moments, the song and the act of singing it soothed them all. "Oh, so true!" Moline cried, hugging Alma. Pauline stood up, careful not to wake Angelina, who was still sleeping in the swing, and went to the steps to sit beside Jose. "What a wonderful song for all of us. You're a good man and a good father."

He couldn't respond. His throat, his tongue, his eyes and ears, even his hands, seemed padded with grief. They sat silently for a while, until Alma said she was hungry, and Moline took her inside to feed her. Angelina woke up and wanted to go home to sleep in her bed, so Jose lifted her from the swing and carried her in his arms to their house.

Jose tossed and turned all night. His pillow was wet with tears, and his bed clothes were damp with perspiration. It was not yet daybreak, but he couldn't stay in bed. He went down the dark hall to Angelina's room, bent over her, and lightly caressed her small back. She was curled up under her pink blanket, wrapped like a rosebud waiting to bloom. Again, tears stung his already swollen eyelids. Would she have the chance to bloom?

Afraid he might make some sorrowful sound and wake her, he returned to the hall, through the tiny kitchen, and out onto his small porch. There was a slight drizzle. The wind had turned cold, and in his mind was a question as dismal as the pending dawn.

What good was he to Angelina? He could clear a field in a day, put up a fence in a week. In even a few seconds, he could play yet unheard music on his guitar and sing words that simply came to him as if from God. But he was not God. He could not cure his daughter and could not fathom a reason for his beautiful child's affliction by such a dire disease. "God has seen you through many things," he reassured himself. "And He will see you through this too." But were they just words?

He held onto the damp wood banister and looked up at the sky—a pale gray sky with the pine trees sketched across it as if drawn in pen and ink. A flock of white birds flew out of nowhere, flew in unanimity as if of one mind, and settled in the top of a single tree, the tallest pine. Probably a hundred birds, he thought, perched all at once among the needles. But now, in the dark shadows of the tree, they seemed no longer the white, living birds that moments ago sailed high and strong through the sky. Now, they were inanimate black ornaments, still as stone on the branches like spent pinecones, soon to fall and burst and spill their seeds for small, hungry animals to devour. Why that tree, chosen of all the trees for miles around? Why had light become dark and white become black? And why was he, only Jose, here to see it? Who gave such a command that these specific things should happen to him? It could only be God. Had God changed their once vibrant lives, Angelina's and his, into static, black stone ornaments? But why?

Jose despaired and almost lost his faith.

He squeezed his eyes shut and tried to pray. For quite a while, he stood there on the little porch, trying for a sense of peace, but no peace and no prayer came—only his confusion. Then, he heard the door behind him squeak open and turned. Angelina, his angel, stood in the doorframe.

At that very moment, her face was lit up by the rosy, gold light of the coming sun. "Oh, Papa, look!" She pointed at the sky. "Look quickly!"

He spun around just in time to see the flock of black birds become white again, and to hear the rustle of hundreds of wings lifting once more to the sky, aiming for the rose-colored sun.

There are bridges on the rivers,
As pretty as you please;
But the bow that bridges heaven,
And overtops the trees,
And builds a road from earth to sky,
Is prettier far than these.
—Christina Rossetti

Chapter Twelve

Alma

Not far from the Broussard land stands a high hill with rocks and boulders leading up to the crest, nearly like an ascending stairway to the sky. The people of the town call it Bethel Mountain, though it isn't tall enough to deserve the name. When Alma and Angelina were younger, after Angelina's many stays in the hospital, they often went to sit cross-legged in the clusters of pampas grass on the far edge of the old pasture and look up at the mountain, chattering happily. But on one occasion, Angelina was very quiet.

Alma asked, "Are you happy to be out of the hospital?"

"Yes," Angelina answered, though she didn't look happy. She looked tired. Her face was pale, nearly ghostly, and she didn't smile.

"What did the doctor say?" Alma asked, afraid to hear the answer.

A tear slid down Angelina's cheek. "He said he'd see me next time, so I know I'm not healed." One tear multiplied into many, and her voice choked. "I thought God would heal me this time. I was certain of it." Her right hand closed into a fist.

Alma touched it, opened it, and spread her own fingers between Angelina's, so tightly that Alma felt the pulsing of two hearts, one weaker than the other. "You might be healing right now and just not know it. Aunt Pauline says sometimes things get worse before they get better."

"But why?"

Alma shrugged. "I don't know. That's just what Aunt Pauline says. She says if you can't have what you really want right now, then think of something else you want. Is there something else you want, Angelina?"

Angelina looked up, her eyes fixed on the hill shimmering in the soft, orange light of the late afternoon sun. "One day, I want to climb that mountain and stand on the top of it. I want to see what's up there. It may be something wonderful."

Alma squeezed Angelina's hand and stood, pulling her friend up beside her. "I think I know what's on the top of it. And it is wonderful!" Of course, she did not know; it was only her childish imagining of a made-up father waiting there for her. "Let's go climb it now!"

"Okay, but I don't know how far I'll be able to go."

"We'll only go as far as you can. Then we'll turn around. And if I need to, I'll carry you."

Angelina laughed. "You can't carry me, Alma. I'm taller than you are."

"Well, I'm stronger, and Aunt Pauline says the strong should carry the weak. But who knows? You may not get tired at all."

So, they took on the hill, and halfway up, Angelina began to grow pale.

"We should turn around," Alma said. "It's too much for you."

"No! I want to see what's on top," Angelina replied between several short huffs of air.

Alma was worried. "Oh, there's nothing up there. We should go back."

"You said it was something wonderful, and I want to see it. I can make it to the top, Alma." She started uphill again.

"Wait! Let's just sit and talk about what it is. We can make it anything we want: castles, clouds, a rainbow. Anything."

And so, they sat together under a pine tree halfway up the hill that had become their mountain, visualizing it as a road from Earth to Heaven, and imagining what might be at the very top.

Angelina smiled. "I can see Dr. Roberts in his white lab coat pronouncing that I'm healed."

Alma looked up at the tangerine-colored sky where there hovered a cloud resembling a gate, just above the mountain top. "I can see my handsome father in his suit and tie."

Angelina set her eyes on the cloud. "I see a beautiful gate of gold, and one day we'll both walk through it." Then they lay on their backs, side by side, looking up. It was nearly dark before they left the pasture; the first of many musings they would have there, nestled side by side beneath Bethel Mountain, their eyes on the gate of gold.

Self-love forever creeps out, like a snake,
To sting anything which happens to stumble upon it.
—Lord Gordon Bryon

Chapter Thirteen

Mal

Mal laughs as Edmund runs out of his house, high as a kite and blubbering something about dinner with his wife, where she tried to manipulate him as usual. Of course she did; Edmund is such an easy target. But Ginnie would never gain the upper hand—not when Mal has been conniving against fools like Edmund since childhood. And of course, he perfected the art of manipulation at seminary.

No one at the university knows that Mal once entered the seminary—at his mother's request—to discern becoming a Catholic priest. His time there wasn't anything he would spread around. He hadn't stayed long—his departure was mutual between him and Fr. Caldwell, the Director of Vocations, who told Mal in no uncertain terms that he didn't have a calling. That was the third time he was brought to the director's office for unruly behavior. By then, Fr. Caldwell had lost the cardinal virtue of patience. He said that Mal wasn't a whole person, that there was something missing in him, something spiritual.

Of course, Mal knew that. He was incapable of dedicating himself to a god he did not believe in. The essence of spirituality was order, and Mal thrived on chaos. What he craved, what he saw as his purpose, was to create the greatest amount of havoc in the least amount of time for the simple-minded god-followers at Holy Trinity Seminary. He intended to get back at his mother, a frigid woman who didn't want him around, for having sent him there to find an answer to the question: *Quo vadis?* Where are you going?

He knew where he was going before he arrived, as well as what it would take to get there. After all, he had an itch to scratch, an obsession to defame anything deemed "holy." Within a few weeks, he was reaping the rewards of his efforts, until Fr. Caldwell ended it.

"Malcolm, I have discussed your continuing behavior with the rector and vice-rector." The priest drummed his fingers on his desk. "And we believe your ailment is a narcissistic mental disorder."

Mal had done much more during the few weeks he'd been at the seminary than had been reported; the director just didn't know about the consecrated hosts he'd gotten hold of and desecrated, tearing them to pieces and feeding them to some pigeons, or the time he'd donned a purple stole and sneaked into a confessional. He got so high on the penitents' sins that he could barely say to them, "Go in peace. Your sins are forgiven," without breaking into a laugh. He had also touched some of the other seminarians. That's all they were: affectionate touches. Or did he purposely want to scare them? Some of the more timid god-followers knew of these things but kept them to themselves, not wanting to ruin him, they said. He only smiled, thinking how gentle and stupid they were. But it enraged him that he, Malcolm J. Hawkins, had just been told by a Catholic priest that he was practically diseased!

He tried to control his anger when he told his side of the story—that he couldn't help what he'd done, that he was not responsible because he had many problems, mostly at home. When he began to list off the reasons why it wasn't his fault, but rather the fault of his heartless parents, the priest dismissed his comments as "nothing but excuses" and told him to take responsibility for his actions.

While Mal seethed inside, Fr. Caldwell stopped drumming his fingers. "The problem with narcissists like you is that they don't believe *they* are the problem. You have an inflated sense of your own importance, and you lack empathy. When is the last time you thought of someone else, Malcolm?"

The question caught him off-guard, so he played the victim. He always did that when he was in trouble, and usually it worked. He could fool most people because most people *had* empathy. "Maybe I need some help."

"Well, we can find you some assistance, if you want. But not here. You are not meant to be a priest. However, we do have access to a Catholic psychologist who may be able…" The director paused again as if what he said would matter to Mal, which it didn't. "To develop your better side. Everyone, no matter what they do, has a better side, a loving side that may not have been developed. Would you like me to call the psychologist?"

Mal squeezed a tear and, as meek as Jesus, he nodded yes. When the psychologist called him, he agreed to an appointment, but he had no intention of following through. Instead, he went to stay with his older sister, who by then had an apartment of her own. She'd always been the one to look after him, even during the short time his parents were together. People who said love was real—Mal knew it wasn't—would say that his sister loved him, but that was only because she was far, far below him in intelligence, even though she was some sort of scientist. Equally dumb was the name their parents had given her—Charity. It had been his mother's name, too, but his mother showed little charity or attention to either of her children. His mother was happy to have his bumbling sister take charge.

Mal was actually Malcolm J. Hawkins III, named after his grandfather, a hot-headed and outspoken Georgia cotton farmer. Back in the 1930s, just when Georgia farmers were experiencing good crop yields and prices, Malcolm I woke up one day and rode like Paul Revere from farm to farm to warn the other farmers, "Watch out, boys! Bad times is coming. I done had a dream about destruction!" Days later, a tiny insect called the boll weevil came in from Central America and began moving rapidly across the Cotton Belt, eating up the cotton fields. Oh, how that incensed the first Malcolm! "Before I let them bugs eat up my home, I'll burn the fields down myself and kill 'em!" People who had no intention of following his advice nevertheless admired his spunk. And when he actually did it—burned his fields—they put him up for a spot in the state legislature, which he won in a landslide.

Mal's father, Malcolm II, was as hidebound as the old man. A graduate of Yale Law School, he'd been much cleverer than Mal's detached mother, but was even colder. Mal had few memories of his father; he'd left the family when Mal was five years old and Charity was ten due to an affair with the wife of his so-called best friend. His mother couldn't wait to tell Mal and Charity about the affair, couldn't wait to call his father a swindler, nothing but a hungry insect that ate up their home. She kicked him out, told him where he could go, then made it known that she'd never cared about him anyway. She said she felt finally "free" from a man concerned only with feeding his own urges.

One of Mal's most vivid memories, just after the divorce, occurred on the Fourth of July weekend. His father and his new wife took Charity and Mal—along with his own aging father, Malcolm

I, who was out of the legislature and into a wheelchair by then—to the sugar-white sands and jade-colored waters of Panama City Beach, about an hour from Bethel. "To celebrate my new life," Malcolm II said. "And for some Fourth of July family fun."

After they unpacked in their high-rise rooms, Malcolm II told Mal and Charity to take the elevator down with Malcolm I, then roll him to the condominium pool so the old man could enjoy the beautiful beach and the fireworks to come later. Mal didn't want to push the wheelchair to the pool, so Charity did, and once there, the old man did not look at the beach. For quite a while, he looked at some giggling teenaged girls in red, white, and blue string bikinis, their bottoms practically bare. His face grew redder and redder until he was enraged enough to holler, "Is that all you silly girls think of your American flag? Well, if that's all it is to ya, why don't 'cha just burn it up like the rest of them ingrates on TV? Yeah, go on and burn up the flag of freedom! See where you are then."

The girls kept giggling and passed on by.

For hours afterward, Malcolm I nodded off in his old, stained golf hat with a long pelican feather sticking out of the band. The feather was compliments of Mal, who'd found it on the beach and stuck it in the sleeping old man's golf hat, laughing and calling him Yankee Doodle. Of course, Charity told Mal to stop, that he was being disrespectful, but Mal kept up with his wild hyena laugh, intermittently poking at his sleeping grandfather's cap and shouting, "Yankee Doodle! Yankee Doodle dandy!" Finally, Malcolm I cracked an eye open, put a hand to his cap, and found the feather. He looked at it for a second or two and said he liked it alright but with one exception. "Son, I'm a Georgia boy. There ain't nothing at all Yankee about me. And don't you never forget it!"

About that time, Malcolm II came out with his new wife and called Mal a fool. Mal, even at five, vowed he would never forget or forgive the insult. From a young age, Mal made lots of vows like that, vows that he would never let any personal injury to himself go without being paid for. He once put a poisonous spider in mayonnaise on two pieces of bread and took it to Charity to eat after she refused to lie to their father about Mal stealing money from his wallet. The spider didn't kill her though. She didn't even get sick.

His father jumped into the condominium's pool with Charity and Mal then called for his new wife, who'd been relaxing in a chaise lounge, to bring him a cigarette. He was leaning against the side of the pool smoking it when Charity, dense and chunky even as a ten-year-old, in her own red, white, and blue-striped bathing suit, looked up and saw an owl perched on the second floor balcony rail.

"Oh, Mal," she called to him. "Look at the wise old owl!" The tone of her voice was sweet, as if she wanted to stroke the bird's back, but Mal knew what she was trying to do—take charge of what he saw and did. He would not let her. Even if he hadn't seen it first, the owl was his.

"Come down here, owl!" Mal commanded in his loudest voice. "Right now!"

The owl did not move.

"The owl's not going to listen to you. See that?" Charity pointed up to an American flag hanging from a high pole and waving its shadow upon the pool's surface. "That owl is free. You can't tell him what to do. He can stay where he is if he wants to." Then she pushed her paddle board into the flag's shadow and stood up on it. "Look, owl, I'm walking on water!" She started singing, "Oh, say can you see, by the dawn's early light…"

The owl didn't seem to notice. It just kept staring and did not move.

"The owl doesn't care about you!" Mal yelled at his sister. "He's looking at me!" Then Mal did a somersault in the water to get more attention from the bird and maybe see it fly up and away, imagining that if he had a gun, he could shoot it in the air. But the owl sat still and staring. So, Mal did another, and then another somersault, splashing water upward toward the owl so it would notice.

It only gaped at him and did not move.

His father began to laugh. Then his new wife, still sunbathing in the chaise lounge by the pool, laughed too. "Fool!" his father shouted. "Can't you see that owl's not real? It's stuffed. Somebody tied it to that railing."

Mal felt humiliated. He glared at Charity. "She's the fool. She said it was real. I knew it wasn't."

Charity did not flinch; she was used to his animosity.

"Okay, you're both fools." His father took a drag off his cigarette and got out of the pool. He turned to his new wife. "You stay with them. I'm going to the bar."

The trip had not come close to a celebration.

Then, when Mal was fourteen, his mother signed him up for the seminary so she could be even freer than the divorce had made her. But Mal's misbehavior kept her from total liberation, which is what he had planned from the start. His goal in the family was always to agitate, especially his mother. Any discomfort he could bestow on her, such as her embarrassment when he was dismissed from the seminary, was like the winning point in a video game.

Now, here he is, twenty years later, a Doctor of Psychology—not at some big Ivy League school where he should have been though. He was forced to take a job at a washed-up university in a little dump of a Southern town overrun with God, grits, and guns. He had several interviews beyond Bethel University, but no one had seen fit to hire him, even though he'd been the best choice for each job. So what? He thought he could have a little fun in the town of Bethel, and he has. And the best is yet to come.

His sister, Charity, always talked about how being kinder to people could give him peace, but that isn't something he wants. Chaos fits him much better. He is sure she still wastes her energy praying for him as she did after the seminary sent him home. To be honest, he felt *something* watching her on her knees like that, on her knees for him. But it was triumph, not peace. He'd conquered his pliable sister. Most people, like Charity, could be conquered. He would always win.

We are always paid for our suspicion, by finding what we suspect.
—Henry Thoreau

CHAPTER FOURTEEN

Edmund

Edmund rolls over in bed and watches Ginnie dress in a pair of over-washed, baggy red pants, the same color—and about the same shape—as his grandfather's old, dead-in-the-field, sun-bleached tractor. He knows she's putting them on as a kind of flag, claiming the weekend as her own before she has to rise and dress as a Bethel University teacher again.

She knows he hates it when she dresses like that. What she really means to do when she puts on the discolored pants, the stained T-shirt printed with "Roll Tide," when she leaves off her makeup and braids her hair into pigtails, is to drive a nail into his pride, squashing any remaining thoughts that she might try to please him. He, of course, is always professional. Weekend or not, he always wears a suit and tie in public, the same as he wears to teach his sociology courses. His body is fit. He maintains a gym habit, still runs, and eats the right food—all the things that Ginnie ignores.

"The weight is showing on you." He shoots the first volley in an increasingly tiresome battle. Something inside his head tells him to stop and say no more. *Why are you belittling her? You sound more like Mal than yourself. Stop it!*

The battle is not between himself and Ginnie. The battle is between himself and his own fear of losing her. Looking at her in the faded pants, again he recalls her frequent appointments with the dermatologist and how, after each visit, Ginnie goes on and on about what a marvelous doctor he is.

She has said nothing about the doctor this morning, yet jealousy overwhelms him. "It surprises me that even a one-legged skin doctor would find you attractive enough for an affair." He says it with menace, as if he has proof, which he doesn't; and as if he doesn't love her, which he does.

She turns her face toward him, and he can see how badly he has hurt her. Why does he insult her? The way he just described her is nothing like what he really feels. Sometimes, he feels as if there is someone else speaking through him. He would never have noticed the few extra summer pounds she gained if Mal hadn't mentioned it at one of their sessions. Always, he wants to make love to Ginnie. Sometimes, even during his lectures, desire for her halts his thinking, causing him to lose his place. Sometimes, he stops talking and calls for students to sum up in writing what he's said thus far to remind himself where he left off.

He looks at her with regret and longing as she explains that she empathizes with her dermatologist and has never thought of Dr. Burke in a sexual way.

Then, all at once, her eyes narrow. She swipes a hand through the air and suspends it above the crown of his head. Her fingers curl as if they hold a gun. "I know who put that garbage into your mind—Mal Hawkins, the foulest man I know!"

He shoves her hand away. "Not true."

He remembers the day he told Mal he was getting married. He hadn't told him anything about Ginnie before. He wonders now why he had not, but there had always been something about Mal, about the way he touched his shoulder as he entered his house, a squeeze that had seemed too intimate yet somehow comforting. Maybe like a father's hand should feel? Edmund had gotten little comfort from his own father, so he'd let that small intimacy go, and then finally welcomed it. It was a fine line though. He'd heard one or two wisecracks from students who also visited him—Edmund assumed for the same drugs and advice Mal gave him—about Mal's propensity for men and distinct dislike of women. So, on the night Edmund told Mal about Ginnie, he was careful how he said it.

He did not say the word "engagement." Instead, he told Mal, "There's someone I like a lot."

Mal glared at him. "Who would *that* be?"

Because of Mal's accusatory tone—a tone that actually sounded like his own father—Edmund simply said, "One of the actors in *Our Town*, the student play I'm in. I mean I have only one line, but Dr. Patton encouraged me to participate."

"Well, be careful of actors. Sometimes they're just pretending to be who they want people to think they are."

Edmund ignored the statement, but something told him it related more to Mal than to Ginnie.

Ginnie stomps to the bedroom dresser and snatches up their wedding photo: Ginnie, slim and beautiful in a wedding dress, her loving eyes set on Edmund; and Edmund, in his tuxedo of black and white, his eyes aimed away from Ginnie toward the silver border around the periphery of the photo, as if someone more important has just summoned his attention. He recalls that the "someone" was Mal Hawkins, who offered himself as Edmund's best man.

"It's a vileness that's always been in him, Edmund. Open your eyes before you're completely blinded by that man." She tosses the photograph on the bed beside him. "Mal Hawkins is the problem between us; you just won't admit it. He masquerades as a sweet little songbird, ever ready to sing to you—or bring you anything you want. But—and there aren't many folks you can say this about directly—he's a flat-out false friend, and anything you accept from him will kill you. The man needs to be in an asylum, not teaching at the university. Even on his deathbed, your grandfather tried to warn you about him."

The old man was still trying to warn him when he awoke that very morning while Ginnie, a silhouette in the early light, was still tightly shrouded in a sheet on her side of the bed. *You know where that bird's carrying you, don't you, Edmund? To the thorn of impalement. Take charge. Change your ways. Now!* Old and tiring words from the grave.

Ginnie's flesh-and-blood words seem no better. Her attempt to manipulate Edmund's every move—Mal's assessment, in just those words—aggravates him as much as the preacher's voice in his head.

Edmund yawns. "I'm not going to talk about Mal anymore."

"Fine!"

Planning to avoid her the rest of the day, he takes a suit and tie from the closet.

"Where are you going? It's Saturday."

"I'm going to the university post office to check for mail."

She sighs with disgust, turns, and strides to the living room.

He leaves without saying goodbye.

At the university, he goes through an entry hall that angles into the faculty lounge and stops in front of the hall mirror to straighten his tie.

Two familiar voices come from the lounge—Mal and Dr. Patton, Edmund's boss. "Ineffective teachers with poor people skills can ruin Bethel University's reputation," says Mal.

"Yes, there are some in my department who have poor people skills, and poor judgment, as well." Dr. Patton laughs. "But most of them have tenure. Nothing we can do about that! Now, the ones without tenure? Well, I give them rope for a while. They're still learning."

"So, you're happy with your staff?"

"I am."

"What about Edmund Gillan? Is he one of those you're giving rope to?"

Edmund's heart stops. What is Mal trying to do?

"I like Gillan," Dr. Patton replies. "But yes, I have given him some rope. He's smart and knows his subject. He has potential."

"You don't think he's been guilty of poor judgment?"

Another snag in Edmund's chest. Is Mal going to tell Dr. Patton that he's hooked on drugs—drugs that Mal gives him? But that would implicate Mal himself.

Dr. Patton laughs again. "No, I don't. I would say Edmund has excellent judgement, especially in his choice of a wife. I hear she's become a great teacher, just as I knew she would."

Mal's voice smacks with hostility. "If you like arrogance."

Dr. Patton's voice tenses. "Hey, lay off the Gillans, especially Ginnie. She's trying to do something good for the university with her new program."

"What? Shoving her phony religion down her students' throats?"

Dr. Patton pauses. "And what have you been shoving down your students' throats for years? Do you think I don't know? As of now, religion is not illegal. But cocaine is. So, I'd watch my mouth if I were you—if you want to keep your job."

Dr. Patton storms out of the teacher's lounge. Edmund ducks around the corner and heads for the post office. He picks up two pieces of junk mail and throws them both into a garbage receptacle in the parking lot.

As he drives home, he considers the risk Dr. Patton took in calling out Mal's crimes. He even smiles a little, thinking that now Dr. Patton might even replace Ginnie as number one on Mal's "get rid of" list.

The smile is quickly replaced by a knot of worry. Should he be concerned about his job? Does Dr. Patton know he willingly takes cocaine from Mal? How would he? Unless Ginnie told him. Just how close is she with his boss?

Put it down, Edmund, or that green-eyed monster will destroy you!

But he cannot put it down. At home, he decides to be blunt. He asks Ginnie, "How well do you know Henry Patton?" A headache starts at the base of his skull and slithers like a snake to his temples.

She shrugs. "Oh, I've known him for years. He was a friend of my parents. Henry actually suggested my new course as a way to test the waters for a religious studies program. He wants the university to stay grounded in truthful values. Why do you ask?"

"I was just wondering." He rubs his forehead.

She quirks an eyebrow at him. "Why now? Has he said something?"

"What would he say?"

"I don't know—maybe that you're doing an excellent job and that your students are very fond of you? I think he likes you a lot. At least, that's what he told me."

"And what have you told him?" Edmund's head pounds from trying to shut out his grandfather's voice.

"I told you, we're friends. I've probably told him a lot of things about you. Good things, Edmund, so don't worry."

He isn't sure he believes her. Just one more cog in the wheel of his already troubled mind.

God has our entire lives in the palm of his loving hand.
We can rest secure about our past, present and future—for He loves us.
—Mother Angelica

CHAPTER FIFTEEN

Jose

When he reached Miami those years ago, Jose was filled with the excitement of building a new life for himself, but the first thing he needed was a job. Since he would be considered illegal, his best bet was to find an ethnic neighborhood of Cubans, make friends, and ask for help. He checked newspaper ads for jobs in Little Havana, found one he thought he might like at Lopez Landscaping, and then went for an interview in a small office beside a two-story house. Mr. Lopez, a happy-looking, rotund man wearing gold-rimmed glasses, looked Jose up and down and seemed pleased. "I run the business with my wife," he told Jose. "And we have many Cubans and other Hispanics working for us. We're looking to hire only those men we can leave on the job and trust to get the work done. Are you such a man?"

"I am," Jose responded, expecting Mr. Lopez's next question.

"Do you have a social security number?"

"I… I do not."

At that moment, a woman Jose assumed to be Mrs. Lopez, as rotund as her husband, entered the room through an open door behind the office. As if she had been watching Jose and heard the conversation, she asked, "What is your name, and where are you from?"

"Jose Alvarez. I was born in Mexico, but I came here from Cuba."

She eyed him up and down, just as her husband had, and said with a fast smile, "I was born in Mexico too. My family left years ago because of the corruption. I wonder if anything has been done about it. Do you know?"

Jose swallowed hard. "I believe the corruption has been…lessened now."

"I like this boy." Mrs. Lopez patted her husband on his shoulder and then left by the door in the back, not quite closing it behind her.

"Alright then. But the most I can do is three to four months." Mr. Lopez shrugged apologetically. "I am required to submit the proper tax forms, W2s, I9s, etc., and social security information. If you're undocumented, your paperwork will be bogus."

"But you will hire me for three to four months?"

"Yes. For only a few we do this. We can find you a social security number, and we will submit it, but in three to four months, we will get a letter from the Social Security Administration explaining that your social security number does not match any of their numbers on file. They call it a 'No Match' letter. We will have to let you go then."

Three to four months would have to do for now. He could save a little of his pay, trusting that when the No Match letter came, God would provide his next step. But where would he live?

As if she'd heard his thought, Mrs. Lopez again entered the office. "We have a room for rent for a small amount. It was my son's, but he has left us now and has a family of his own. If you would like it, we can deduct the payment after you've earned your first paycheck."

He could have hugged her! "Yes, thank you."

And so it happened, a job and a place to live. The job was enjoyable; Jose had always loved plants and flowers. He worked hard for the landscape company, which Mr. Lopez appreciated, as did Mrs. Lopez, who doted on him. She once even called him, "*Mi hijo*," my son, and said Jose reminded her of him. Everything seemed to be going well. He was even able to enjoy some of Little Havana, full of businesses and restaurants, museums and theaters, plus a colorful nightlife.

One night, at a beer house in Little Havana, he was celebrating his good fortune alone when he met an attractive bartender, a blond woman with blue eyes who spoke with an Irish brogue. She was a little older than he was, but he could see she liked him by the way she followed his every movement, listened to his every word. She said her name was Annette, and that she would call him Mr. Tall Dark and Handsome. That night, he never gave her his name, and she never asked. He was young, then, barely out of his teens, and naturally, he was flattered when she said she'd like to get to know him. He knew very few people and was anxious for conversation with someone other than his fellow landscape workers. So, he waited for her while she poured him beer after beer until her shift was over. Then he offered to walk her home.

Unsteadily, they made their way to a small apartment a few blocks from the beer house. Once there, there was little conversation. She immediately pushed him down on a lumpy bed, flung herself on top of him, and began to kiss him. He knew he needed to leave—because she was drunk, too, because he'd never had sex before, and because he knew it was all wrong. But he did not leave. Afterwards, he felt terribly guilty. He didn't plan to see Annette again; in fact, he promised himself he would not.

Three months later, just when he was worried about the arrival of the No Match letter, Annette showed up at the door to his tiny room. Standing in the doorway and still calling him Mr. Tall Dark and Handsome, she told him she was pregnant, and since he was the father, she needed money for an abortion. At first, he felt angry. Then he began to tremble and had to hold on to the doorframe. What she wanted to do was wrong. But he had been wrong, too, in having sex with her. The only innocent in the whole affair was the baby. "I will not kill my own baby!" he shouted just as he glimpsed Mrs. Lopez in the hall, clutching his daily fresh towels. He knew she had heard. Everything that had seemed good was now going in the opposite direction.

He ushered Annette out of the doorway into his room and then closed the door. Her demeanor softened, and her eyes filled. She set a hand on her stomach. "A baby will keep me from making a living and paying my rent. I have only myself, no other family to help me. I don't know what else to do." She began to cry. Jose did not like to see her cry, especially when he was the cause of it. And he did not think that she really wanted to get rid of the baby, so what could he do to solve this? There had to be some better solution. And suddenly, an idea entered his mind, but whether it would work or not depended entirely on Mr. and Mrs. Lopez and the No Match letter. He sat Annette in a chair and told her to stay there for a few minutes, then left to find them.

He did not have to go far to find Mrs. Lopez; she was only a short way down the hall, still holding the fresh towels. She stayed where she was until he reached her, then handed him the linens and said at once, "I heard everything. What can I do to help, mi hijo?" The most beautiful words he'd ever heard.

He was afraid of her answer, but he asked anyway. "Has Mr. Lopez received the No Match letter yet?" He knew that when the letter came, he wouldn't be able to continue working for the landscaping company, and that would ruin his plan.

"No." She touched his shoulder. "But when he does—if he does—there is still a way, mi hijo. Mr. Lopez will see to it."

He hugged her. She softly kissed his cheek as if he were truly her son come back to her, and said, "Do not worry."

He offered to take care of Annette if she would give birth to the baby; then afterwards, he would raise the child. Annette seemed happy to agree, and for six months—after no letter came, and with Mr. and Mrs. Lopez's agreement—Jose gave Annette the cot in his tiny room while he slept on a blanket on the floor. She was not an easy person to live with. Mrs. Lopez didn't fall in love with her as she seemed have done with Jose. But as the baby grew inside Annette, Jose was amazed at what was happening to her and to the child within her. When he saw the sonogram and was told the baby would be a girl, he knew he would name her Angelina. An angel from God. Annette did not want him in the delivery room, so on the day Angelina was born, he first saw her in the nursery, wrapped in a pink blanket. He asked the nurse if he could take the baby to see her mother. When Annette saw him come into the room, she quickly said, "No! I don't want to see her. I don't *ever* want to see her, or you, again." And she hasn't.

With both love and fear in his heart, Jose took Angelina home to the Lopez house, a tiny human life he would take care of forever. He knew it would be hard on Mr. and Mrs. Lopez to have a newborn in their house, so he told them he would find another place as soon as he could. Of course, Mrs. Lopez objected.

"Staying for much longer wouldn't be a good idea for me or the baby," Jose told her. "And not good for Mr. Lopez if I should get caught. I think I should leave Miami altogether."

Mrs. Lopez swallowed hard, and her lips began to tremble. Finally, she said, "We will help you do whatever you want, mi hijo."

Praying the rosary daily on his mother's beads, he trusted that God would show him the way. Looking back now, he sees it as another miracle, the way God's plan worked for him and his baby daughter.

Not long after Angelina was born, Mr. and Mrs. Lopez called him into their living room. He came at once, holding Angelina in his arms. A red-haired woman he did not know sat on the brown sofa, her hands crossed in her lap. Mrs. Lopez introduced her as Sr. Mary O'Hara with Catholic Social Services.

"What a beautiful baby," she said right off. "You are a fortunate man, Mr. Alvarez." She opened her hands and held them out as if she wanted to hold Angelina, so Jose laid her in the woman's arms. Sr. Mary shifted a bit on the sofa, then went on. "Mrs. Lopez has told me of your plight. I think I can help you. We have adoption services for anyone who—"

"No!" Jose reached to take back Angelina. "I'm not just anyone. I'm her father. I will take care of her."

"But how?" Sr. Mary asked, giving up the baby to Jose.

"God gave her to me, and He will show me how." He said the words with anger but calmed quickly and turned to Mr. Lopez. "I'm going to leave Miami."

"But you have a job here with us," Mr. Lopez said. "It will be hard to find another. For now, I have taken care of your documentation. We'll help you find a new place to live, and you can keep your job here. You've been such a good worker." He turned to his wife. "And Mrs. Lopez is very fond of you."

"You have both been wonderful to me, and I'd like to stay,

but I think I should find a job in another place. After all, I have a child now, and the No Match letter is certain to come in the months ahead."

"There are things I can do. I could…"

Sr. Mary interrupted. "Mr. Lopez, you do not want to get yourself into trouble." She turned to Jose. "Where would you like to go?" she asked, as if any place was possible.

"I'm not sure. I don't know much about American places, but wherever I go—" He looked down at Angelina, tightening his hold. "She will go with me. I will not give her up."

They told him how hard it would be. Who would take care of the baby while he worked? And he would have to work. They told him that if he truly loved her, he would allow her to be adopted by someone who could do all that. At once he was afraid. Could they somehow take Angelina from him? Was that legal in America? But Jose did not relent. He was her father, he repeated. No one else will ever be her father. He could see that Sr. Mary was touched by his words, so he spoke directly to her. "I love this child with all my heart. I would die for her."

Sr. Mary stood. "Excuse me a moment," she said, taking a cell phone from her purse. "I need to make a phone call." She left to go out on the small front porch. She closed the door. It seemed to Jose that she was gone for hours while he stood in the living room, holding Angelina closer and closer. Was Sr. Mary calling the police? Would they come to take his baby? He would fight them if he had to, even if he ended up in jail. But if they put him in jail, he could not take Angelina. His mind swirled, one thought crashing into another.

Mrs. Lopez offered him tea. He said no. Then Mr. and Mrs. Lopez chattered to each other and to him, but he did not hear.

Finally, the front door re-opened. There were no police, only Sr.

Mary, who was smiling. "My brother, Fr. Billy O'Hara, pastor of Sacred Heart in Bethel, Alabama, will take you and your baby."

God's plan, in which Jose had trusted, had come to pass.

We shape our dwellings,
and afterwards our dwellings shape us.
—Winston Churchill

CHAPTER SIXTEEN

Alma

Alma's mother and aunt seemed to see the old house in which they lived and the land around it as a beautiful domain of certainties, where all three of them—her mother, Aunt Pauline, and Alma herself—were born and still lived.

"Faithful," Aunt Pauline said of it. "It has a great soul."

"Yes," Alma's mother responded. "Always has."

The twins did not appear to notice any of the interior variations that had occurred over the years, though there were many—paling paint, unsteady stairs, doors that stuck or would not close correctly. Or that the flowers, especially azaleas and camellias, along with weeds, overpowered the yard around the house. They did not seem to mind the overpowering. The imperfections were like lines slowly embedded into the face of a beloved, but their home still smiled at them.

On occasion, though, when events occurred that were out of their control, such as violent storms, predicted tornadoes, unpredicted diseases, or rare winters when temperatures drastically dropped, the twins faced the possibility that vulnerable living things—people, animals, and plants—could disappear. They could die.

In contrast, Alma, and especially Jose, were continually aware of that possibility. Angelina's health could shift at any moment and often did. But always, she recovered and came home a little stronger.

Last year, as the end of autumn approached and winter was in the air, Angelina was hospitalized with another infection and high fever. Usually, such events lasted only a few days. But this time it was weeks. Angelina was much thinner and deeply depressed when Alma visited. "I think I've been given an early death sentence."

"No!" Alma responded quickly. "That's not true. You will be healed one day. You are an angel. People like you are too good, too beautiful, to be given an early death sentence."

"Except, who makes the rules, Alma? Not you and I."

Of course, they were God's rules, Alma thought. But surely, God did not want Angelina to die. She'd donated blood to Angelina. Hadn't it helped? She knew from Jose that sometimes it did not—not for a while anyway. So, Alma said nothing more, only stayed with Angelina and held her hand in silence until Jose came in. He kissed his daughter, and she said, "Don't worry, Papa. I'll be fine."

Then a nurse peeked in the doorway to say that visiting hours were over and Alma should leave. "Are you sleeping in the chair tonight?" she asked Jose.

He nodded yes.

"I'll bring you a blanket then."

Later, Alma stood on the porch with Aunt Pauline, overlooking the yard with its abundance of flowers, and farther out, the land with its still-green grass and trees.

"How was Angelina?" Aunt Pauline asked.

"Very depressed. I'm worried about her, and so is Jose."

It was chilly, and Aunt Pauline shivered, buttoned up her blue cardigan, and said, "Well, I've heard that cold air affects leukemia patients. And winter is coming soon." Then she set her sight on the camellias in full bloom and added, "Winter causes so much beauty to meet its death. But God's world has its own rules."

It was odd. The second mention of rules in one day. Still, Aunt Pauline had a penchant for saving beautiful things from death. And three days later, just after Jose called to say that Angelina was being released from the hospital, she had a chance to do it.

Pauline, Alma, and Moline were watching The Weather Channel on television, happy over Angelina's release, when the meteorologist forecasted that it would be well below freezing that night. Aunt Pauline exclaimed, "Oh no! Here it comes. The camellias will not make it. They will be destroyed!"

All three bundled up quickly and went outside to see what they could do.

Aunt Pauline squinted from beneath the purple hood of her coat. "Oh, just look at those camellias, Moline! How in the world could anything be more perfect? We have to save them."

Alma's mother turned up the velvet collar of her coat so that her hair—highlighted pink at the time to match Chancee's latest look—stood out to Alma like a serving of cotton candy. "They are gorgeous, Sister, but I do fear they'll never live through the night."

"Well, we can save some of them. At least, we'll try. Moline, you and Alma start picking as many blooms as you can. I'll get some sheets and light blankets to throw over the bushes." Aunt Pauline hurried back inside the house. By the time she returned with the coverings, Alma and her mother had picked camellia blooms until their arms overflowed.

"You both look like brides," Aunt Pauline said.

"Well, you should know," Moline laughed. "Three times a bride."

"Better three times than no times, Sister."

Alma sighed. Tonight their foolishness was irritating. She was still thinking about Angelina and the possibility of *her* early death.

Moline turned to Alma. "Go get all the vases you can find out of the storage room and fill them with water for flowers. Use the pots and pans from the kitchen if we don't have enough."

Alma gathered every receptacle she could carry while Moline and Pauline threw white sheets and blankets over the bushes. Alma thought the yard looked as if it were a graveyard haunted by ghosts, and, for at least a week, the inside of the house resembled a funeral parlor. The camellias outside survived, though, and continued to flower, almost enough to replenish every bloom that had been taken into the house.

However, the next fall the bushes were attacked three times by separate diseases of petal, leaf, and root. Petal blight hit them first, small brown spots that quickly enlarged until the entire bloom was ravaged by dark brown veins. Infected flowers dropped within two days into an ugly array of death. Then leaf gall disease hit. The once-lovely waxy leaves became enlarged and fleshy with small greenish-white galls on the undersides that eventually turned rust-colored. Finally, the worst disease of all, root rot, took over. Entire bushes wilted, the foliage became brown, cankers appeared, and sap oozed out of the stems.

"I give up!" Pauline said then. And she made a different choice than previously. She gave every one of them an early death sentence. As if the camellias and their diseases had become too much to deal with, as if the whole yard would be destroyed if she allowed them to stay, as if the once-perfect bushes had become fallen angels, she called on Jose to dig up every bush and abandoned them forever, as she had each of her three husbands.

Alma teared up when she saw the barren spaces that were left.

She thought Aunt Pauline should have been more patient, that with a little more time, the bushes might have survived, like they had before, and like Angelina did, despite her bouts with leukemia's demons. "Why did you just give up?" Alma asked her aunt.

"It's a lost cause and a waste of time. Nature has its own rules about life and death. We have to accept that and let go," Aunt Pauline replied, snatching a tissue from the box on the kitchen counter to wipe her own tears.

It was not Alma's way to let beloved things go. Planted years ago by her grandparents, before their twins were born, the camellias were one of Alma's earliest and fondest memories. Even as a toddler, she was fascinated by the beauty of the camellia blooms in the fall and their deep green leaves all year long. They surrounded the screened porch where, in her grandfather's lap, she sat nightly with him in the old metal rocker, her grandmother rocking in the glider next to them. By that time, her mother had begun working at the dentist's office, and after work, she usually went to a favorite bar. Aunt Pauline usually went to bed early, so Alma ended the day on the porch with her grandparents.

Even now, she can sometimes hear the squeaking metal chair that wasn't a rocker but rocked anyway when it was needed to put a little girl to sleep. Her grandfather sang to her in a quiet voice, deep and husky from too many cigarettes. *Froggy went a courtin' and he did ride—uh huh.* After he finished his song, she kept her head against his chest, listening to the beat of his heart perfectly timed with the rhythmic squeak of metal. She was not asleep, though, and remained sensitive to his movements and his voice.

She still has a vivid memory of his twisting toward her grandmother in the glider and hearing him whisper, "Do you think Moline will ever tell us who Alma's father is?"

The glider stopped. "Honey, I don't think she even knows. We may as well say Alma doesn't have a father."

Alma has never let go of those heartbreaking words.

Years later, when she was in the last week of elementary school, the class's summer project was to make pretty cards for the upcoming Father's Day in June. "Just tell your father how much you love him," her teacher, Miss Wilson, told the children. "And then decorate it with drawings of things he likes."

Alma raised her hand. "What if you don't have a father?"

"Everyone has a father, Alma," Miss Wilson said, but she quickly looked embarrassed. "Maybe he doesn't live with you, but you could get your mother to mail it, couldn't you?"

Alma nodded. Yes, she would do that. She didn't know what things her father liked though, so she decorated it with hearts and hands and angels, and she thought her Father's Day card was beautiful. She was proud to take it home and show it to Moline.

At first, her mother appeared angry, and then her eyes filled, and her voice choked. "I don't know who to send this to, Alma. I'm sorry, but you don't have a father."

"Miss Wilson said that everyone has a father."

Her mother's anger returned. "Well, your father is a lost cause! Just think of Jose as your father. You and that sweet, sick girl are like sisters, after all. For heaven's sake, just give Jose the card. It's not that big a deal."

But Aunt Pauline stepped in, as if she realized that it was a big deal. As if she meant to save a beautiful thought. "Of course, you have a father, Alma. Miss Wilson was right. It's just that your father is far away."

"Then how can I send him the card?"

"Give it to me. I'll send it, and I promise you, he will get it."

Although Aunt Pauline's promises were often unreliable, Alma believed this one because her mother suddenly hugged Aunt Pauline, and they both began to cry. Their tears made it credible. Maybe her father wasn't a lost cause. Maybe she would meet him someday. But one thing she was positive about, she would never let him go,

After that, the only thought she gave the card was to imagine it in her father's faraway hands, in some distant place where he was smiling because her beautiful card had touched his heart.

False face must hide what the false heart doth know.
—William Shakespeare, Lady Macbeth

CHAPTER SEVENTEEN

Edmund

After a long day of teaching, as another headache pounds relentlessly through his skull, Edmund doesn't think about his resentment of Ginnie nor the conversation he heard in the faculty lounge when he worried about how much Dr. Patton knew. He does not even think about Mal's potential to be disloyal. All those worries vanish in the wake of his craving for the drugs; either cocaine or marijuana will do. He shoves aside Ginnie's nagging voice in his head that says he's become addicted and decides to cut his last class short and drop by Mal's on his way home. That way, Ginnie won't know.

Mal doesn't waste time on small talk. He sets a closed bag of cocaine on the coffee table and sneers at Edmund. "Which one do you think Ginnie is having an affair with—her dermatologist or Dr. Patton?"

The question hits Edmund like an unexpected arrow. Why would Mal ask such a thing? He doesn't remember saying anything to Mal about Ginnie having an affair with either man. Ginnie explained the reason for her closeness to Dr. Patton. Maybe he has nursed a little doubt, probably because he is somewhat jealous of his boss, but he has never said anything to Mal about it. And most of what he said to Ginnie about Dr. Burke flew from his lips without real reason—only a parroting of Mal's suggestions set in Edmund's drug-muddled mind. More and more, Edmund is saying things he hasn't thought through.

"She's not having an affair with either one!" he answers decisively, as if Ginnie is looking over his shoulder. "If I indicated that, I didn't mean it. Sometimes I…don't mean what I say."

"Oh, I think you do mean what you say. You want to berate Ginnie, not because of anything she's done—at least, not anything you know about—but because you believe she's smarter and more successful than you. For people like you and me, Edmund, that's a battle flag."

"What do you mean, like you and me?" Once, he might have been flattered by the comparison. Instead, he stares at the unopened bag of cocaine.

"I mean, she is an egotistical woman. Aren't there times you feel as if you could shoot her for what she does?" He quickly adds, "I'm speaking figuratively, of course."

Edmund sees the disdain in Mal's face and knows he should leave his house, but the cocaine is on the table in front of him. He has to have some. He has to. His feet won't move until his body has been fed with it. He peels his eyes from the cocaine, glances at Mal, then back to the cocaine. "Yes, I suppose sometimes I could shoot her."

Mal smirks.

Edmund grinds his teeth a moment. "Except I love her. I don't mind that she's smarter than me."

Mal narrows his eyes. "You don't mind being bullied?"

"I don't see it as that."

"Not yet, but you will." Instead of opening the bag of cocaine, Mal crosses the room and opens the front door. "I think that's all for tonight, Edmund."

Edmund returns home on edge without the cocaine he craves. Pain and irritation spike through him at the thought of Ginnie confronting him, which he expects.

Instead, she meets him at the door with a kiss and a hug, and the troubles between them evaporate.

"Follow me, husband."

She leads him to the kitchen where she has cheese, crackers, a bowl of grapes, and two glasses of wine spread out on the kitchen table. "We finished reading *Macbeth*," she says, motioning for him to sit at his usual place across from her. "It was the first choice for my course, a perfect example of how an author like Shakespeare relies on God in his work."

As he takes his seat at the table, he brushes a hand across her shoulders—straight, strong shoulders, he thinks, like he ought to have, but he is still a "slumper," another derogatory term used by his grandfather.

He sighs and focuses on her. The wine helps the pain subside just enough. He picks up a cracker and a piece of cheese, thinking first of his grandfather's histrionic faith and then its direct opposite in Mal. "What do you mean by 'he relies on God'?"

"I mean that Shakespeare keeps before his audience the consciousness of the choice between good and evil, which is at war in the soul of every human being. Each of us is both a child of God and a sinner, Edmund. If my religious studies program is approved, all the courses will highlight that fact."

Edmund swells with pride for his wife. He pictures her standing confidently in front of her class saying those words. She's doing something no one else has attempted at the university in these politically correct times. Obviously, she believes it is working.

"Good literature can change people, you know."

He sees enthusiasm in her eyes, and he envies it. Enthusiasm is another quality Ginnie has that he doesn't. These days, except for their lovemaking, the only thing that truly excites him is the prospect of cocaine.

She reaches across the table and puts a hand on his. "My students even want to perform the play! Can you imagine that? They suggested we get some of the teachers involved too, which I thought was a marvelous idea." She gets up, stands behind him, and puts her cheek against his, and an arm around his shoulders. "I'll be directing," she whispers in his ear. "I think your role should be Macbeth himself."

He laughs. "You've got to be kidding!"

"I'm serious. You used the play in your master's thesis, didn't you?"

Her fervor brings him into her passion for Shakespeare's creation. Maybe he can indeed play Macbeth.

As quickly as the excitement rises, the idea turns bitter. What if he, as the actor, disappoints Ginnie as the director? She will show him up again. "No. It wouldn't work. I haven't acted since we did *Our Town* years ago, and even then, it was a bit part."

"Yes, you dug my grave," Ginnie giggles. "But you know Macbeth well, and how conflicted he was. You'd be great!"

"As great a man as Macbeth?" he asks facetiously, because he does know the play well and never once admired Macbeth. In fact, he thought the character was written to personify evil. While writing his paper, the voice of his grandfather agreed. *Lucifer himself rebelled against a king! He broke the order God established, and it led to chaos for humanity!* On his completed paper, his professor commented that Macbeth was not evil personified, as Edmund presented him, but a man who, out of selfish desire, chose evil. He reminds Ginnie of that.

She rubs her fingers into his shoulders, relieving some of his tension. "I think you were more correct than your professor because Macbeth wasn't forced to choose evil and kill Duncan. If he had tamped down his selfish desires, he might have chosen otherwise."

"He could have. Except he wanted to be king himself."

"Yes. But his 'wanting to be' wasn't evil. The thought became evil when Macbeth acted on envy and his overwhelming desire to have the power of a king. The means he chose to have it was to kill another man, which is what destroyed him."

Edmund grits his teeth. The man wanted what he wanted, no matter what he had to do to get it.

Ginnie adds, "Macbeth made a free choice to murder."

Edmund thinks about it a moment and slowly nods. Macbeth was a disturbed man, and Lady Macbeth wore the pants in the family. Both had surely played a big part in leading him to it. "True. Macbeth made a free choice to murder."

"So, what do you think, Edmund, about playing Macbeth? Our first practice is tomorrow night. Just come try it." She kisses his lips then leads him into the bedroom, where, of course, he acquiesces.

With Ginnie in his arms, so close to his heart, his own falseness flies like a venomous bat through his head, leaving behind the words of Lady Macbeth's lesson in hypocrisy, "False face must hide what the false heart doth know." He often starts arguments with Ginnie about Dr. Burke, her dermatologist. Always, she talks about the doctor in an admiring way that incenses Edmund because he feels she's hiding something from him. But he is being two-faced. For years, Edmund has been hiding something from Ginnie.

It happened during his first year as a graduate student, just after their engagement, when they promised to love only each other.

And it happened one night after he'd been to Mal's for advice. For the first time, Mal offered Edmund cocaine. Edmund was hesitant to try it; he wasn't used to drugs then. But Mal encouraged him. "You'll be surprised at how good you feel."

Afterwards, he didn't feel good; he felt great, with a huge sense of empowerment that told him he could do anything he wanted. The downside was that he couldn't seem to remember how to find his way back to his student apartment, so he stumbled into a bar then ended up in a motel room with a blond woman. She was older than he was, and if she hadn't been wearing a mini-skirt and red patent leather boots, she might have reminded him of his mother—he still missed his mother terribly. The reminder was not because of what he saw in the blond woman's face; he could barely focus then. It was because, like his mother, she cleaned up another of his many mistakes.

"Sugar, you've made a mess," the blond woman said after he'd turned over his drink at the bar. "Let me help you." Then she grabbed a few napkins and sopped it up. There had been a band playing an old Chancee Wile song, "Daddy Don't Preach to Me," that the woman seemed to love because she climbed up on the long bar and started singing it along with the band—*No, Daddy. No, Daddy. Don't give me no sermon*, and then started prancing up and down the bar in her red patent leather boots. After she tripped and fell, still singing, into his arms, everything went downhill. Edmund didn't recall much of what had happened in the motel room, except he thought he'd taken off her red patent boots, and that she'd had bright red matching nail polish on her toes.

On his way home those years ago, he promised himself that he would never again take the cocaine that caused him to lose his in-hibitions and betray Ginnie. If Mal ever offered the drug again, he would not accept it, no matter how good it made him feel. Then, as soon as he opened the door to his small apartment, the first thing he saw was a copy of *The Love Song of J. Alfred Prufrock,* a poem assigned in his first undergraduate English class. The professor assessed it as an examination of the tortured psyche of an overeducated, neurotic, and emotionally stilted man. In reading it back then, Edmund had seen himself as that man, an alienated man, judged by others and condemned. And he knew Ginnie would judge him too, judge what he'd done that night, if she ever learned of it.

Lying beside her now, he's thankful she hasn't learned of it. Then he makes his excuse. The whole thing was completely different from a sustained affair—it wasn't a real betrayal. It was only the one night, and he'd only been engaged to Ginnie then. He hadn't known the woman, not even her name. He's never seen her again and hopes he never will. But Ginnie knows her dermatologist well, maybe too well. And Dr. Burke? He doesn't fool Edmund. True, the doctor seemed mild-mannered when Edmund first met him at Mal's infamous "End of Summer Party," but by now, Edmund has seen the man in action.

Yesterday, Ginnie called him on his cell to say that her car wouldn't start after her dermatology appointment, so he'd have to come pick her up. "I'll be waiting in the office," she said. When he got there, she was making a follow-up appointment with a girl at the reception desk while Dr. Burke, in his starched white jacket, stood with another assistant behind a high counter in the front office, all smiles and good looks.

"Your wife is a joy to treat," he told Edmund and then turned to his staff. "Isn't she, guys?" Naturally, they agreed, while Ginnie beamed then went over to the counter to give the assistant her insurance card. The innocent-acting doctor reached over to pat her shoulder as she left. "See you next time, Ginnie."

Tonight, as he studies her sleeping face, Edmund has a second thought about his visit to the dermatology clinic. He recalls seeing the doctor stroke Ginnie's shoulder, not pat it. Dr. Burke left his hand there too long to call it a pat. Could it have been the replay of a former, secret caress? At once, his head hurts and his stomach tightens, while Mal's question from earlier tonight spins like a toy top in his head: *Which one do you think Ginnie is having an affair with, her dermatologist or Dr. Patton?*

Ballet is not just movement, not simply abstract.
It's something beautiful.
Sometimes there's this feeling in the movement
that makes me want to cry.
—Nina Ananiashvili, *The Ballet Book*

CHAPTER EIGHTEEN

Angelina

Angelina sits alone on the lowest swell of the high hill looking down at the house she shares with her father. She remembers having no other home except the house on the Broussard farm. She likens its image to one of the stark white eggs she often gathers with Alma; inside the fragile shell is a womb, a point of reference toward life itself. The *house* is important, not because it is the building in which she lives, but because it is, itself, an idea. It is *home*. Unlimited by perimeters and colored only by shadows from the high hill, home is essential. The land around it is essential. The people, within and without, are most essential of all. For they are the ones through whom the idea passes. And it will continue to pass through them, and far beyond them. Earthly bodies are only rented for a lifetime; what comes afterward is eternal. Angelina believes that, and it gives her hope.

She loves the farm, loves the Broussards, especially Alma, and mostly, she is happy with her life. Because she was so young when she was first diagnosed with leukemia, she was unaware for many years that she could die from it. Now she understands that her life may not be a long one. When she asks her father about dying, he says, "No! You will live through this storm of affliction and for a long time afterwards." But there is such pain in his eyes, and he trembles when she speaks about it, so she no longer asks him, *When will I die?* Or, *What is dying like?*

The only person she talks to about death is Alma. More than a good friend, she's a soft pillow, one that Angelina can tuck between her ear and shoulder, someone she can hold on to. Alma listens. She doesn't tell Angelina not to cry at the thought of death. Instead, she says, *Cry when you need to, and I'll cry with you.*

The first time they cried together had nothing to do with Angelina's leukemia. They were painting a newer sign for the chicken farm. As they painted, they talked about Angelina's mother and then about Alma's father. "I wish I had known my mother," Angelina said.

"I wish I had known my father too."

They held each other for quite a while, without words, because each knew something of the other's loss. And then, Alma pulled away and smiled. "Since we don't know them, we can make them up."

"No, Alma. We can't just make people up. If they're not here, they're not real, so what good does it do to pretend?"

"It's not pretending exactly. It's your idea of how you'd like them to be. An idea is real, isn't it? Just a different way of seeing something. I'll help you, Angelina. What would you want your mother to be like?"

"I would want her to love me like your mother and Aunt Pauline love you. What would you want your father to be?"

"I would like him to be like *your* father, and to love me like Jose loves you."

Then, all at once, the realization came to Angelina. "Maybe we already have what we want, just in a different way."

"Maybe we do," Alma said, and they hugged, and then cried again.

Many more times after that, they laughed as young girls will do, hugged each other as sisters, and cried—especially those times when Angelina's disease worsened, and the prospect of death loomed over her. Before Alma could give her blood to pull Angelina through, it had been their tears, shed together, that helped her—that show of empathy, one for the other, that comes from deep within the soul.

Yet sometimes their common tears did not come from an experience of sadness at all, but from an expression of beauty. A red-orange and purple sunset viewed together as they climbed halfway up their high hill. The laugh of a baby girl belonging to a stranger who let them hold her and pass her between them while they pondered what it would be like to someday be a mother. A song Papa composed, music that pricked their hearts with emotion. The brilliant painting of a smiling, elderly man and his bright-eyed wife, her silver hair draping across his shoulder. A beautiful ballet—its gracefulness, its symphonic eloquence, its human yearning. The first time Angelina watched a ballet on television with Alma, Aunt Pauline, and Alma's mother, she said, "When I am cured, I want to be a ballerina."

"You don't have to be cured to be a ballerina, Angelina. You can be a ballerina now," Aunt Pauline said. "Ballet will show you how to move through your life like a lady, especially when life is not kind. Maybe you and Alma should take lessons."

"Oh yes, Aunt Pauline," Alma said. Alma's mother rolled her eyes, but Angelina could tell she thought it was a good idea too. So, Aunt Pauline made certain that both girls took ballet lessons. She signed them up with Miss Ursula—Bethel's best, and only, ballet instructor, an older, gray-haired woman from Hungary who had once danced professionally with the Hungarian National Ballet yet somehow ended up in Bethel, Alabama.

Their lessons became a team project. Before their first meeting with Miss Ursula, Moline took them shopping for black leotards and pink shoes and little pink zip-up bags to put them in because Alma's mother wanted the girls to have all the advantages a former star ballerina such as Miss Ursula could give them. And every Thursday afternoon, Jose drove them to Miss Ursula's studio, waited in his truck for their two-hour lesson to end, and then drove them home.

Angelina loved the lessons, and Miss Ursula as well. In a month, she and Alma had gained a sense of discipline in learning new positions, coordination, balance, and how to control their bodies in motion. Miss Ursula said both had the bodies of ballerinas and that they were progressing well. She wanted them to see the upcoming production of *Swan Lake* to be performed in Mobile, a ballet that had been danced for over one hundred years. "Still, t'ere's no more beautiful ballet t'an t'is one," Miss Ursula said in her thick Hungarian accent. For two weeks, the girls repeated her statement, mimicking her accent, until Aunt Pauline and Alma's mother put their hands over their ears and told them to stop. Then, on a Saturday afternoon, while Papa looked after the farm, Aunt Pauline and Alma's mother took them to Mobile to see the full production of *Swan Lake*.

Angelina was immediately drawn into the ballet and its story. She didn't say a word during the first act, mesmerized by the exquisite costumes, the gorgeous combination of blue and silver lighting, and the backgrounds that went from foreboding to joyful. Throughout, it was easy to see the ever-present threat of violence and pure evil juxtaposed against beauty, grace, and love.

"The dancer who plays Odette looks exactly like a swan," Angelina whispered to Alma during the second act. The ballerina was in a white tutu and feathered headdress.

"So does her evil twin," Alma whispered back when the same ballerina swirled on stage in the opposing role of Odile, in a black and gold tutu with a spiked tiara.

Moline said, "You know Prince Siegfried's future was decided for him. No one should have their future changed for them by a magician's trick. I'm glad he rebels to follow his heart. Exactly what I would do!"

"Unfortunately, that's true, Sister," Aunt Pauline whispered back a little too loudly. "It's just what you would do!"

Angelina usually enjoyed the twins' banter. She thought it was funny, but now, what Moline said about the prince's future struck her as serious. She agreed with Moline. She saw the same contrast of light and dark in her own life, the evil of her disease playing out against an abundance of love from her father, Alma, and the Broussard twins. She saw the innocence of Prince Siegfried and Odette in danger of being destroyed through a magician's trick by the dark and malevolent Odile, just as her own life was in danger of being destroyed by leukemia.

By the last act, all four were crying over the deaths of Prince Siegfried and Odette, the Swan Queen, as their spirits ascended into the heavens above Swan Lake. It was the most wonderful thing Angelina had ever seen. The triumph of good over evil gave her great hope. "One day," she whispered to Alma on the drive home, "I'm going to dance the role of Odette in *Swan Lake*."

Alma touched her arm. "You will be wonderful!"

Angelina looked at Alma. "Do you think death is really as beautiful as it was in the ballet?"

Alma shrugged. "I don't know. But I do know heaven is beautiful, and it's the place we're all made for."

"Yes. Except we have to die to get there. It's dying I'm afraid of."

"No, Angelina, don't you dare think about dying! You haven't gotten your pointe shoes yet." Alma put an arm around Angelina. "You're going to be the best ballerina the world has ever seen!"

Nothing is but what is not.
—William Shakespeare, *Macbeth*

CHAPTER NINETEEN

Mal

As he gets ready to leave for another day at Bethel University, Mal looks in the mirror above the chest of drawers in his bedroom and sticks out his tongue. His squirrel-colored hair is on the verge of turning gray, but his skin is still taut on his face, as if the years have ignored it. His tongue? Of course, it is not to be trusted. Manipulative words swim strongly from his mouth as if they are true. Clearly, they are not, but who will dare to tell him so? He's never encountered much opposition, not since he was dismissed from the godly seminary, and he spears any inkling of it with what the senseless might call ungodly ways. He has taken many brainless students under his wing by filling their bellies—and oh yes, their minds—with the lure of immediate gratification. First, he rids them of their inhibitions and then masks their personal truths with lies. It isn't hard. Most people will lie to attain a pleasure for which they long.

His silly apprentices long for the immediate gratification of drugs. But as an admired psychologist, he has long been privy to plenty of other means to sway a person toward the toleration of excess. Inciting greediness, revengefulness, freeing sexual urges, and provoking a craving for power are only a few of his favorites. And here at the university, he doesn't have a pious priest in charge to stop him—only the sanctimonious Ginnie Gillan.

His head pounds at the thought of a new Religious Studies degree in the College of Arts and Sciences. Even worse if she is in charge. Mal doesn't even want to consider the consequences. He knows a program like that, with the right professors, could change the minds of many students—even some of his own.

Of course, there are certain traits he looks for in his students—his apprentices, as he calls them. People with anxieties who find rage difficult to control, act impulsively, and have a hard time fitting in. Edmund fits the bill, but he's also a hard sell due to the controlling voices of his dead grandfather and his grandfather's God. But Mal is fixing that with the cocaine.

Unfortunately, Edmund's wife also tries to control him. Ginnie, the great teacher of wholesomeness and virtue. And she's making major headway. Amazingly, her students love her, while she gives them nothing tangible at all, only platitudes based on...What? A worn-out, so-called supreme being? If Mal wants to continue to oversee Edmund's mind, then it is time to dislodge Ginnie from it. Already, with her silly classes about a god in literature, she has become a threat to Edmund, and an even greater threat to Mal as the master of his itching, mindless students. Naturally, evil will judge its own. It needs no higher power to calculate for it. Because there is no god with a capital G. No God of perfection. If there were, there would be no defectiveness, no wickedness in man, and he, Mal, would never have been born.

Mal owns several guns, but the Bersa Thunder .380 is his favorite, the gun he showed to Edmund. He's a proficient puller of triggers, but any dislodgment of Ginnie cannot be done by his own hand. He never works that way. Always—dare he say it again?—evil needs a pawn.

He finishes dressing and drives to the university. Passing the auditorium to go to his classroom, he hears the play practice going on, so he peeks in. Edmund has just ended his lines as Macbeth in scene three of Act I.

My thought, whose murder yet is but fantastical, shakes so my single state of man

That function is smothered in surmise,

And nothing is but what is not.

They are Mal's thoughts exactly. He smiles, thinking he's like Macbeth, a man who knows that life has no spiritual meaning, which leaves all actions open to a world of confusion. No mental measurements, no standards for behavior exist because there is no God to put them there. Good and evil do not exist for Macbeth or for Mal. Both covet what they want without regard for any other human being. If he can make his student worshipers believe that "Nothing is but what is not," then they need no respect for order, no respect for hierarchy and a king called God. Goodness is cancelled. So, a person could literally get away with any so-called sin. Even murder.

He approaches Edmund as he walks from the stage. "You're actually playing Macbeth? How suitable for you and Ginnie! I suppose she's playing Lady Macbeth?"

"No. She's directing."

"Oh, of course. She would be directing." Mal glances around. "Where is she?"

"She had to check on something. She'll be back in a minute."

Mal smirked. *The fool playing Macbeth.* "Well, Edmund, how

do you like playing a man whose wife sees him as full of human kindness, and yet he commits murder?" He waits, then answers for Edmund. "Methinks Macbeth is quite a conflicted man."

"That's the point, isn't it?" Edmund replies just as Ginnie comes up behind him and puts a hand on his shoulder.

She glares at Mal. "Yes, that is the point. Macbeth is at odds with himself."

Mal chuckles. "To murder, or not to murder, and yet, he does murder. That is *my* point."

Ginnie buzzes in his face like a carpenter bee. "I don't care what *your* point is. I would appreciate it if you would leave."

He knows she is challenging him, which is both aggravating and exhilarating. But the exhilaration can't compare to his adoration of the hatred he feels for her.

He decides to accept her challenge. He is growing tired of Edmund. The fool is too easy to manipulate. "Ah yes, man is so good, and yet so evil, *n'est-ce pas?*" He laughs and heads for his classroom.

Standing behind his classroom podium for several moments, Mal considers the faces of his students. Young faces, but not innocent faces, except for one older woman about his age who simply sits in on the class. He doesn't know her name. He's never asked, though somewhere in the dean's office is a list of those few who signed up to audit his class. She isn't there for a grade, so he doesn't care who she is, but she has bright blue eyes that remind him of his silly sister, Charity; and like Charity, her eyes seem to question everything about him, from the tie he is wearing to the truth of what he says. If it wasn't for the woman, this class would be his favorite. Surely, these students are the most malleable. But here she is again in the first row, ready for him like Charity would be—a phony St. Michael with a sword of righteousness raised to defend the world against "the wiles and wickedness" of the devil.

"Well, bring it on, both of you!" he mutters to himself and then begins the lesson in his sturdiest voice—a direct attempt to battle Ginnie Gillan. "Today, we'll consider good and evil. Raise your hand if you believe in it."

Hands go up. Mal nods approvingly and continues. "According to a recent poll, more than eighty percent of people believe in good and evil, including ninety percent of Republicans and seventy-five percent of Democrats. Only twenty percent, however, believe that evil is born; fifty percent believe it is created by society, and thirty percent cannot decide."

He notices the older woman doesn't raise her hand, but her bright blue eyes remain focused on his face. She must be in the thirty percent of the poll. The undecided who just sit and listen. The "lukewarms" he likes to call them.

"It is *my* belief," Mal says, as if his is the only belief that matters, "that the concepts of good and evil are utilitarian excuses used in religion, in politics, and in societal families for the purpose of keeping human beings under the thumbs of the powerful. In themselves, good and evil are not real."

Immediately, the older woman's hand rockets straight up. He takes a breath and, charged with adrenaline, nods for her to speak.

"Your belief completely ignores that each singular human being makes his own decisions multiple times a day. Not everything is decided for him by religion, politics, or society. A person can definitely choose good or evil. I do it myself frequently. Don't you, professor?"

He sees that she is not lukewarm—no, not lukewarm at all—but he won't let on that she's ruffled him, though his former adrenaline high is gutted. He wishes she would just go away, but he must answer her question, aimed at him personally. "Of course, I make decisions. I'm talking about concepts."

Again, her hand shoots up. And again, he nods.

"But decisions *are* conceptual, and completely nonphysical. I would say that decisions are spiritual because many of them have much to do with the well-being of others."

A boy on the front row raises his hand but doesn't wait for Mal's nod. "The well-being of others is good, isn't it? And what is not done for the well-being of others is not good and can be evil."

The boy's voice is too confident. The blue-eyed woman is winning. Mal has to turn this discussion around. "Then what else is good? And what else is evil?"

The hand of the youngest girl goes up. "God is good."

Inside, Mal groans.

The boy sitting next to her—without even raising his hand—chimes in. "Satan is evil."

Yes, Bethel is truly a place of God, grits, and guns. Mal straightens his back and stands as tall as he can behind the podium with a forced smile. "This course is about human nature, not God. Making decisions does not require a belief in good and evil. Good and evil do not exist when human nature wants the best way to scratch an itch. The only pertinent question then is, Can I get away with it?"

Several heads turn to watch as the blue-eyed woman rises with an audible huff and abruptly leaves the class.

So what? The blue-eyed woman must have seen he was right. Just put a rock of crack, or a porn movie, or a shifty way to make a buck in front of any one of the students before him now, and it would be obvious. Their god is whatever feels good at the moment. Yes, the god of most people is their own pleasure.

A few weeks later, Mal can't resist going to the production of *Macbeth* for no other purpose than to see Ginnie Gillan fail.

Unfortunately, the production is a hit—first performed for the faculty and then twice for the public because the faculty liked it so much. There are nightly standing ovations for both Edmund and Ginnie, and Eleanor Burke, of all people, who plays Lady Macbeth.

Mal sits stiffly in the audience for all three performances. Of course, he's read the play, but he's never seen it on stage. In his mind, he criticizes each performance and keeps notes. The dialogue about man's propensity for evil enthralls him. And though he does not rise during the first two standing ovations, he does at the third. He has to give it to Shakespeare. The man knew how evil works.

"Will you walk into my parlor?" said the spider to the fly;
'Tis the prettiest little parlor that ever you did spy.
—"The Spider and the Fly," Mary Howitt

CHAPTER TWENTY

Edmund

Ginnie calls Edmund to say she has to work late, but there is uncommon excitement in her voice; he can almost see her smiling. A pause, and then, "Aren't you going to ask me why?"

"Okay. Why?"

"Well, I have some planning to do because—" She stops to giggle. "Oh Edmund, Sam has approved the Religious Studies degree program!"

"That's great! I'm proud of you." And he is. Instead of tensing with envy, he feels joy for his wife wash over him.

She has some planning to do with Sam, but after she meets with him, she's going to brainstorm for next semester's literature course by making a list of excellent authors who were spurred by their faith in God. "Next term, I'll assign each of my students a different author to report on, and then each will give an oral report to the class on why they believe their author has been placed on the list. That way we can cover more territory. I'll be home around ten…so keep the bed warm."

Excitement fills her voice, but Edmund knows she's really telling him not to go to Mal's. The old insecurities begin to creep in. Will she use her new success as one more way to control him?

"Okay." Then he abruptly ends the call.

Afterward, he stares at the wall a few minutes, thinking about her good news. He loves her and is happy for her. But what about himself? Where does he fit in her obvious rise at the university? He needs to talk to…someone, and who else is there?

So, Edmund walks to Mal's house. He won't stay long. He'll be home before Ginnie.

In his mind, a short way down the sidewalk, his grandfather stands before him, blocking his way. He points a finger at Edmund and says, *Hell is murky!* The old preacher wouldn't have known the words belonged to Lady Macbeth in the play's fifth act, but he had certainly known about hell. He thought he had the ability to see evil in others, and said he had the gift of presence to purge it out. However, he had not seen any evil in belittling his own grandson.

Edmund keeps walking past the invisible presence of his grandfather.

About halfway to Mal's, he recalls that as a boy, he always felt there must be something inside him that deserved the old man's insults and wondered how he could get it out. Then one day, the old preacher had some pamphlets printed to hand out at church entitled "How to Save Your Soul from Hell." Edmund saw them in his grandfather's office and thought about looking, but he didn't want to believe in hell. He didn't want to believe in anything his melodramatic grandfather believed in. And then he remembered the scorching summer morning when his grandfather stood in his Sunday pulpit waving a handful of the new pamphlets, until a few of them escaped and got caught up in the whirring of the tall fan behind the lectern. The pamphlets flew wildly about the congregation like white paper birds.

Edmund was sitting in the front pew beside his grandmother and caught one of them, as did several other people around him. His grandfather noticed and said excitedly, "People, if one of those pamphlets flew right to you, the Lord meant you to have it. He means you to know how to battle what's inside you. He means you to go to heaven and not hell. And on that piece of paper are your instructions."

Immediately, Edmund wanted to get rid of his pamphlet; throw it on the floor, or sit on it, or lay it in his grandmother's lap. Instead—because he wanted to know "what was inside" him—he opened the pamphlet and read the only words there: Follow the Good Book.

Then his grandfather went on. "We don't have nothing to do with how we get into this life, people, and I don't expect we're gonna have much to do with how we leave it. But where do we go after that?" He laid down the remaining pamphlets and raised up his Bible. "Well, that depends, brothers and sisters. That depends. Because it ain't like we're not responsible for the stuff in the middle, all the stuff we do between life and death. Every miserable thing we do, brothers and sisters. We will all be held accountable."

Edmund pushes the memory away.

At Mal's house, he knocks on the door.

"Come in, Macbeth." Mal grins when he opens the door. "I think the part fits you."

Edmund sits on the sofa. "I didn't want to be in the play. Ginnie wanted me to, so I did."

"Exactly why the role fits you. How are Ginnie and her dermatologist doing, or is it Ginnie and Dr. Patton now?"

He doesn't want to talk about that. His head throbs, and his grandfather's voice is still in his brain. *Every miserable thing we do, brothers and sisters. We will all be held accountable.*

He pushes the voice away. "Fine. I mean, Ginnie's fine. Patton is only her friend, and I'm trying to forget about her dermatologist." The thought of Ginnie together with either of them infuriates him, though. "In fact, Ginnie's more than fine. The degree program in religious studies has been approved." He watches Mal's face redden.

Mal springs from his chair. "I'll be just a minute." He leaves the room and returns with the Bersa Thunder .380, which he sets on the glass-topped table.

"It's a nice one," Edmund admits. "You've shown it to me before."

Mal grins, his face still red. "Oh yes, I'd forgotten." He opens the desk drawer next to him and sets the gun inside. "But I haven't forgotten this." From the same drawer, he pulls out a plastic bag and spreads out a few heaping lines of cocaine and then stands back, as if he's just fed a hungry dog from which he'd intentionally withheld food so he could get a grateful wag of its tail.

Edmund doesn't want to be grateful to him. He doesn't want to admit that Mal might have hold of his collar. Ginnie and his grandfather are enough to contend with, so he tries not to appear too pleased with Mal's offering. After sniffing a little, he steers the conversation away from Ginnie and back to the subject of his grandfather. "I need to get rid of the old man's voice. It's getting worse."

The old preacher's warnings are becoming more frequent, and he reminds himself that Mal is very accomplished, the president of the Alabama Regional Association of Psychologists. If Mal says cocaine is the answer, it has to be true. After all, his name is attached to several research papers. Edmund hasn't read any of them, though he's been meaning to read the most recent one, "The War Between Chaos and Order." He's been told it is a paper in which chaos wins.

"Tell me about your grandfather," Mal says.

Edmund thinks he's already told him enough over the past years, but he takes a labored breath and repeats the story. "The man who raised me—a holiness preacher—was a holy tyrant, a tall, hungry-looking figure with a prophet's unkempt beard who constantly cornered me, demanding that I justify even the smallest endeavor. First, he would ask me, 'What is its nature, Edmund?' And next, 'Is it sinful?' But before I could offer an opinion, he'd caution, 'Think carefully now. A mistake could cost you eternal life.' Sometimes the grilling took hours because he wouldn't let up until I gave him the answer he wanted. Then he'd pat me on the back and say, 'Only the holy are happy.'"

Edmund doesn't say so to Mal, but, oddly, revisiting those days, he often feels a measure of satisfaction, even certainty, that he and his grandfather might have been pursuing genuine Truth. Maybe the old man in his head, the old man Mal disparaged, *could* save his soul, because despite his dependence on Mal, Edmund never truly doubted that he had a soul, and that it needed salvation. After he met Mal, he lost any gratification he'd found in coming up with correct answers to please his grandfather or his grandfather's god. He'd traded it for the sheer delight that came from deriding the old man and his message.

Mal's dark eyes pinpoint Edmund. "What do you think your grandfather wants you to do?"

Edmund runs an impatient finger through the drug on the table. He is tired of talking, but he goes on. "The thing he said most was, 'Fix yourself, boy, lest you miss the promise of something grand.'"

"Well," Mal begins in a fatherly voice, "you could take his advice—be open to doing something grand, and solve the problem of Ginnie too. You know, kill two birds with one stone?" Mal pauses as if waiting for a response, but Edmund considers that something off-balanced is occurring.

"Are you listening?" Mal's voice is stern. "There is one easy measure that could produce something grand, just one easy measure with Ginnie." No mention of his grandfather now.

"Oh?" His eyes roam toward the white powder. As the first sniff begins to take effect, he covets more. A flash of thought kicks in, that Mal might be trying to provoke him into trying something more sinister than drugs, but he snorts another line and asks, "What easy measure is that?"

With a satisfied smile, Mal leans back on the plush, red cushions of his chair and cocks his head. "An act of masculine ferocity. You've heard the old wives' tale of scaring a person to stop his hiccups? Just frighten her a little. Besides, that grandness you talked about? It's there. It's just repressed. You need to let it out."

"How?"

"I'll loan you the gun. As long as you…are careful to cover yourself. Don't you dare mention my name. Don't you dare. Keep this between you and your grandfather and your wife, all right?" The psychologist rises to reopen his desk drawer. His clay-colored skin skulks its familiar trek down the sharp bones of his face as he finds the revolver and offers it to Edmund once more. "Come on, Edmund, I'm helping you out here. It's a noble gesture on my part, just for you. We've talked countless times about avoiding the old professor's trap—your inability to take action. Won't it be grand to take charge?"

"Yes, grand, but—"

"For now, just put the gun in your pocket!"

He does as Mal orders because he can't stay much longer. He needs to get home before Ginnie arrives. He leans forward and snorts more of the cocaine.

Mal continues. "By the way, did you hear that Ginnie's derma-tologist is getting a divorce? He must have a girlfriend somewhere."

In the drug-induced mellowness of the moment, Edmund disre-gards Mal's provocative words.

An hour later, he's safely asleep in bed when Ginnie returns home.

You cannot swim for new horizons
until you have the courage to lose sight of the shore.
—William Faulkner

CHAPTER TWENTY-ONE

Alma

Alma sits on the steps outside Jose's house, remembering the day just shy of three years earlier when Angelina tried so hard but did not succeed in climbing Bethel Mountain. She turns to gaze at sunlight cast across the high hill, but drifting clouds cause the light to move from tree to tree, boulder to boulder, as if not to play favorites. The intermittent light leaves behind dimness, a reminder of numerous unsuccessful attempts to rid Angelina of her leukemia. And yet, success has remained possible. Today, Alma is waiting again for success, waiting again for Jose to bring Angelina home from the hospital in his red delivery truck. Waiting for the miracle.

When she sees the truck winding its way home, Alma hurries to meet it and puts a hand through the open window on the passenger side to touch Angelina's shoulder, but her friend does not turn toward her. Her eyes remain fixed on whatever she sees beyond the windshield. Alma looks in the same direction and notices Bethel Mountain shrouded in the haze of a large cloud settling above. Alma senses something in Angelina's demeanor that warns her to ask no questions, at least not right now. She greets Jose instead. He gets out of the truck with a small suitcase to take into the house. "Wait there," he says to Angelina. "I'll just set this inside the door."

Angelina turns to Alma. "I know you want to ask how I am. It's just like before. They say I'm in remission. So, I suppose I'm fine, at least for a while. Dr. Roberts said if I can stay in remission for a full three years, he'll call me cured."

Angelina's never stayed in remission that long, but to encourage her, Alma says, "I think it will happen."

Angelina shrugs her shoulders. "If not, he mentioned the possibility of radiation, or even a stem cell transplant." At once, she appears thinner, her blue eyes almost indigo, more serious, and there's despondency in the sound of her voice as if she's lost all hope of being cured. Because of the doctor's reference to advanced treatment?

"Papa brought my paints to the hospital so I would have something to do besides worry. I painted a picture for you while I was gone. I'll show it to you in the house."

Jose comes out of the house and around to the passenger side of his truck. Angelina struggles to get out, and Jose offers her his arm, but she pushes it away and steps down on her own. Jose appears surprised, even a little hurt. It's not at all like Angelina to oppose help from her father.

Inside, the girls sit at the dining table Jose constructed years ago from yellow pine, and Angelina pulls a sketch pad from her duffle bag, opening it to a page. She tears the page from the pad and hands it to Alma—a watercolor painting of two girls with long blond hair who look like sisters. In front of the girls is their mountain, and leading up to the top of the mountain is a path bordered by trees and laid with different colored rocks of many sizes. The rocks are numbered from one to ten in Angelina's perfect calligraphy. On the crest of the hill is a scrolled gate, painted gold, and above the gate, the half-circle of a rainbow around which, again in calligraphy, are the words *Heaven's Gate*.

"It's beautiful, just what we imagined," Alma says.

"In the hospital, all I thought about was climbing Bethel Mountain. I wanted the gate to be real. Of course, I know it isn't, except on paper."

Jose strokes the top of his daughter's head. Did she tilt it a little to avoid his touch? Alma isn't certain. "Let's celebrate that Angelina is home," he says. He takes a carton of ice cream from the freezer and sets it on the table, then retrieves three spoons and bowls.

Angelina pushes her bowl away. "I'll celebrate after I've climbed Bethel Mountain, only when I've stood on the top of it."

"But why?" Jose asks. "Climbing a mountain is hard. You're not ready for that kind of struggle."

"I am ready, and I'm going to do it. Tomorrow."

"Let's see how you feel tomorrow. You may need to wait a day or two."

"No, I don't need to wait. I'll be ready tomorrow." Angelina's tone is defiant, almost as defiant as Alma's mother's tone toward Aunt Pauline when her twin expresses opposition to Chancee Wile.

"I know you want to try, Angelina. You have your heart set on it, but it won't be easy, and you may—"

"Stop, Papa!" she hisses at him with narrowed eyes. "Don't say another word."

Jose looks puzzled and even more hurt as she goes on.

"Yes, I do have my heart set on it. I know it won't be easy, and I know I'm sick. But in a way my sickness has made me stronger because I already know how painful it is to struggle for something I want. I'm used to it. So, I will climb that hill tomorrow, and I will stand on the top of it."

"But why suffer when you don't have to?" Jose asks. "Tomorrow, you don't have to."

"Papa, I *want* to. You know yourself that nothing comes without a struggle. Wasn't it you who once said that suffering plus faith equals salvation?"

She turns to Alma then, speaking to her as an older sister might. "We're too old now to simply draw up a storyboard of our life and then just imagine it's going to come true. If we want it to come true, we must make an effort and suffer through it. So many times, I've simply imagined I would wake up one day and be healed, but it doesn't happen that way."

Alma doesn't argue, but she doesn't agree that a storyboard is useless. Isn't every human life created in God's imagination, coming to fruition through His ongoing storyboard? And didn't that same storyboard send His own son to earth for the greatest of reasons?

Angelina turns to Jose. "Unless I put forth every effort, a healing may never happen. So, yes, I will try the hill once again. And I'll succeed. I will get to the top this time. And no one can do that *for me*, Papa. Not even you."

Jose remains silent and looks at his daughter as if he perceives something brand new in her. "Well then, go ahead. Climb your mountain. You are right. You already know about battling hills, and so far, there is not one you haven't beaten."

Alma is surprised at Jose's words. She thought he'd put his foot down and tell Angelina she couldn't go.

The next morning, Alma and Angelina meet at the mountain, the sun just peeking over its crest. Each has a small backpack, a towel, and bottles of water provided by Jose. At first, they climb with little effort, until the heat of the sun beams hotter on their backs, and some of the rocks become unstable beneath their feet. Angelina stumbles and scrapes her knees. Alma helps her up, but now, Angelina grapples with each step as blood trickles down both her legs. Suddenly, she laughs as if she's thought of something comical. "I have a question, Alma." She points to her bleeding legs. "Whose blood do you think this is? Mine or yours?"

Alma laughs too. She takes out her towel, wipes the blood from Angelina's leg, and pretends to study it. "Hmm. Hard to tell." She smiles. "So, we'll call it 'our' blood. And since we're halfway up now"—she rubs the towel on a large, gray rock, leaving a blush of red behind— "we'll mark the spot with it."

"Yes!" Angelina says. "Today, it's 'our' mountain, marked by 'our' blood."

"And today is the day we get to the top of it."

But soon, as Angelina continues to climb, she struggles again, perspiring profusely and growing pale. To keep from stumbling, she grabs hold of the low branch of a pine to steady herself.

"Maybe we should go back," Alma says. "You might fall and really hurt yourself this time."

"No!" Angelina lets go of the branch and takes off with Alma close behind her, then turns to looks at her friend. "Are you going to catch me if I fall?" Before Alma can answer, Angelina grins. "Don't worry, Alma. I won't fall. We're going to make it this time."

An hour later, they reach the top of the mountain, one right after the other. Of course, they don't find a golden gate, only delight in what they have done. Angelina sits, slumped over her knees, clutching the sides of the last rock she climbed. Exhausted, she lets out a breath and smiles. Her face is shining from perspiration, wet as the tiny chicks they'd watched working so hard to break from their shells and step into a completely new existence.

Storyboard or not, Alma cannot help but imagine Angelina stepping into new life, minus leukemia. Gate or not, Alma sees her friend standing before the scrolled, golden gate, Heaven's Gate, basking in the colors of a rainbow above it. She pictures herself there, as well, holding the hand of her father.

"I'm aching all over, but I think it was worth it," Alma says.

Angelina stands and looks around. "Oh, yes! It was worth every painful step. Up here, all is peaceful. There is no sound except the wind, and we can almost touch the sky." She looks down to the pasture, the house, the road leading to Bethel. "All the chaos below us, leukemia included, seems of no consequence now." With her face painted in sunlight, she says, "I am filled with hope for both of us, Alma. We conquered a mountain. If we can do that, then it's possible for you to find your father, and for me to get well for good."

No! I am not Prince Hamlet, nor was meant to be;
Am an attendant lord, one that will do
To swell a progress, start a scene or two,
Advise the prince; no doubt, an easy tool,
Deferential, glad to be of use,
Politic, cautious, and meticulous;
Full of high sentence, but a bit obtuse;
At times, indeed, almost ridiculous—
Almost, at times, the Fool.
—T.S. Eliot, *The Love Song of J. Alfred Prufrock*

CHAPTER TWENTY-TWO

Edmund

He hid the gun Mal gave him in the bottom of his running bag, which he keeps in the closet. He doesn't think much more about it until morning, driving to the university. He is seized by a horrible headache, a red-hot burning in his stomach, and a swirling of emotion concerning Mal's words and the jealousy they continue to arouse in him. *By the way, did you hear that Ginnie's dermatologist is getting a divorce? He must have a girlfriend somewhere.* Of course, Mal meant that the girlfriend is Ginnie. What if that's true? Will Edmund be the laughingstock of the university? What will they say about him—that his regal wife is too good for him? That he is truly a fool? What will his students say? Especially the kind girls who thought him a hero. He is nobody's hero. Especially not Ginnie's. She says she loves him, and shows him love, but still, he's not sure. She may think she'd be better off without him. She'll more than likely get a promotion and a raise for developing a new degree program, while he will remain far beneath her as an adjunct professor. Is he envious of her, his own wife?

An older lady in the car in front of him slams on the brakes at the stoplight, and he almost runs into her. He is furious, wants to open his window and yell something demeaning. Then comes his grandfather's warning. *Anger produces disorder and chaos. Calm down, Edmund! You'll alert the noises again.*

Oh yes, the noises inside him, something he did not tell Ginnie about when he was trying to be honest. He did not say that clanking and crashing noises often assault his mind, fabricating enough fear inside him that cannot move or act or even think of anything else. He did not tell her that his mind is filled with paper doors like those in a young child's book, or that those paper doors open to pictures so grotesque that he must mentally paste them down so he will not see what is behind them. He did not tell her that when they make love, he is sometimes afraid she will devour him, leaving only his brittle bones, so easily broken. How could he possibly tell her these things? If he does, he is certain she will call him a lunatic and leave him on the spot.

The traffic light changes to green, and he and the older woman continue. Oddly, both turn into the university parking lot. If she has something to do with the school, he's thankful he didn't yell at her. She isn't a professor, though, and she doesn't look like a student, but older people with certain interests sometimes monitor a particular class for no credit. The university welcomes that. The woman goes into the building while he's gathering up his teaching materials. In the hall, he notices the woman again, entering Mal's classroom. Then he runs into his boss.

"Good morning, Edmund," Henry Patton says. "Where's your better half? I thought you two rode together." Of course, he would ask about Ginnie. The headache and red-hot burning in Edmund's stomach worsen.

"Not always," he says and keeps walking. "Our schedules are different today."

"Edmund, wait."

Edmund stops and turns immediately.

Patton approaches and stands close to him, as if what he's going to say is confidential. "I think there's something we need to discuss. A couple of miscalculations that may be putting you in dangerous territory."

"What miscalculations?"

Patton's face reddens, and he speaks guardedly. "Well, first, I have no interest in Ginnie except as a friend. I still think of her as the little girl I knew. For that reason alone, I feel close to her. I believe you and she make a lovely couple, so there's no reason to be jealous of me."

For the second time this morning, Edmund is furious with a woman, and this time it's the woman he knows intimately. No one except Ginnie could have told Dr. Patton that Edmund is jealous of him. As usual, Edmund does not know what to say, or how to say it; he only knows he must curb his anger around his boss. He tries to smile and slough it off. "Oh, I'm not jealous. Mostly, I was teasing Ginnie, but I wish she hadn't said anything about it to you."

Henry Patton looks surprised. "She didn't say anything about it. Mal did." For a few seconds, they stare at each other quietly. Then Henry continues. "Mal himself is the other miscalculation I wanted to mention to you. From my own observations, no one else's, and because I care about both you and Ginnie, I must tell you that I think Mal is leading you down a false path. I think you should listen to Ginnie."

Now he is certain this is Ginnie's work. When things don't go her way, she calls for backup, just as she did when her course was briefly cancelled. Of course, she and Patton have talked! Naturally, she told him that Mal was a bad influence because she hates the man and always has. And now, here stands his boss, with whom he can do nothing but agree, passing on Ginnie's instructions. He can feel her devouring him and gnawing on his bones, at the same time believing that she's helping her husband by keeping him away from Mal. Had she told Patton about the gun too? Yes, she must have. Of course, that would be after she told him about the drugs. She has ruined him! The clanking and crashing noises assault him again, filling him with fear until he cannot move. He tries to paste closed a paper door, now opening before him, showing him the distortions of death and hell. But he is not successful.

"Are you alright, Edmund?" Dr. Patton asks, his voice echoing, as if coming from a deep well.

"Fine. I'm fine," he says, as his teaching materials fall from his shaking hands.

"Let me help you." Patton bends to pick up the fallen folder, its papers scattered.

"No! I'll get them myself." Edmund gathers the papers quickly and hurries to his classroom, looking back to see Dr. Patton studying him as if Edmund were a social experiment. The sociology of—what? Absurdity? Obsession? Inhibition? Maybe all of them, he thinks as he enters his empty classroom. He closes the door and looks at his watch; he will have no students for another half hour. He sets the now-rumpled folder on his desk, collapses in the chair behind it, and tries to breathe in and out, but the sound of his

breath keeps repeating Ginnie's name in his mind until he feels betrayed by the woman he loves—just as his mother betrayed him
by not keeping him safe, just as Mal betrays him when he closes
his house to him, just as God betrayed him, years ago, when He
allowed his family to be killed, his childhood home to be sold. Even
God had not been faithful. And now, Ginnie has given away his
secrets to Henry Patton.

When the buzzer rings for class to begin, Edmund hears it only
as a clanging noise in his head. And when the room fills with students, Edmund does not see them or hear them. He sits in front of
them, silent for at least fifteen minutes, until one of the kind girls
who'd thought him a hero touches his arm and whispers, "We're
here, waiting for our class." Only then does he stand, open the folder with his crumpled notes, and in a trembling voice, begin.

The question is not how to get cured, but how to live.
—Joseph Conrad

Chapter Twenty-Three

Moline

Moline enters Alma's room and sits beside her daughter on the bed as she puts on her usual school shoes. "Forget school today. We need to get on to the hospital, sugar. Jose called. Angelina needs your blood."

Hurriedly, Alma shoves her feet into the shoes and stands, ready to go. "I knew it was happening. She was so pale and weak yesterday, so sick. It's like she's trapped in the old barbed wire fence and just can't get out."

"Well, that's why you're going to the hospital, isn't it? To get her out."

"But what if my blood doesn't help this time? What if she doesn't go into remission?"

"It's always worked before. Hush up while you're ahead, baby." Moline puts an arm around her daughter's shoulder. "Of course, we all know stuff can happen. And if does, it's alright to cry, even throw a hissy fit. It's alright to fall to the floor and kick and scream. But when that's over, you'll get up, girl. You'll put on your lipstick—despite what Pauline says—and go about your business. This is life, after all, and it is a risk. Sometimes it will hurt and won't go the way we want it to. But you and I? We won't quit living because of it."

Pauline often calls Moline as reckless as Chancee Wile, and maybe she is, but she's tough, too, with the endurance to persevere until she wins, no matter what it costs her. Moline has no doubt that if Chancee ever got leukemia, she would beat it and make it known to the world that she did it by her own human power. But Angelina is different. She has been tutored by Jose. Instead, she relies on the greater power of God.

"Will you come with me, Mama? Alma asks. "Like you did the first time?"

Moline doesn't hear Alma. She's deep in thought, looking into Alma's blue eyes and wondering. Did Alma's father have blue eyes, too? Did Alma have his mouth and nose? Because they were not Moline's. In fact, there wasn't much about Alma's face that resembled Moline. And what was inside Alma's head and heart—goodness and kindness—did not come from her either. Alma's father must have been a good man, someone loving, who wouldn't hurt a fly. Because that's who Alma is.

"Mama?" Alma touches her arm. "Are you listening? Will you go with me?"

"I was just thinking about…yes, of course I will. Just let me call work and tell them I'll be a little late."

A half hour later, the polished floor of the hall shines in front of Moline and Alma, capturing their blurred images and echoing the sound of their footsteps. The entrance to the hall looks exactly like the exit, Moline thinks. Angelina's hospital room is on the second floor. Room 202. If there were no numbers on the doors, she could lose her way in this place where beginnings and endings occur in the same split second, where faces and pain come and go. And where, for Angelina and Alma, the start of a dream takes place over and over again.

They see Jose in the waiting room, his place of choice during transfusions. They go in to give him a hug, then head for Angelina's room. Moline takes a breath before she opens the door. Angelina looks colorless and her breathing is shallow, like on every other day she's needed a transfusion. Moline is certain Alma's heart is aching, but her daughter smiles at Angelina and kisses her forehead.

"I'd like to stay with my daughter while she donates," Moline says to the nurse. The nurse nods and says, "Let's begin."

Alma's blood is taken directly, withdrawn from her arm by means of a hypodermic syringe, then passed through a plastic tube to a collection bag to which sodium citrate has been added in order to prevent Angelina's blood from clotting. It is passed by gravity from a container down through a plastic tube and into a vein in Angelina's arm. Sometimes it takes two hours, sometimes a little less. Moline watches her daughter quietly follow through with what Pauline would call a worthy risk. Yes, a worthy daughter—another gift from her unknown father?—and her worthless mother.

Both girls remain quiet for a while, Angelina looking up at the paneled ceiling, a fearful look, an anything-can-happen look. Finally, Alma looks over at Moline. "Don't worry, Mama. By now it's all routine."

Angelina gives a cynical smile. "Yes, routine," she says, then closes her eyes.

Moline knows that uncertainty will remain with Angelina as long as she is not pronounced "cured." She also knows that routines are frequently broken, by good fortune or bad. In that moment, Moline's eyes set on Alma, so good, so noble. And something quivers then rises inside her. Is it contrition? A yearning to scour herself, like cleaning the refrigerator to get rid of anything spoiled? All at once, she no longer wants to give in to those "less than good" things in her life. But can she change them? Yes, it is true that Alma has no father, and a mother who is a nutcase at times. These are chaotic things caused by Moline. Things that have brought disorder to Alma, as well as herself. Moline cannot physically repair them now. But she can, at least, mentally confront them.

So, Moline uses her imagination, possibly the only thing Alma has inherited from her mother. She pictures her mind as a sieve, like the colander she and Pauline use to wash dirt and grime off vegetables from the garden. And she sees herself, one day, washing away the disordered things in her life, until all her chaos flows down a drain to nowhere, and she is left only with order, sparkling and clean and valuable.

Of course, the thing about imagining a resolution is that no one else can see it unless it is carried out. No one else can carry it out except the imaginer. So, procrastination often gets in the way.

It is in the solitary mind and soul of the individual that the
battle between good and evil is waged and ultimately won or lost.
—M. Scott Peck

CHAPTER TWENTY-FOUR

Jose

J ose glances at the clock. Two hours until he needs to drive
to Bethel Hospital for visiting hours. Despite her success in
climbing the mountain with Alma, Angelina has had another
relapse that required another transfusion. He is grateful to Alma for
sharing her blood with his daughter. They are truly like sisters by
now, he thinks.

His heart feels full because Angelina is again in remission, though
she won't be strong enough to come home for another few days. But
what does that really mean? It does not mean she is cured. It does
not mean the disease that has overtaken her will not return. And
yet, that is his prayer, and he trusts in it. After all, he tells himself, I
am here because I trusted that I would be able to provide for myself
and my daughter. So, he will continue to trust until the word *remission* becomes the word *cured*. They only have to be patient, and it
will come to pass.

Before he leaves for the hospital, he means to tackle the two huge, dangerous sago palms leading up to the side porch of the Broussards' home. Theirs is a nice house, although in all these years, he's only seen the kitchen and living room. His is a nice house, too, he thinks. Perfect for him and Angelina. His house is small and old, probably built a half century ago for a tenant when the Broussard place was a sustainable peanut farm. When he and Angelina moved in, the little house was not in good shape, but now it seems to sparkle—new paint inside and out, and furniture he built with his own hands during the time he had off from the chicken business.

He helped Miss Pauline establish the business, starting from scratch. He thought they worked well together, putting a business plan in place and working backward from the number of eggs they planned to sell each week to how many chicks they needed to meet that goal. During her prime, a laying hen would, on average, produce three to five eggs a week. At first, they planned to sell ten dozen eggs a week, so they did the math and began with thirty chicks, thinking they would be able to sell to several of Bethel's small grocery stores. With their heads together, they figured out pricing and decided to raise the chickens on pasture rather than caged. Not only did it make sense with the many empty acres of land that the Broussards owned, it made for better eggs with a deep, rich orange yolk. So, they advertised the difference. Soon they were selling twenty dozen, then thirty, then forty, and the number continued to increase. Angelina and Alma helped paint a sign on the doors of the red delivery truck Miss Pauline bought for the business. This time, they spelled the words correctly: *Broussard Farm, Fresh Orange-Yolk Eggs. Wholesale or Just You.*

He wishes his family could have seen it, his American house and the business he runs. He wishes they could have known Angelina, and that he and his daughter have a happy life here. He wishes they were not all dead—his brothers, his mother and father. Then he stops himself; wishing won't change what is. His father laid out the path for their family when he opened a door to corruption and led Jose's brothers through it. And that corruption was the death of all of them, except his mother who died last, from grief over the sons and husband she'd prayed for.

She'd prayed for him too. In his younger years, Jose rarely saw her without a rosary, her hands moving over the beads, her lips moving in silence. He'd always considered himself strong, but seeing his mother turn her family over to God made him feel protected and stronger, even as each member of the family died and was buried. He did not attend their funerals. He did not cry for them, especially not for his mother—though he never failed to think about her—because she was headed to eternal life.

When he contemplated the choices his father had made, choices that affected all of their lives, he at first felt anger. But mostly, he felt vulnerable and alone. Maybe that was why he wanted Angelina so much, wanted to raise her himself in a home where he could be a good father and shelter her from harm. But he hadn't been able to perfectly protect her, not from the awful disease of leukemia. He was a man of faith and always would be, but he had come to realize that each life has its own crucifixions, and that for every human being—often through no fault or personal corruption of their own—simply living in this world is perilous, especially without a strong foundation of home.

The twins' house is set on a strong brick foundation that, unlike the rest of it, still appears almost new. The white planks above the foundation are peeling in a few places. The sturdy steps that lead up to the side porch are almost hidden, covered by the only large shrubs left in the yard—two prickly sago palms with ominous fronds that seem to reach out and frisk anyone who tries to enter the porch from the outside. Recently, Jose noticed long scratches on

Alma's arms and questioned her about them. "The palms did it," she told him.

Jose became concerned. Sago are thorny plants that can be toxic. He led Alma immediately to Miss Pauline, who at once doctored the scratches with alcohol so they wouldn't get infected. When Alma winced from the sting, Jose winced too. "I will take them down. It should never be painful for someone to enter their own home, their place of safety."

He glances at the time again, to be sure he won't be late getting to the hospital, then takes the large clippers in hand and walks to the Broussard house to clip the hazardous bushes from the side porch steps. As he knew they would, the treacherous fronds slap back at him, cutting his cheek until it bleeds. He wipes off the blood with the back of his sleeve and continues until half the fronds are gone. He takes off his work gloves and sits on the steps to rest for a moment, looking toward his little house in the distance and remembering Annette, Angelina's mother.

Over the years, he sometimes wondered if she lied about his being the father of the baby she was carrying—a baby she'd wanted to abort and have him pay for. The thought has bothered him for years; it is entirely conceivable that Angelina is not his daughter. He knew Annette had been familiar with one-night stands; he could see it when he met her. He is not a stupid man. But back then, he'd been barely twenty and gullible. He does not like the thought of having been played, and yet when he considers all he's gained because of a likely lie by Annette, he feels nothing but gratitude. Maybe Angelina isn't the child of his body, but she is the child of his heart, the most important person in his life, and he will love and protect her no matter what.

When she was in elementary school, she asked him about her

mother, and if she looked like her. Then she smiled and said, "Because I know I don't look like you."

So, he made up a fine lady, one he saw in his wishful mind as real. "Oh yes, you look just like her. She was beautiful and kind. You would have loved her."

"But why didn't she love me?"

"She did love you, Angelina."

"Then where is she? If she loved me, she would be here, wouldn't she?"

"She would, if she could, but…she can't." His eyes filled, and he couldn't go on.

Angelina jumped to the only conclusion she could come to at that time. "Oh, Papa, how did she die? Did she have leukemia too?"

"No. No, she didn't have leukemia. It was…a different sort of disease." Then he gathered her in his arms. "Mi niña, can we talk about this another time?" His voice and his heart were breaking over the lie. Even his arms trembled as he held her.

She kissed him. "Yes. At least I know she loved me."

Again, Jose puts on his heavy work gloves and begins to slash what's left of the menacing, overgrown appendages of the sago palms as if they were the cause of Angelina's leukemia. A fury rises within him each time a poisonous frond falls to the ground. In an angry, rasping voice that does not even sound like his, he eggs himself on. "Get rid of it! Destroy it!" He does not wonder or care that the bushes might be vulnerable in winter, and surely not that such a close cutting may stunt their growth. He only cares that they will no longer prevent the entering of a house that belongs to people he loves. When he is finished, he wipes the perspiration from his face, ignores the blood coming through the cotton of his long sleeve shirt and the sting of bleeding scratches on his face.

He cleans up the mess and hauls it off, leaving each of the perilous sago palms stripped and naked to the trunk and perhaps in danger themselves. He heads back to his own house to shower, after which he will drive to the hospital, and he and his daughter will once again stand up to her disease. No matter what it takes to protect his Angelina, he will do it, as long as he can.

I confess I have yet to learn that a lesson
of the purest good may not be drawn from the vilest evil.
—Charles Dickens

Chapter Twenty-Five

Alma

After missing her first day at work because of Angelina's transfusion, Alma dresses for her new job as a salesperson at Dillard's, which isn't something she wants as a career, but it will help her save money for nursing school after she graduates and keep her around people so she can practice her bedside manner. "A bedside manner is important if your goal is to be a nurse," Aunt Pauline told her. "A nurse has to be kind and loving. So, you'll have to seek out and study kind and loving people"—Aunt Pauline gave a slight tilt of her head toward Alma's mother— "because those qualities don't come naturally to everyone."

Alma's mother didn't hear the comment because she had a towel wrapped around her head. She'd just washed and dyed her hair and was busy painting her nails bright red.

Alma used to wonder if her mother ever noticed anything of importance besides herself. Did she ever notice a new day or new season? Or the desolation of winter that comes with bare branches and dead leaves on browning grass yet gives way to the greenness of spring, never failing to usher in gardenias and magnolias? Or the gold-orange heat of a summer sun and the garden's fresh vegetables they harvest for their table? And especially, Alma's favorite, the season of fall, when the land moves in a rustling wind as if breathed upon, spattering the high hill in tiny dots of color like a pointillist painting or a postcard sent to impress. Oh yes, when God created the seasons, He gave a lesson to human life that rebirth is always possible, in fact, intended. For a long while Alma thought that her mother missed out on that part of life's wholeness.

But then, last winter, Alma, Aunt Pauline, and Alma's mother had been standing together by the window, in silent awe of the unusual snow falling on the land around their house. They rarely had snow in this part of Alabama, but that day, everything glistened: the trees, the grass, Angelina and Jose's house in the background, even the new fence. Alma thought about how God created each snowflake to be different just as He created each person to be different from anyone else. He made them individuals with their own distinct personalities, talents, and dreams. She recalled from a school lesson that each snowflake has six sides and is made up of some two hundred crystals—each tiny one! She hadn't seen any of that with her eyes and yet trusted it was true. Amazing, she thought, that such a small piece of snow could be so intricate, so unique, and yet all of them together created the one immaculate phenomenon happening in front of their eyes.

She glanced up and smiled at her mother and aunt. Even then, the faces of the twins were not the same. Aunt Pauline's appeared peaceful, but her mother's expression surprised her—wide-eyed and awestruck, very uncommon for Moline. Her mother had truly noticed something apart from herself.

Breaking the silence, Moline turned her face from the snow to Alma. "Did you know your name means 'soul'?"

"No, I did not." Alma continued to gaze at the snow. She wondered why her mother had thought of such a profound word as soul, when before, she had not appeared to think profoundly about much of anything.

"Well, it does." She turned to Aunt Pauline for affirmation. "Alma's name means 'soul,' doesn't it, Sister?"

Aunt Pauline seemed startled, too, at the unexpected seriousness of her twin. "Sister, the word is of Latin, Italian, Hebrew, and I believe Arabic origin. And it means 'nourishing,' 'kind,' and you're right, 'soul.'" Aunt Pauline liked to show her intelligence by giving more information than was asked for. She put an arm around Alma's shoulder. "You have a lovely name, and it's perfect for you."

"Yes, I'm glad I named you Alma," Moline said to be certain she received the credit. "I started to name you Chancee, after Chancee Wile, you know. But when I looked at your little face, I knew you'd be nothing like her. Of course, I was correct."

Okay, Alma thought, the mother she expected had returned. Thanks be to God she'd not been named Chancee Wile!

The thoughts of snow skitter away with the heat of the day on her skin. She's filling out employment papers for her new job at Dillard's. Signing her name, she thinks how dreadful it would feel to sign the name Chancee Wile! Then she hands the paperwork to the manager, and he directs her to a counter.

"We've all had a first job," a middle-aged woman named Rose says, patting her hand after she shows Alma what to do with the sales receipts. "No one here expects perfection, just that you do your best, sweetheart." Right off, Rose reminds her of both Angelina and Aunt Pauline. "Her best" is what she plans to do at Dillard's.

Her first customer is a boy who appears to be a little older than she is—the handsomest boy she's ever seen, which makes her nervous. He says he needs a bracelet for his girlfriend, that it's her birthday. Since it is August, she tells him that the August birthstone is peridot. "Would you like to see a bracelet with peridot?"

He laughs. "What's a peridot?"

She thinks he might be teasing, but his laugh relaxes her. She smiles as she takes out a bracelet with the greenish yellow stones and hands it to him. "Here. The pamphlet says it's known to the Egyptians as the gem of the sun. It's formed deep in the earth's magma and erupts to the surface through volcanoes, plus it's been found in meteorites and comet dust."

"Comet dust? Wow!" When he smiles his eyes are bright, and green as the peridot stone.

"Yes. I think comets are amazing, thousands and thousands of years old. One day they show up as a surprise and then disappear again for another several thousand years before they return," she says, remembering a conversation with Aunt Pauline.

The boy gives her a serious look, almost a look of warning. "I think that's the message in them. They're always around, whether we see them or not."

Alma agrees. "A lot of things happen that we don't see."

Then comes another smile from the boy, and she notices his perfect white teeth. "Well, if you have a sturdy tripod and a camera with a good telephoto zoom lens, you can take pictures of comets. I've done it myself."

She grins at having read him correctly. He knows more than he lets on. "Are you an astronomer?"

"Only an amateur at present, but it's my major at the university. Do you like astronomy, too?" He is still holding the bracelet and fingering its stones.

"I like what I've read about astronomy. My friend Angelina and

I love to look at stars and the constellations. There's a hill we climb where the top of it brings them so close!" She thinks how much Angelina would love talking to this boy who knows the heavens.

"Where's the hill? I might be able to show you my favorite constellation, Scorpio. It's viewable in August. I could bring my telescope and camera and then photograph it."

"Scorpio?"

"Yes, and there's a legend that goes with it. Do you want to hear it?"

"Sure."

"Well, in Greek mythology, Scorpius represents a scorpion sent to get rid of the great hunter Orion, who was so arrogant he wanted to kill every animal in the world just because he could. Scorpius was small, but he went after Orion anyway, and there was a great battle."

"Scorpius was courageous."

"Yes, he got a place in the heavens for that, but so did Orion. The goddess Artemis, who favored Orion, placed them on opposite ends of the night sky. Scorpio can still be seen today, endlessly chasing Orion. I could show you that too."

Alma smiles. "I suppose that story tells us to care for all creatures, large and small."

"Like I said, I could come to your hill and show you and your friend. Maybe over the weekend?"

She doesn't have a chance to answer him; another customer with a question comes to the counter. When the customer leaves, Alma turns back to where the boy was standing, but he is gone. And the bracelet she showed him is gone, too. She looks everywhere, thinking she may have misplaced it. But it is nowhere to be found. Then an alarm goes off, and the head of the jewelry department rushes toward her. "What happened here?"

Her hands are sweating now. "I don't know exactly." Her voice trembles as she says, "I believe the boy I was waiting on took it."

The head of the jewelry department looks as if his head might explode until Rose, the kind, middle-aged woman Alma spoke to earlier, comes to soothe the situation and remind their boss that he had a first day too. "I remember it well." Her eyes pinpoint his. "Do you?"

At once, the young department head calms down.

At home, Alma nervously tells her mother and Aunt Pauline what happened. Moline gasps. "Did they fire you on the spot?"

"They didn't fire me at all. The head of the department just said I ought to learn a thing or two about people. He said some people will be really nice just so you'll trust them; but then, they'll take everything they can while your back is turned. He said I shouldn't trust anybody who comes into the store—that I should always keep my eyes on them."

"So true, so true!" Aunt Pauline sighs. "Trusting can be hazardous."

Moline nods. "Yes, it can. You shouldn't be so naïve, Alma."

"But we have to trust, don't we? And we're supposed to care about others."

Aunt Pauline turns to Alma. "Do you think, when he stole the bracelet from Dillard's, that handsome boy cared about you, or about how much trouble it would cause you?"

"I don't know. Maybe he thought about it later. Maybe he was sorry—"

Moline interrupts. "I wouldn't count on his being sorry, Alma. You need to be aware that there are people in this world who do harm to others, either for their own benefit or because some person or some circumstance pushes them into it." Moline stops for a second, a dreadful expression on her face. She puts her fingers to her mouth as if her own words remind her of something sorrowful. Then she recuperates and speaks with passion. "I'll tell you one thing for certain, Alma. That boy *knew* what he was going to do when he walked up to your counter, and he used your inexperience to do it. So, next time, don't be so naïve. Never let down your guard."

Aunt Pauline sets a hand on her twin's shoulder. "Well, I declare, Moline! There are times when you actually make sense."

We are all born mad. Some remain so.
—Samuel Beckett

CHAPTER TWENTY~SIX

Edmund

Early Friday morning, Edmund stares at Ginnie with a piercing glare after confronting her about betraying his addiction to Henry Patton. Ginnie denies it again. She tells him Henry is a perceptive person and can see things for himself.

Then Edmund rants about her dermatologist, that the doctor is getting a divorce because he has a girlfriend, like Mal said, and Edmund is certain she is the girlfriend. Once again, she denies it. She goes on and on about the wrong decisions Edmund is making because he listens to Mal. About the drugs. About his lying. About the loss of meaning in his life. And more.

His heart pounds violently, his head so full of her voice, he thinks it might explode. He tries to raise a hand to his temple to relieve the pulsing, that rushing sound like an advancing tsunami, but his hand trembles uncontrollably and he cannot.

Then he hears the noise, a detonation that seems to originate from somewhere outside himself, a loud and vulgar vibration like the violent burst of a worn-out tire. And finally, minutes of absolute silence.

He has no recollection now of what he yelled at Ginnie, or what she said to him, but at last, she is quiet and still. Her head rests against the back of the white, secondhand sofa, one leg extended, the other tucked beneath her. Her sky-blue eyes are turned coldly toward him. Waiting for him to say he's sorry? Of course she is. He wants to apologize, but anything he says now will go unheard. He knows her. She will not respond until she's paid him back in some way.

But he is sorry, maybe even the "sorriest person in the state of Alabama." Yes! He remembers now. Just before the noise, she flung those words at him along with her wedding ring. He was trying to open the front door to get away from her repetitive list of condemnations—that Mal was taking him over, that the drugs were warping his mind, that his jealousy of Dr. Burke and of Henry was out of control—but his hands were too sweaty to turn the brass knob. The air conditioner wasn't working. He felt as if both the house and Ginnie intended to smother him. So, he turned toward her, yanked off his wedding ring, tossed it on the floor next to hers, and stomped them both.

"So what if Mal gives me a few drugs? You know the kind of headaches I have!" He stood straight, inches away, pointing a finger in her face. "Who do you think you are for putting me down? I could have had any woman I wanted. I didn't have to pick you!" Of course, he did not believe that. They were "battle words," Mal's suggestion, but he went on. "I'm not jealous of a one-legged skin doctor or my boss. I am not out of control!" He repeated all those lies to her, and more—before the noise.

Now, fingers of sunlight steal through the slatted shutters behind the sofa, slip across her face, caressing her cheeks, touching her mouth as if kissing her. He remembers how sweet it is to kiss her, and he wants to, but her lips are closed to him. He's glad her lips are closed; she can't call him "a lunatic" again. She used to call him "wonderful," "baby," and "the answer to my prayers." She used to stroke his face and look at him as if he were a splendid gift. Today, she said there was foulness inside him. She said she wouldn't make love to him anymore until what he loved most was her.

He extends a palm toward the sofa where Ginnie is sprawled—a conciliatory gesture, but she doesn't appear to notice, so he slams the end table with his fist and three framed pictures wobble out of place. He returns them to proper order. The first was taken by his father on the day of his Baptism. In it, he is wrapped in a lacy, white garment in the arms of his mother. Her long, dark hair falls over the crown of his head. A few streaks of gray reveal that he was her surprise baby, her last child when she thought she'd never have another. Staring at the picture, he can see how dearly she loved him.

The second picture is of his First Communion in which he is meticulously dressed in a blue blazer and red-striped tie, standing in the center of the front row because he was the shortest child in the class. He was smiling at his father, who took the picture, and at his mother, dabbing her eyes with a tissue. Edmund was the last of her children to receive his First Communion. Just behind him in the picture stands the kind priest, and beyond the priest, Jesus on the wood of the Cross hung on a wooden wall. Afterward, they went to the church hall for orange juice in paper cups, bacon and eggs, and sweet rolls. He sat between his lovely Catholic mother and his father, the son of the old preacher, who wouldn't change his mind about anything. Beside his place at the table, he laid the missal the kind priest gave him, with its mother-of-pearl cover impressed with a gold chalice. He remembers the handwritten words inscribed inside the front cover: *God loves you, Eddie. He will love you despite what you do because God's love never relents.*

The last picture, taken by his mother, is of his father standing behind what was left of the full-flowered dogwood tree his mother planted in their backyard when she inherited the big white house in Montgomery. The dogwood lies horizontally on the ground. His father, in a red plaid shirt, had just cut it down because it had become diseased. Minutes after she took the picture, his mother cut a vase-worth of branches with white-petaled flowers, centered with crowns of gold stamen. She poured some water in the old heirloom vase and handed them to him. "Edmund"—she never called him Eddie, as the priest had—"put these on the dining room table." It was Good Friday, and his father's parents were coming for Easter Sunday. The old holiness preacher, a warrior for Jesus Christ, was always out to get Edmund.

Now, Ginnie is out to get him too.

He needs air. He needs to get away from Ginnie's judgmental words and glaring eyes. Her spite and the pictures on the table have increased his headache until it grips like a vise around his ears, behind his eyes, down the bridge of his nose. He can barely breathe. He tries the front door again, strengthening his grip on the doorknob. At last, it opens to a withered yard of dead grass where a lone loggerhead shrike picks through the dry dirt with its hooked beak, chasing after a brown lizard. As Edmund hustles down the walkway toward the curb and his car, the bird flies away.

He notices the pines on the other side of the street are an odd, night-colored green. They seem pasted to the sky. Two elongated contrails of airplanes converge above the pines in an X which, when he looks again, assumes the shape of a cross. He recalls the wooden cross on the wall in the church of his childhood. Again, he recalls the inscription the priest wrote in his First Communion missal: *God loves you, Eddie. He will love you despite what you do because God's love never relents.*

The pale yellow lines fragment and distort into lips, opening like a mouth, and he hears his name, *Edmund,* as if he's being called to repent for something awful.

He yanks open the car door and gets in, dismissing the illusion. It was only an X, not a cross—not an omen. *Grandfather, get away!*

The humming of the car's air conditioner reminds him of the stirring of fans in the holiness peddler's church. He sees himself in the pew, slipping away, little by little, from the old preacher's words in the pulpit. "Oh, you've done it, Edmund. You've done it now! Beg for forgiveness. Change yourself, or you'll never climb the ladder to eternal life."

Beside him on the seat is a neat stack of jackets, several sweaters, and the old winter face mask he'd used for hunting with his grandfather. Ginnie gathered them up the previous day and told him to take the stuff to the Bethel Rescue Mission. He studies the face mask, thinking she's trying to do it again, trying to control him again, disguising her disapproval of hunting with a good deed. His hand closes into another fist. He will not get rid of that face mask! He will wear it! He pulls it on and shoves the rest of the stack of clothes to the floorboard, slams the accelerator, and skids off.

The tires of his car squeal like the wild hog he was finally able to shoot as a boy on his grandfather's land. They'd been after deer, but the old man determined from the rounded tracks around his deer feed that hogs were eating the corn instead. He meant to get rid of them. They waited in the deer blind for hours until a hog came. "You take that devil down," the old man whispered to Edmund. "And this time, don't flinch and foul it up!"

He hadn't flinched. He hadn't fouled it up—then.

Like his grandfather's voice, the squeal of the hog resounds in his head. He tries to block out the memory, but a whirring takes over, louder and louder, like the vulgar detonation he heard that morning, and then like sirens warning the town.

The confession of evil works is the first beginning of good works.
—St. Augustine

Chapter Twenty-Seven

Moline

The previous year, Moline agreed to begin the RCIA program with Pauline as her sponsor but dropped out after a few weeks when she learned she'd have to make a general confession to Fr. O'Hara. Actually, she liked the priest. He'd been to dinner at their house several times, and he was very jovial, not holier-than-thou like she'd expected. Once, he even admitted he "sort of liked" one or two Chancee Wile songs. Still, she couldn't imagine herself listing off for him all the sins of her life. That would take hours.

"I'll do it sometime, Pauline, but not now," she said to her twin, who gave an exaggerated sigh and stood slump-shouldered before her as if Moline was a heavy burden.

"Sister, think about Alma, your innocent daughter."

"She's going to Mass with you, isn't she? I've seen to that."

"You've seen to it? No, Jose and I have seen to it."

"It's not the right time for me to become Catholic. Maybe next year, or…"

"Sister," Pauline said, "there's no righter time than now to better yourself. One day, you're going to do something you're so ashamed of that you'll never get rid of it. Unconfessed shame never disintegrates. It petrifies."

Of course, by then, Moline had already done that "something." For years, she'd kept it hidden, even from herself, pushed it down deep, refusing to remember it. Every time its recollection started to rise, she shoved it back into its hiding place. But it never stayed there; it kept creeping out in vague black-and-white nightmares she didn't understand but from which she would wake with her heart audibly pounding and her brain silently screaming, "Sinner!"

After a multitude of those nightmares, she finally agreed to complete the RCIA program with Pauline and took some of her shame to Sacred Heart Church. Still, she couldn't say she was in good standing. She had not confessed her most dreadful sin, the sin of her nightmares.

One Sunday morning, Alma was already waiting in the car for Pauline, ready to pick up Jose and Angelina for Mass. "I wish you'd come with us, Sister," Pauline said, passing Moline as she hurried to the car. "You shouldn't keep missing Mass."

"Not today." How could she receive communion when she was an awful, unconfessed sinner? Pauline was right—what she'd done was petrified within her now, like the ancient rocks formed within the base of a very old mountain, irretrievable unless the entire mountain be demolished. She feared demolishing the mountain, feared forcing herself to remember and have her life ruined by her misdeeds. Not only her life, but possibly the lives of Alma and Pauline as well. She could put up with the nightmares, but remembering was the one risk she could not take.

After Pauline and Alma left for Mass, Moline looked into her bathroom mirror, searching her face for any easily correctable flaws.

She did this often; too often, Pauline said. But this time, she wasn't looking for external flaws but rather her interior self. What was behind her mirrored image?

She recalled the question Pauline asked the last time she saw her twin looking into the mirror. "What does God see?" But Pauline was righteous. Too righteous, and Moline told her so.

Pauline responded with a huff. "Either life is a matter of eternal significance that has a bearing on what comes before and after, or else there's nothing much to it. And if *nothing much to it* is the case, then Moline, you might as well continue with whatever makes you feel good." When she raised her eyebrows, Pauline added, "But beware—the feeling won't last."

For a long while, Moline continued with whatever "felt good."

Alone in the house on a Friday afternoon, she checks the mirror again and sees her flaws, and deeper down her secrets, dirt she'd swept time and time again into a safely cloaked pile. Sometimes the mound of muck grew larger, strapping her with stinging bands of guilt until she became so tied up inside, she couldn't move even a finger. She meant to get rid of the muck, that ancient sin that sat like an overweight black cat in the back of her mind, green eyes blazing, tail swishing back and forth, waiting to pounce, to make such a ruckus that the woman behind the mirrored image would be exposed.

She promises herself to talk with Fr. O'Hara. Just a talk, though, not a confession, and preferably in an empty church where no one else will see her.

She finds Fr. O'Hara finishing with confessions and sits in a pew near the altar, simply breathing. A tiny ray of sunlight puddles on the pew just in front of her. She reaches for it as if to grab her place in something bigger—just in case the something bigger turned out to be more important than she was. Immediately, her hand and arm are immersed in the glow. She feels as if the regular Moline has absconded, leaving behind only the part of her the sun has lit.

Oh, how long is she going to have to wait on Fr. O'Hara? Moline does not like quiet or inertness. She sees herself as a person of energy, and the chances she takes as energetic too. Was it a mistake to come here? Is she taking life too seriously? She doesn't usually choose to be serious. A person doesn't have to be all serious—shouldn't be, really. People were created to laugh and have fun. She thinks of leaving then, not waiting for Father because she, Moline, is just fine.

Then her eyes turn upward to the crucifix hanging on a panel of purple velvet above the marble altar and she feels the sting of guilt.

She knows she isn't fine.

Fr. O'Hara touches her shoulder. "Are you coming, Moline? The confessional's empty and you're the only one here."

"I just want to talk, Father. I don't want to confess."

So, he sits beside her in the pew, a big man with an Irish brogue who—except that he has no beard—reminds her of Santa Claus with his shock of silver hair and rosy complexion. "What do you want to talk about?"

She turns to see that there is no one in the church except for the two of them. Then she says, "I want to talk about who I am and why."

"Who do you think you are, Moline?"

"I'm not a good person. I mean sometimes I do good things, but I…"

Fr. O'Hara grins. "Do bad things? Well, join the human race, Moline, my dear. God made you to be who you are, exactly who He wanted you to be. He loves you, but He will not force you to love Him. He gave you a free will so that you can choose to love him or not, and follow his commandments or not."

Moline doesn't like to be commanded to do anything, and she tells that to the priest.

"God does not care if you like it. He is the ultimate judge, and he wants things his way, because he made the world. If you want to do it your way, then be prepared for whatever comes."

"God sounds a little too controlling to me."

"He *is* controlling. He controls night and day, doesn't he? He controls which animals and plants grow on the Earth and which do not. He controls who is born and who isn't; and for that matter, what a person looks like, which eyes and hair and skin color they have. He loves each of them as if they were his only child, and has a purpose in life for each one, calling them beautiful, whether they are attractive to other human beings or not." He pointedly eyes Moline, as if he knows of her frequent visits to the mirror.

"Have you been talking to Pauline about me?" she teases him.

Fr. O'Hara remains serious. "That is the point, Moline. Life is not all about you. God wants order in the world, not chaos. He wants order from every human being. He wants them to choose it. Again, that's why we have commandments."

"But I like freedom."

"Well, you have it. The freedom to choose between order and chaos, good and evil. And the freedom to get rid of your sins. Just think how amazing that will be."

Amazing, yes. But a lot to take in—not that she hadn't heard most of it before from Pauline. And before Pauline, their parents, who'd been devout Christians and peanut farmers all their lives. Well, she had heard it, but she hadn't listened. Now, she wants to be amazed, to tell her story to Fr. O'Hara and feel at least somewhat free. She can't tell all of her story, not the part she blocked out—the part she cannot, or will not, remember—but this time, all that she tells him will be true.

She begins with leaving her parents and the farm because she didn't feel like going along with what they wanted, when it wasn't what *she* wanted. She wanted pleasure, not hard work on a peanut farm. Whiskey and sex gave it to her, and, back then, it didn't matter who she drank with or slept with. She needed a job, so she got one, a job at the dentist's office and an apartment. Days, she dressed in pink polyester and made appointments. Nights, she made sure her hair was as blond as she could get it, painted her nails crimson, put on her mini-skirt and her red patent leather boots, and went out to the bars to have a good time. Usually, she came home drunk with someone she'd met at the bar. She never asked their names, never told them hers. In the morning, when she woke in a rumpled bed—empty of a man by then—she simply got up, changed the damp sheets, and got ready for another day of work at the dental office.

Of course, it all came back to bite her. She returned to the farm pregnant and unmarried. Pauline, Catholic and penitent after tossing three husbands—and after learning that Moline was having a baby—returned to the farm as well. Their parents did not know what to make of either of their daughters. To use Fr. O'Hara's word, it was chaos.

Everything changed when Alma was born. Moline's baby girl was all any one of them needed to come together. "How can we not cherish innocence?" the twins' mother asked, standing over Alma's cradle, stroking her tiny fingers. Pauline embraced Moline, and Moline cried tears of joy. And then, their father lifted Alma in his arms and took her to the rocker on the side porch, where in his rough, deep voice, he sang to her.

After their parents died, Pauline said, "I don't know how our poor parents lived through either of us."

Moline, still trying to cover up what she was on the inside, quipped, "They *didn't* live through us. Remember?"

"No, they did not. We may have caused their early deaths. For once, you're right, Sister."

"Pauline, I did not say we caused their deaths. I only said they died." Of course, an argument ensued, and afterwards Pauline cried over her sins, as was typical, and Moline left to find a bar that was still open.

All this, she tells Fr. O'Hara, and also that during that time, the only thing opposing the chaos was Alma. "Alma was simply goodness. The worthiest thing that ever happened to me. But I have never felt worthy of her." Tears puddle in her eyes. "Do you know some people called Alma a bastard child to her face? Adults, who ought to know that a child doesn't pick her parents."

"Has she asked about her father?"

"Yes. But since I honestly don't know who Alma's father is, I picked the best of the men I remembered being with. I didn't remember the sex, only the handsome man in a nice suit and blue-striped tie. So, I set him in my mind as Alma's father. Whatever his name was, he was kind and a gentleman. I picked him because Alma deserves the best."

"Yes, she does." Fr. O'Hara gives her hand a pat. "I have another appointment to get to. Next time, I'll expect you in the confessional. After all, it's absolution you want, Moline, not conversation."

He is right. She desperately wants absolution. And yet, she leaves feeling better than when she came in. She even supposes that making up a father for Alma, though it was a lie, wasn't so bad.

After she returns from speaking with the priest, she continues her thoughts of Alma, wishing Alma was home instead of at her job at Dillard's. Moline wants to talk to her, tell her how much she loves her. Maybe even reveal more of her father—from Moline's imagination, of course.

She feels drawn to go to her daughter's room. She's read that a young person's room reveals much of who they are and what they want out of life. So, she climbs the stairs and opens the closed door, stopping in the threshold to take it in. The two windows are open, and a breeze gently blows the thin cotton curtains Pauline made for Alma years ago—pink, printed with white rosebuds. And a little young for her now, Moline thinks. The bed is made, as always, and there are original paintings on the wall signed by Angelina. One is of a mountain with steps to its crest. The crest is labeled Heaven's Gate. A mason jar of water sits on the dresser beside a statue of the Sacred Heart of Jesus that Pauline gave her.

Moline notices more drawings, in a neat stack on Alma's desk, and goes through them. They are not drawings by Angelina but by Alma. One is a title page, perfectly printed: *I See My World As Greater than the Sum of Its Parts*. All the rest of the drawings are of the same handsome man—some of his face, some of his hands, and even a very scientific drawing of his heart. There are other drawings of him too, walking in a suit and tie with a pretty girl who looks like Alma. Beneath the drawing are the words, *I want the world to see me with my father*.

Moline gasps. Could Alma have met her father without her knowing? She looks more closely at the drawing and smiles, then smiles again, until the smiles burst into laughter. The drawing actually looked like "the kind gentleman" she set in her own mind as Alma's father.

She recalls Fr. O'Hara's words: *God controls who is born and who isn't*. She thinks of the millions of babies born every day all over the world. How lucky she is to have Alma. God wants Alma to be here because he has a purpose for her. And maybe that purpose is to be Moline's child. Maybe too, just maybe—like the priest said—God loves Moline enough, despite the awful things she's done, to give her his very best of daughters, with a father who, even if he is unknown, must be just as good. Yes! A prince of a man from whom Alma's good virtues must spring.

There's a part of you missing. Some men can't see the color green,
but they may never know they can't. I think you are only a part of
a human. I can't do anything about that. But I wonder whether
you ever feel that something invisible is all around you.
—John Steinbeck, *East of Eden*

CHAPTER TWENTY-EIGHT

Edmund

Still wearing the hunting mask, Edmund turns the steering wheel right and then left with no thought about where he's going. The sweat running down his face and back irritates him, and he desperately wants to end the whining in his head. He reminds himself that he's his own man, that he's in charge, and that he'll allow no one to do Edmund K. Gillan wrong. Oh, they'll try; he knows they will.

Who are "they?"

He's made a numbered list in his mind. Dr. Burke, Ginnie's soon-to-be-divorced dermatologist, is the first one on it.

He passes the Rescue Mission but doesn't remember the clothes Ginnie gave him to donate, only that she once volunteered there. An old man sits in a straight back chair in front of the mission. He waves a hand as Edmund passes. Edmund presses the accelerator and passes Hubble Hardware, where his grandfather once took him to buy a hammer and nails to fix their broken fence; Radio Shack, where he bought his first pocket radio with headphones; Pretty Pearl's Beauty Parlor, where he restlessly waited for the hairdresser to lift the hairdryer from his grandmother and comb out her steel-colored hair; and finally, Gunter's Guns, where he stood beside his grandfather as he bought the Bersa Thunder .380. On the side of the building are washed-out painted letters that read, "Heaven's Gate." He remembers his grandfather liked the old name, Heaven's Gate, the biblical Bethel, where Jacob dreamed of a ladder ascending to heaven. Over the years, his grandfather gave many sermons about the struggles of climbing that ladder.

Edmund recalls one in particular that he heard as a boy. The week before his grandfather preached it, Edmund nearly killed a schoolmate with his fists. All he recollects about the beating now is that he saw the kid take something from his desk, something that belonged to Edmund. At once a whirring sound, like that of a running blade saw, began to cut through his head. "Thou shalt not covet!" Edmund yelled—the over-used words that came from his grandfather's mouth anytime the old man perceived in Edmund an inkling of longing for anything other than God. With every splintering blow, Edmund hollered, "Thou shalt not covet!"

Yet there were moments during his childhood when Edmund was certain he felt God's desire for *him*. God's longing to covet *him*. And he would shout back, "Thou shalt not covet!" Immediately, he would be sorry he said such a thing to the God to whom his grandfather said Edmund belonged.

Now, in his mind, he sees his grandfather pointing a finger, stiff as a gun, toward his entire congregation, but Edmund knows the old man's voice is aimed only at him. *Do you think you're at Heaven's Gate? Do you think God wants you enough to allow you to climb the ladder? Well, you'll never climb it unless you're pure as fallen snow. Unless you leave room for God's wrath, not your own. Repent!*

Edmund takes another left and passes the dermatology clinic where his grandfather's old church with its Highway to Holiness sign once stood. He pictures the one-legged Dr. Burke inside the now reconstructed church, coveting Ginnie. Maybe he's deciding how to position her on his examination table the next time she begs him to fix her acne-pocked face. Maybe he'll set his eyes and mouth inches from hers, trying to take what doesn't belong to him, while Ginnie smiles with misdirected sympathy. Then he pictures Ginnie at home, probably still quiet on the couch, counting the hours until her next appointment with the doctor. He means to teach them both a lesson for messing with what belongs to him! He listens for his grandfather's voice and hears nothing except the bothersome squeals of the hog. He sees himself standing over it as it quivers and dies, recalling the pride he felt in killing it because the varmint wanted what wasn't his.

After that, it's as if a part of him is missing. He's unaware of anything he passes, even unaware of his own thoughts, as if he is not the driver but the automobile: a changeless, mechanized vehicle set on autopilot, incapable of turning around on its own. He thinks fleetingly of the accident in Montgomery in which his parents and siblings were killed. Yet he survived! The timid shadow, the forgettable family member, survived. Why? The doctors said the accident probably didn't alter his brain, but he knows it did. Why did it have to be him? Why did it have to be his family? He's angry, so angry he could bust up the world. At once, he vividly recalls—as if it is happening now—the boy at school, crying as he hit him; the thieving hog, quivering as he killed it; and Ginnie, finally quiet, after calling him an incurable, drug-addicted lunatic. All of them were trying to put him down into his weakness. But this day, this Friday afternoon, he will not let them!

Such is the human race. Often it does seem such a pity
that Noah and his party did not miss the boat.
—Mark Twain

CHAPTER TWENTY-NINE

Mal

Mal slams the door to his classroom and locks it from the inside. He has a habit of standing at his podium in an empty classroom to ruminate over past grievances, no matter how slight or how long ago. This time, he is going over his conversation with Henry Patton in the faculty lounge. He remembers every word; it did not go as he intended. Why? Ginnie Gillan, of course! To get at Ginnie through smearing Edmund, the fool, has always been his plan. Ginnie is the one he wants to get rid of. But his triangulation hasn't even gotten him to first base with Patton. He can't understand why Ginnie is so well-liked, or why Patton and the others think she is a great teacher when she is so pompous. Even Edmund, her own husband, is beginning to see her pomposity thanks to Mal.

Behind the podium, he gives the empty classroom a churlish smile as he thinks about his success with Edmund. The first time he met the fool, he smelled a fuel that invigorated him, someone to twist and use, someone to admire him and desperately need him. And then he met Ginnie, his immediate adversary who, in Patton's eyes, is Ginnie the Great Teacher.

He can't stand by and let her greatness spread to the ends of the earth, can he? Not Malcolm J. Hawkins, the Greatest Manipulator in Bethel, and maybe the whole world if he has the chance to show himself. His scheme hasn't worked with Henry Patton, but it has with many others, and of course, Edmund is still in play.

Maybe, Mal thinks, he has chosen the wrong role with his boss. Maybe he should play the victim with Patton. He is good at that when he can't get what he wants any other way. He can give reasons why Ginnie is jealous of him, trying to ruin him because of his popularity and the popularity of his courses that don't accord with her own beliefs. No one doubts the students like him; he has many little drug-seekers who fawn over him nightly. But playing the victim is his least favorite persona. People like Malcolm J. Hawkins are not victims. They *have* victims, especially isolated people with no real support system, or someone like Edmund, the fool, with a messed-up mind. People like Edmund are more than fools; they are tools. But his wife, Ginnie, is not; she is a bona fide threat to Mal.

Still at his podium, he shouts to the empty room, "How dare Henry Patton challenge me? He deserves anything that's coming to him! Anything I can bring!"

A knock on the door interrupts him. Is he speaking too loudly? Mal steps from behind the podium and opens the door to see the blue-eyed woman who sits in on his class. She looks around the classroom and, seeing no students, she says, "I thought we had class today."

We? This woman is nowhere near a part of his class. She is a piece of destruction. "No," he says politely. "We don't have class today."

"My goodness," she giggles, "I must have my days mixed up. But I heard you speaking, and so I thought—"

"No, there is no class," he repeats.

She doesn't turn around to leave.

Out of curiosity, and because one needs to know his enemies, he says, "I know you sit in on my class, but I don't believe I know your name."

She doesn't answer. "Dr. Hawkins, I find your class…enlightening, but I feel there's a key component missing in your own psychology."

Oh, she is just what he does not need! "What do you mean?"

"Not what, but who. God is missing. Your appreciation of God, Dr. Hawkins. And it may cost you your soul."

Always, she reminds him of Charity, with a precision he cannot abide and wants to destroy, just as he destroyed Charity's room when they were children, turning over all her orderly bookcases and stomping her precious books, smashing her figurines of angels until they were only miniscule pieces of porcelain strewn over the floor. But his favorite destruction of things she cared about was what he'd done to the green and yellow parrot she loved named Buddy. She always stroked Buddy, gave him lots of attention—too much attention, according to Mal. Every night, she moved Buddy's cage to a quiet, dark corner of her room so he would sleep well, and every morning, moved him back in front of the window so he would have lots of light and not get depressed. She taught Buddy to mimic her words too. Especially, *Buddy loves Charity. Buddy loves Charity,* until Mal was sick of hearing it.

He tried to teach the bird to say, *Nobody loves Charity. Nobody loves Charity.* But it didn't work; the parrot would only scream and flap its wings and try to bite him whenever he came near. So, one day, when Charity was at school and he was home pretending to be sick, he took from the cabinet a chocolate bar, toxic to birds, and gave it to Buddy. The parrot died two days later—from seizures and an attack on its central nervous system, the vet said.

He looks at the blue-eyed woman and wonders which toxin would work on her. Then he smiles at her, as the Head of the Psychology Department ought to do, and turns away from her without a word, leaving her in the threshold of his classroom, still standing in the open door. He takes the back way out of the building just to be rid of the sight of her and heads home.

In chess, as in life, a man is his own most dangerous opponent.
—Vasily Smyslov

Chapter Thirty

Edmund

Edmund keeps driving, not knowing where he will end up. He needs to get away. He ran away once before, when he was eleven years old and had been orphaned for a year. He stole money from his grandmother's purse to buy a ticket on the Greyhound bus headed to Montgomery, where he remembered a once-happy life with his parents in the huge white house surrounded by hot pink azaleas and lots of land. His mother inherited the house from her own parents. She could have sold it for a lot of money, but she didn't. Instead, she went to live there with her husband, son of the old preacher, and her five children. Edmund, her sixth child, was born there.

He remembers every detail of the house and every square of its many acres that were once a cotton plantation. His mother told him the house was finished in 1822 by her third great grandfather, who had an architect build it for her third great grandmother's birthday.

The beautiful Greek revival had tall pillars on the front porch and large rooms with enormous chandeliers. His room was upstairs, on the back of house, overlooking the family cemetery.

Edmund recalls how much he loved living there, not because of the size and beauty of the house but because of the old cemetery that he saw each morning from his window and visited each day as a child. He thinks of his mother's voice explaining to him who was buried there—sons and daughters of the American Revolution and their many children who fought over hundreds of years to build the new nation of America. She spoke of those who rebelled in the Civil War and those who struggled in its aftermath, and finally she turned her face to the big-roomed house with its chandeliers. "And my people, who survived long enough to build this house, our home." Then again, she set her eyes on the graves. "We pray they are gone to heaven now, or at least to purgatory and not hell," she told him as if she could see beneath the slabs and found nothing there, found them gone.

In his boyish mind, a doubting mind, he pictured himself beneath the earth opening the lids of each casket to see if his mother was correct, that those buried had somehow vanished and made it to heaven; yet all he saw in every tomb were bones. He looked up at her then, at her beautiful, trusting face, and asked, "How can we know if God sent them to heaven or to hell?"

She put a hand on the top of his head as if to touch the brain inside and said, "We can't know. We can only see the outside of a person, but God sees our mind, our intentions, and everything we do, Edmund. But it's not God who sends us to heaven or hell. We determine where we end up by what we do here on earth. It's why we pray for each other."

The time he ran away from his grandparents, he was in the bus

station when the Montgomery police found him. He was thinking of the old house, recalling his mother pointing out graves and
wondering if he would end up in heaven or hell. His grandfather
sent alerts to every police station in south Alabama when he found
Edmund gone, and finally the police called the old preacher. The
old man came, dragged him back home, and set him in the circle of
a spotlight that angled down from the roof of his house. "Sinner, if
you want eternal life, make amends!"

Edmund was so mad he wanted to shoot his grandfather. He
calmed down after his sweet-hearted, soft-spoken grandmother for-
gave him in secret, her breath warm and soothing on his cheek,
reminding him of a puppy's nudge. "You've separated yourself from
God, Eddie, but He wants you to return and be united with Him
again. That's what your grandfather wants too. He wants you to
return." Then she baked oatmeal cookies and asked him what else
he could expect from his grandfather, a preacher, who wanted his
grandson to gain the promise of a grand home in heaven.

Edmund's thoughts shift to Ginnie.

She said something once, when she was talking about the plans
for the new degree program and also haranguing him about his drug
habit. "Most people long for that moment of grace that will turn
them or better them or lift them up to a higher place in the eyes of
those they love." She glared at him then, waiting for his response,
tightening the tie on her robe until he wondered how she could
still breathe. She finally went on: "But some people"—she stared at
him—"also forget that the price of restoration sometimes takes the
pain of a crucifixion."

"Right. But who wants to be crucified?"

She seemed regenerated that he had spoken and began at once
to explain, but it came out as an accusation. "To a certain extent,

crucifixion happens to each of us. Suffering can even help us do the right thing, when everyone—or someone—is telling us to do the opposite."

"Oh, now we're on Mal and the drugs again?"

"Edmund," she said quietly, as if she had suddenly become a kind mother advising her child, "you need to get rid of him. He's not your friend. If you don't get rid of him, he'll ruin your life and our life together."

"Our life together? That's supposed to be a threat, isn't it?"

Then it occurred to him that Mal had implanted in his mind that whatever Ginnie said or did was a threat to him.

For several moments, she only looked at him, and in those moments, he recalled how it was when they were newly married, how they rarely passed each other without touching and saying, "I love you." At that moment, he wanted to start over and make it all better. He wanted to take responsibility, to lift himself to a higher place in her eyes because he did love her, but he didn't seem able to stop himself from pointing a finger back at her whenever she said anything he did not want to hear. And he did not want to hear about Mal, or the drugs, or how she was developing new programs for the university while he was developing nothing, and in fact, was often not able to remain standing in front of his class and focus on the subject he was teaching.

Was it envy?

Envy had been on his grandfather's list of the seven deadliest sins. *Don't you know, Edmund? Satan came into existence through envy.*

Mal scoffed at the very idea of sin. When they first met, he convinced Edmund to stay away from both his grandparents. Then, at nearly a hundred years old, both died natural deaths, one right after the other. They were buried side by side on the same day at Heaven's

Gate Graveyard. At their funeral, the voice of his grandfather began to haunt him; not in a shout but a whisper, as if his voice rose from the bottom of a deep, sealed well. But it didn't last. The sound of his grandfather's voice continues to ascend as if the old man is stepping up the rungs of a ladder, his voice coming ever closer and closer, louder and louder.

Time and tide wait for no man.
—Geoffrey Chaucer

CHAPTER THIRTY~ONE

Pauline

Movies aren't the only thing the twins watch on television. They like the nightly news, mostly due to the influence of Pauline's third husband. He wasn't nearly as bad as the first two. He'd been a banker in Birmingham and liked to keep up with government regulations. Tonight, the twins are sitting side by side on the sofa watching the House of Representatives debate the funding of Planned Parenthood. The Committee is using the five-minute rule.

Moline bristles. "What is the five-minute rule?"

Pauline likes explaining things to her sister in the manner of her third husband, the one who first brought her to Catholicism and then converted her into an ardent Republican. That husband loved the news! Pauline had to sit quietly while he watched because he did not like interruptions. Neither does Pauline, so she waves a limp hand at her sister, a sign to be quiet. She likes to explain, but not in the middle of things.

Of course, the sign doesn't work. Moline asks louder, "What is the five-minute rule, Pauline?"

Pauline gives an audible sigh, just as her third husband used to, then twists toward Moline with her arms across her chest. "Okay. Pay attention. In Congress, when the House sits as the Committee of the Whole, a member offering an amendment can speak only five minutes in its favor, and an opponent of the amendment is allowed to speak five minutes in opposition. Equal time. That's how it's supposed to be, then the debate is closed."

"I don't like that rule."

Pauline lets go of her third husband's persona and becomes herself again. She pats her sister's hand. "I know, Sister, but it's only a procedure to make things fair and equal."

Moline gives a grunt. "Fair and equal?"

"Well, sometimes it turns out that way. Just look at you and me."

"Sometimes," Moline admits, "but I still don't like it."

Pauline was born only five minutes before Moline, but that little bit of time made all the difference. Even five minutes is important to a child. Because of Pauline's additional five minutes on earth, Moline never had equal time. Pauline at once became the favorite. She never admitted to Moline that she knew she was the favorite, but throughout their childhood, she'd been aware that their parents' attention to her was greater than their attention to Moline.

From the time she entered first grade until she graduated high school, Pauline brought home nothing but As, while a C was the highest grade Moline ever made. Their father rewarded Pauline a dollar for every A. She saved her money until the end of each school year; then her father took her to downtown Bethel to spend it on whatever she wanted. Of course, Moline wanted to go, too, with money from her father as well.

"To receive a reward," Moline's father told her, "you must do something that is worthy of a reward." Her parents waited years for her to do something worthy of a reward, but nothing ever happened; Moline was too stubborn. So, the family eventually stopped expecting her to do anything well. Pauline thought that it had shackled her sister in several ways and was sorry it had.

From an early age, Moline craved being noticed, and later, she did anything she could to attract a response. Even a negative response would suffice. She was jealous of Pauline and became the ultimate family problem, picking fights with her sister, only to be scolded and punished. Whatever Moline was told to do, she did not do. All for attention and envy of Pauline. Pauline somehow understood this and began to give in to the fights. She ignored the bruises Moline inflicted upon her and never tattled on her twin. It was hard, but it made her strong—and prideful.

Sometimes Pauline thought of herself as a high-flying eagle and of Moline as a little crow—the only bird feisty enough to peck at an eagle in flight. Pauline had to admit that it took courage for Moline to sit like a crow on the back of an eagle, even if all the while, she was pecking at her twin's neck.

Eventually Pauline came to the decision that she would no longer stand for the bruises. She would not fight with Moline. She had more abilities and could fly higher than Moline, so she would. After all, an eagle was the most majestic of birds, larger than a little crow, and much stronger. Playing the eagle's part, she would open her wings and fly too high for Moline to stay on her back so that her sister would finally let go. She set the image in her mind and carried it through. And it worked. At eight years old, in the middle of a Moline-instigated tousle, Pauline grabbed her sister and hugged her. "Please quit hitting me! Don't you know I love you, Moline? More than anything in the world."

Moline stopped and stared. "Anything in the world?"

"Anything."

Moline broke into tears. She hugged Pauline back, and said, "I love you, too."

From that time on, they were tight as ticks; even their parents said so. They said Pauline had saved Moline from herself, and the family from disruptive envy—until Pauline married her first husband, both of them only seventeen. Moline saw him as competition for her sister's affection, and her jealousy returned. She was more than callous to the poor boy; she was as venomous as the brown widow spider she kept in a mason jar for weeks and then dropped in his shoe.

Of course, Moline denied that she'd done it when she visited the hospital where Pauline sat by her young husband's bed, his leg swollen up like a beer barrel. "I would never do something like that," she told her twin. But Pauline knew she had done it. Always, she knew when Moline was lying. Again, her parents couldn't handle her, couldn't keep her off the streets or out of the bars. This went on for years—throughout Pauline's second and third marriages—until both twins came home, and Moline gave birth to Alma.

"I don't need a baby," Moline groaned as Pauline drove her to the hospital. "I don't want a baby! It's all your fault, Pauline. You're the one who encouraged me." Pauline didn't answer; she knew it was the pain making her twin talk that way. "So, you can take care of it, Sister. I'm certainly not going to."

"Mama and Daddy will help you, Moline. And of course, I'll help too." Actually, Pauline couldn't wait to hold the baby. In her three marriages, she hadn't once gotten pregnant, which was probably a good thing, considering any one of the three father-figures the baby might have had. Her second husband might have been the best as a father, if he'd ever stayed sober, which he didn't seem able to do. When he wasn't drinking, he was kind and loving, but when he was drunk, he was the meanest of men. Naturally, she had to leave him. Well, she thought then—and still does—nobody's flawless. Everybody has their personal sins, and their bad side sits right next to their good side because people are complicated.

The birth of Moline's baby was not complicated. The little girl was born thirty minutes after they got to the hospital. Pauline was in the delivery room with her sister for the miracle. And it was surely a miracle! Instantly, love shone in her sister's eyes for the tiny little person she held in her arms. There was no more talk about not wanting a baby.

"Want to hold her, Pauline?" Moline asked.

Pauline gently took her. She placed the baby's small, warm body in the crook of her elbow, and when she stroked the soft skin of a brand new person, Pauline felt as if she was holding something of God in her arms. And then, it was so obvious! This time, the person who would save Moline from herself wouldn't be Pauline but this God-given child, Alma. Pure and simple.

Hell is the ultimate expression of the value of human liberty.
To deny it is to say that liberty is incapable of resisting grace,
or that sin is finally so absurd as not even to deserve punishment.
—M. Jouhandeau, quoted by Arnold J. Benedetto, SJ,
Fundamentals in the Philosophy of God

CHAPTER THIRTY-TWO

Edmund

Edmund unexpectedly finds himself driving on a newer side of town. Minutes later, he's in the parking lot of the Bethel Mall. He cannot account for where he's been. He thinks he may have stopped the car at some point to go into the dermatology clinic. Yes, he thinks he pulled in there to confront Dr. Burke. He doesn't remember facing him though. The doctor must have been too busy to see him. He needs a break, needs to get away. His watch says it's four o'clock, but he doesn't know how long he's been here, parked away from the mall entrance in the shade of a large live oak. He wonders why he's here when Ginnie is at home. Did she send him away? Has he lost her forever?

Oh, you've lost her, Edmund. And now, you risk losing eternal life. Make amends!

He slams the dashboard with a furious fist, and with each hard hit, the old man's words repeat over and over. *Make amends.* That must be why he's here! He should give Ginnie a gift of compensation, a gift of grand proportion. And he's in just the right place. He gets out of his car to go into the mall.

Two women hurry out of the Dillard's entrance, heading toward him. He walks slowly, hoping they'll find their car before he has to pass them, but they speed up until they're close enough for him to hear them and see their anxious expressions.

"What I wanna know is, who's in charge?" The woman shakes her head as if speaking of something too horrible to be believed.

"Well, today, it's a scary world. Who is in charge of anything these days? You can take all the precautions you want, but things still happen," the other replies.

"Mama said she heard it live on the Friday Big Bam Radio Show, that some guy went crazy and started shooting at everybody in the clinic. Four people were killed for no reason at all. You can't predict something like that."

"Yeah, just innocent bystanders doing their jobs, and some nutcase in a face mask walks in with a gun."

"What's worse, he got away! Who knows if they'll ever find him?" She exhales a depressing sigh. "We live in a dangerous world."

Edmund agrees with the woman about the world being dangerous. When the two are behind him, he rearranges the set of his suit coat. One side is weightier than the other, as if that pocket holds something heavy, but it doesn't concern him now. He enters the store to find what he came to find, something much grander than Mal suggested.

At the jewelry counter in Dillard's, his hands are jittery. He observes them shaking as he goes through his wallet to hand the girl a credit card for the necklace she's shown him, his gift of amends to Ginnie. He's startled by a scream behind him—a crying baby, pushed by his mother in a stroller. They pass quickly but the scream remains, triggering a memory of many people screaming, yelling, running, and the recollection of a blast, more than one blast. His hands are trembling so much now that his fingers seem unable to keep hold of the plastic card. It falls on the glass counter.

"Uh oh," the girl with blond hair says. She cautiously picks up the card with pink-painted nails as if raising a bandage to see if a wound has stopped bleeding. "Want me to swipe it for you?"

Young, pretty, and neatly dressed, she's trying not to look at his quivering hands. She's probably around sixteen, and more than likely, this is her first real job. He notices the glass counter's shine and her purse positioned neatly on the floor behind her, next to a bottle of Windex on top of a folded paper towel. He is meticulous too, so he appreciates that about her. He gives an affirmative nod, and she swipes the card through. "You'll have to sign the receipt, sir." She offers him a pen, holding tightly to the box with the pendant as if he might take it without paying for it. For a second, her blue eyes seem gray—gun-colored. They fix on the center of his tie as if she deciphers something foul in the heart behind it.

Willing his hand to be steady, he nearly snatches the pen, then signs the receipt with jarring strokes: Edmund K. Gillan. Then he feels the need to reaffirm his name. "Edmund K. Gillan," he says loudly, too loudly.

The girl draws back a little, and her defensive movement stirs in him a feeling of pride. Edmund K. Gillan is in charge. Edmund K. Gillan will be remembered. She hands him his copy of the receipt. "Thank you, Mr. Gillan. I hope your wife will enjoy the pendant."

His wife? How does she know he has a wife? Can't she see he wears no wedding ring? It's lying on his living room floor...and at once, the shaking returns.

The girl puts the box into a plastic bag marked with the store's logo and offers it to him. No matter how much he wills it, he can't close his fingers around the bag. And now, the girl is studying his tie again while she holds out his purchased gift—an arm's length away from her breast, as if it's something decomposing and she wants him to go off with it quickly.

Edmund feels nauseous, out of balance. He steadies himself by seizing the counter's edge, his fingers drumming frenziedly. He thinks he's done something terribly wrong. He thinks he ought to go off quickly; he ought not to be here. A confusing light from the ceiling falls on the flawless glass of the counter, and within it is the girl's reflection, all crystal clean and golden. He sees goodness in it. He sees innocence. He thinks he sees what he once was, and what he is meant to be. And it scares him. "You keep the gift," he says to her and quickly walks away.

The human face is, after all, nothing more or less than a mask.
—Agatha Christie

CHAPTER THIRTY-THREE

Alma

Alma stands frozen, one arm straight out like an angled flagpole, her fingers still holding the bag. She watches Edmund K. Gillan walk frantically toward the main corridor of the mall as if certain wickedness tails him. Remembering the handsome boy and the bracelet he stole, she knows she cannot take her eyes off this man.

She stares after him, wondering what to do. She wonders if there is something wrong with him, the way he's shaking. An illness perhaps.

She feels compassion towards him, knowing how disease rakes a body. She has watched Angelina suffer daily. But except for the trembling, the man looks physically healthy—mid to late thirties, about six feet tall, a clean-cut sort of dark-haired handsome in a suit of silver gray with a yellow and navy-blue striped tie and a white shirt. Except for a reddish smear on the slim band of the cuff peeking out of the left sleeve of his coat—maybe from his lunch—the man appears perfectly dressed, nearly immaculate.

She doesn't know much about older men, but standing in front of the counter, under the light from the ceiling, his deep blue eyes and angular face reminded her of the picture she drew of her father—handsome, serious, well-dressed. Of course, she has no idea what her father actually looks like. That was only a high school assignment. Her father has never given her any gifts, unlike this man. Right now, right here, in the very place she is standing, a flesh and blood man, a stranger, has given her a gift like none she's ever received.

For a second or two she follows Edmund K. Gillan with a grateful heart until she comes back to the reality of what she holds in her hand, what he told her to keep. Of course, she ought not keep the pendant; it is valued at four thousand dollars, despite being on sale. She ought to leave her counter and run after him to give it back. With the bag in her hand, she walks through the store and into what she can see of the bafflingly bright tunnels of the mall, but Edmund K. Gillan is nowhere in sight. She can't give back the pendant if she can't find the man who gave it to her.

Still, she knows his name. She can find him if she wants to, in the phone book or online. Even the credit card company might give her some information if she tells them a customer walked off without his purchase. But it's nearly the end of her shift, and she's tired, and there are things at home she has to deal with that aren't nearly as flawless or beautiful as a diamond pendant she can hold in her hand.

Suddenly, she wants it as much as she once wanted her father, as much as she wants her friend Angelina to be cured.

Should she even worry about Edmund K. Gillan? She'll probably never meet the man again. He's only one of those undefined and soon-to-be invisible people like her father, who brush against the life of another for reasons only God knows. But she's a careful girl who questions her every action, plans ahead, and worries about consequences.

Just this morning, she stood in front of her mother wearing a sundress with spaghetti straps, holding a white cotton sweater in her hand. "I can't decide. Should I put this sweater over my dress? With only the straps, it's pretty bare, and it is cool in the mall."

Her mother rolled her eyes. "Alma, you're so cautious. At least you've painted your nails pink, and I'm proud of you. You've taken a little risk for once in your life."

"Thou Shalt Take Risks" has always been the first of her mother's Ten Commandments.

Alma puts the bag with the pendant into her purse—because of her mother, because it is Friday and her shift is almost over, but mostly because she's off for the weekend and there will be time to decide whether or not to look for Edmund K. Gillan.

There is evil in every human heart,
which may remain latent, perhaps, through the whole of life;
but circumstances may rouse it to activity.
—Rev. Dr. Martin Luther King Jr.

CHAPTER THIRTY-FOUR

Edmund

Edmund stops for an espresso at Starbucks at the end of the building's south exit. Inside the wintry chill of the mall, he did not remember that outside, waiting for him, is a gruesome August day, too hot for coffee. When he goes out to the parking lot to find his black sedan, he is slapped in the face by the heat, and the coffee splashes on his hand, burning him. He pours it out violently, as if it meant to hurt him, then throws down the cup and smashes it on the pavement with his sole.

He searches one row after another for his car but can't find it. This time, it's Mal's voice that takes over, reprimanding him: *Did you cover your tracks? Did you take note of the car's location when you got out of it? No, you did not. Take charge, Edmund!* After this morning's argument, he tried to do as Mal suggested and take charge of Ginnie, but she turned her cold blue eyes on him, parted her lips, and called him a lunatic. And then—well, he isn't sure what happened next. He thinks she became quiet, probably giving him the silent treatment as she is prone to do.

He thinks he may have parked his car on the north side, but instead of going through the mall, he walks around the outside of the building that sits like a tremendous brown toad frozen in a dumping of concrete. He searches for a good thirty minutes, up and down the rank of vehicles; still, he can't find it. Then it comes to him that even if he locates his car, he can't go home to Ginnie without his gift of amends.

He was stupid to leave it. There was something about the young blond girl behind the counter that made him want to give her something, as if he owed her, but it is Ginnie he owes. He paid for the grand thing and its promise of atonement, so he ought to return to Dillard's. The fresh-faced blond girl would surely give it back to him.

He turns around for Dillard's, re-winding his way through the automobiles, still keeping an eye out for his own black sedan. Inside, at the jewelry counter, an older woman is bagging up a purchase. He asks her for the blond girl with the pink-painted nails.

"Oh, she left for the day," the woman says. "Can I help you?"

He's not sure how he answers, but he finds himself back in the parking lot. The August sun is going down, coloring the multitude of windshields a liquid gold and shooting luminous, fragmented mirrors that make him squint and sweat. He reaches into his pocket for a handkerchief, and his fingers touch something cold and hard—the gun Mal set in his hand. He doesn't remember taking it out of the gym bag with his running clothes, where he put it after deciding Mal's idea about scaring Ginnie was a bad one. So, why did he take it out? Why? He stands stark still, as if the soles of his shoes have become part of the pavement.

He remembers this morning's violent noise and Ginnie's sudden silence. He remembers hearing the same noise when he entered the dermatology clinic. Yes, he was there. He was there! But he couldn't have used the gun and—no! It's impossible to consider.

He rubs his perspiring forehead, driving his thoughts back to the old pictures on the end table beside the sofa. In his mind, the picture glass lights up like diamonds, and the tarnished brass frames turn to gold. He lowers his head in memory of his parents, the priest, and the missal he gave him. If only he could be like he was back then. An innocent child with none of time's fractures.

He was a father. That's what a father does.
Eases the burdens of those he loves.
Saves the ones he loves from painful last images
that might endure for a lifetime.
—George Saunders

Chapter Thirty-Five

Jose

Those years ago, when Pauline Broussard came to interview Jose at Sacred Heart Church rectory where he and his baby, Angelina, were staying, her chicken business was still just idea. Before Pauline arrived, Fr. O'Hara told Jose, "She's a thinking woman and smart enough to carry it through. It will be a lot of work. Creating something from nothing always is."

"I've started from nothing several times, Father. When I was young, I had everything a person could want in Mexico, but it was all taken from me because of my father's dishonest and perilous choices. Still, he loved me, and for my safety sent me to Cuba. I was alone, so I had to grow up quickly. Cuba was not a good country for me. I wanted to leave, and did, on a small boat to Miami. I know what it is to create a new life."

When Pauline arrived to meet him and saw Angelina in Jose's arms, she reached for her at once and held her tenderly, as a mother would, as she spoke to Jose. "I'm looking for a good man. Someone responsible to help me create this business, so tell me about yourself, Jose. Start with why you are here in Bethel."

He liked her immediately and unreservedly told her his story, though never his real name. All the while, she smiled at Angelina; he wondered if Pauline heard any of it.

When he finished, Pauline set her blue eyes on him. "Jose, you have been through a lot in your young life. God must love you very much to allow you to suffer so. He's been with you, though, and brought you through it all." She kissed the top of Angelina's head. "And He has given you the greatest gift of all, a human life to love."

Fr. O'Hara grinned at Pauline. "Is that a yes?"

"I declare, Father, you know it is!" Then she addressed Jose. "You will manage the chicken farm, Jose. And you will have a house of your own." He felt like crying then, but he did not. He showed his strength to Pauline because he saw she would expect it from then on.

As it turned out, he and Pauline were of like minds, admired each other, and worked well together. And when Alma came along a short time later, and she and Angelina grew closer and closer, Jose felt he had family again.

Friday evening, Jose backs the truck out of the hospital parking lot with Angelina beside him. He smiles, knowing they're heading home with good news. He turns onto a service road that leads to the four-lane highway then glances over at his daughter. She is such a beautiful girl, like an angel. On the day she was first diagnosed with leukemia, he recalls crying inside as he looked at her, wondering how long she would live. In the days afterward, it was only his music that saved him from despair. He wrote a song for her then and still sings it to her nightly.

Much have I marveled at many sunsets
And milky moons passing, vainly seen
Soon did I slide into blue midnight nets
With my deep-loved child of dreams.
Our kindred hearts pierced with pain
Bruised brown in a skin of sorrow;
In fragile fields my faith was lain,
So her strength I sought to borrow.
Yellowed leaves will hang not long
They fall beneath the tree,
Yet she endures her sullen song
And we dare her destiny.

They will continue to dare her destiny. Succumbing to leukemia has never been an option for Jose or Angelina. She holds his rosary in her hand—his mother's rosary.

"God has blessed us," he says. "I am very grateful."

"I'm grateful, too, Papa, but sometimes I've wondered if God really loves me."

"Oh, mi niña, how can you say that? Of course God loves you! We are leaving the hospital behind, aren't we?"

"But I'm not leaving my disease behind. Maybe it's just hiding again. If God truly loved me, wouldn't he take it away for good?"

He notices the bruising on her arms from the hospital's needles and how frail she is. How should he answer? Despite his faith, her question has plagued him too. Many times, he's wondered what sort of love would allow God's children to suffer. And then his own child, his beautiful child, answers the question for both of them.

With the crucifix of the rosary lying flat in her palm, she fingers the corpus of Christ and says, "Oh, I'm sorry for doubting, Papa. It's just that sometimes, I get so tired of pain."

The words come to him as an errant lightning strike into the pink sunset of the afternoon sky. *My Father, if it is possible, let this cup pass me by. Nevertheless, let it be as you, not I, would have it.* Jose pulls over to the side of the service road and cuts off the ignition. He turns to Angelina. "Mi niña, do you think God loved his son, Jesus?"

"I am certain He did."

"Yet God allowed his own son to suffer on the cross. Jesus did not want to suffer any more than you do, or any of us do." Jose touches her shoulder. "We are God's children too. His plan for us here on earth is no less than his plan for Jesus. We are to become saints, to be at home with God eternally. The sufferings of Jesus and the crosses each of us carry show us the way." They were the words of his tearful mother on the day his father sent him to Cuba.

Angelina edges over to hug him, the rosary hanging between her fingers as she puts her arms around his neck and kisses him. "You can start the truck again. Let's go home."

"Yes, let's go home. We have a beautiful life ahead of us, mi niña!"

Fair is foul, and foul is fair.
—William Shakespeare, *Macbeth*

Chapter Thirty-Six

Mal

Through the open kitchen window, Mal hears sirens coming from the four-lane highway. The screaming noise irritates him, so he slams down the window, screaming Jesus's name in vain. Then he goes back to putting mayonnaise on his ham and cheese sandwich. He is still upset with Dr. Patton, as well as the obnoxious blue-eyed woman who confronted him in his classroom. She has a lot of gall talking to him like that. He will call the Chairman of the Board of Trustees and get her barred from his classes, tell the chairman that she came onto him, or that he can see, as the expert psychologist he is, that she is off-balance and possibly dangerous to the rest of his students.

He opens a kitchen drawer to take out a knife and notices an old cell phone in the back of it. The cell phone is not his, and not like any he's ever had, so whose is it? He tries to remember, but all he gets is a sudden flashback to his long-ago days at the seminary of god-followers that his mother sent him to. It concerned a boy named Jeremiah, a weak boy, a discard, with thick glasses and a stutter. Mal smiles. He can still hear the boy scream, "Na-na-n-oooo!" as he pushed Jeremiah out of the open second floor window of his dormitory room, just because he could. Mal felt refueled afterwards. The boy wasn't hurt; he only fell into a hedge and had a few scratches. But then he started running toward the prefect's residence. Mal had to keep him from doing that, and did. He couldn't remember everything he did to him; only that Jeremiah never told on him, not even after Mal was called to the office of the Vocations Director for a few other transgressions. No one except the two of them knew about the incident.

But what did the cell phone in his hand have to do with a discard like Jeremiah, a boy no one would miss if he were not on the earth at all?

Oh yes! He remembers now. The cell phone has nothing to do with Jeremiah. It belonged to a blond woman who came onto him at the Off the Road Whiskey and Stuff Bar out on the county highway. They might have had a good time except for the worthless kid who was paddling his way down the dirt road on a flat board with wheels because his crippled legs didn't work. He'd seen the kid before, paddling around downtown Bethel, grinning at anyone who would grin back at him. Funny thing, the kid seemed happy and even had a following. People actually liked him. But Mal couldn't stand him. The creep was always in his way, grinning and looking at Mal as if he would grin back. Of course, Mal never did. He usually put a shoe to the back of the wheeled board and shoved, sailing him down the street—exactly what he did the night he met the woman who owned the cell phone. She got all rattled over what he did to the cripple. She was going to call the police over something so insignificant. He took the cell phone to keep her from doing that.

He tosses the phone back in the drawer and realizes how tired he is. Usually, he likes chaos, but lately, there are times when he surprises himself by desiring a simple, quiet peace. Though he laps up the praise and attention his students give him, he is glad to be able to sleep and get away from them for a time, so, in the middle of making his ham and cheese sandwich, he decides to take a short nap.

He dreams he is lecturing to one of his classes, and the blue-eyed woman who sits in on them is confronting him. In the dream, he poses the question to his class is, "Is God real?" The blue-eyed woman waves her hand in the air to answer. Her entourage of students has grown alarmingly, and several of them wave their hands too. He knows he will get a lot of God and grits responses—purely sentimental emotion; so, before he calls on them, he expands his question. "If God is real, then why does he allow evil in the world?"

All of the hands drop down. He smiles. The question is always a stumper; there is no sensible answer.

Then, as if she's only been considering what she would say, the blue-eyed woman raises her hand again. He nods confidently for her to answer.

Her voice is as sure and methodical as ever. "No moral evil, and I emphasize 'moral evil,' meaning mortal sin, can ever be willed positively by God; it can only be permitted, and that is because God gave us the gift of free will. The commission of sin is never willed at all by God."

That sounds like his former Vocations Director, and even in sleep, Mal feels his blood pressure rising.

"Physical evils that occur," she goes on, "are willed by God, but never for their own sake, only for the sake of a 'good,' and only as a means to a 'good,' never an end." Then she sits, looking at him for a response.

In the dream—he would never have done it in reality—he raises his voice to the point of shouting. "What a crock of religious propaganda! Sin, what you call evil, exists only because of the belief that God exists. But God does not exist!"

The blue-eyed woman is not deterred. "Then why do we have moral evils perpetrated by human beings who make those choices? Where does free will come from?"

Mal glares at the blue-eyed woman while two or three of his students—his students!—answer at once, "God!"

Immediately, the victorious blue eyes of the woman pinpoint his. She speaks with too much authority. "Professor Hawkins, an intelligent discussion of evil cannot be had amid outbursts of emotion. Perceptive people, like your students"—she holds up both hands, opening her palms and moving her blue eyes around the classroom—"understand that physical evils can be willed because God loves the 'good,' and that moral evils are permitted because God respects human freedom."

All the students applaud.

He rushes from his podium toward the woman. But when they're face to face, he sees the woman isn't the blue-eyed one from his class but rather his aggravating sister, Charity.

That's when he wakes up.

He's hungry, craving the ham and cheese sandwich, which has become a little soggy. He sits at the table to wolf it down, as if it is his last meal. As he chews, Ginnie Gillan and her fool come to mind. He's had success with the fool because he has stirred doubt in Edmund's already fragile mind. He's taken advantage of the fool's worst experiences, turned them into profit for himself, and then turned them into distrust of his wife. He has no doubt that Edmund has taken care of Ginnie for him. He is certain of it. All it required was a little plucking—by a much superior man—of Edmund's fears and insecurities.

Although the fool may have taken a different direction. After all, Edmund K. Gillan is human and real, not some manifestation of memory, or like the bad dream he just had. Still, Edmund has no strong convictions. He is not free enough to overpower Malcolm J. Hawkins's will. Mal has been able to twist Edmund's mind just enough from so-called good to so-called evil. Yes, Mal is confident that by now the suffering fool has destroyed Ginnie.

I am in blood, stepped in so far, that, should I wade no more,
returning were as tedious as go o'er
—William Shakespeare, *Macbeth*

CHAPTER THIRTY~SEVEN

Edmund

After learning that the blond girl at the Dillard's jewelry counter had left for the day—the girl to whom he gave the pendant—Edmund wanders through the parking lot of the Bethel Mall, still searching for his black sedan.

He passes a puddle left by yesterday's rain. A sparkle of sunlight catches his eye, white and nearly blinding. Shining like the pendant he has now lost. The diamond pendant would have been the perfect gift of amends for Ginnie. "I never expected something so beautiful," she might have said—just as she had one morning during the previous winter in Bethel, when she snapped open the shade and found it was snowing. "Edmund, come look! It's so pure and white. As immaculate as a newborn soul before any human weight has pressed upon it." What he would give to hear her say words like that again!

The snow was only an inch deep, but still miraculous for Alabama. The blooming camellias he and Ginnie had planted were no longer blood red but looked a silver-pink. Pine branches bent toward the frozen grass like the silver spruce they'd flocked at Christmas. The steel-colored road in front of their house was frosted over, slick as glass, mirroring a glint of sun, just a fragment of light drawn around the edges of a high cloud. And when he cracked open the window, the air was chaste and clean.

But in a matter of hours, the pink and red blooms turned brown. The grass withered, and cars turned the whitened road to brown slush.

Ginnie said something about it being impossible to maintain innocence and purity in a tainted world, and he agreed. But now? Oh, to seize a glimpse of purity again!

He wants to go home to Ginnie, but he's afraid to face her without his gift of amends. Wherever his car is, he'll leave it and turn to Mal once more. Mal's house is nearby, just across the four-lane that borders the mall. He knows Mal will be home by now.

He takes off in that direction, running, gasping for breath, dangerously dodging the five o'clock traffic with its roaring sounds that mimic the clattering noise in his head. Then comes the bleeping horn of a truck as he runs across the four-lane in front of it. It swerves to prevent hitting him, its rasp like the squeal of hogs.

For what seems forever, he continues to dodge the vehicles flying down the four-lane and finally makes it to the other side of the highway. He climbs the hill that leads to a wooded area then drops to his knees to catch his breath for several minutes. At once, alarms and sirens scream. He sees blood-colored lights flashing and notices the red truck that swerved to miss him lying on its side in the median. The sign painted on its door reads: *Broussard Farm, Fresh Orange-Yolked Eggs. Wholesale or Just You.*

Responders are arriving. He remains kneeling on the hill long enough to see them carrying one body, then another, out of the truck. He thinks one of them is a young girl, a child.

"A child," he says to himself, and his thoughts tumble back to Ginnie. Yes, they often think about a child. He and Ginnie have always wanted one, but it hasn't happened. Another of his failures as a man. He has failed and failed again, in almost everything. His fingers feel weak—even his toes in his shoes feel weak.

His grandfather's condemning voice returns. *Have you not done enough? Did you have to kill them too?* He closes his mind to the senseless words, turns away from the blinding red lights and seething sirens, then takes off running again toward Mal's house. "Help me!" he cries, but to whom? He runs alone.

When Edmund reaches Mal's house, he is perspiring profusely. When he knocks on the door, his hands are trembling. When Mal ushers him inside, the chill of the mall returns. He sits in a chair by the black brick fireplace, still filled with the old ashes of winter, and settles in like a frightened mouse shuddering in a dark but familiar hole. "I have things to discuss," he whispers. "The first thing is Ginnie."

Mal grins. "Did you show her the gun? Did you do something grand?"

Edmund puts a hand into the pocket of his coat and feels the gun inside. "No, not grand at all." He takes it out to give it back to Mal, inadvertently pointing it at him. "Or maybe not grand enough." He thinks of the lost diamond pendant, his would-be gift of amends to Ginnie. But then he sees Mal staring at the gun, the color draining from his face, and the man he has come to for help suddenly looks shriveled and small. Is Mal afraid of the gun in his hand? Does Edmund hold the power now? He smiles; that *would* be something grand.

"Wait, wait," Mal says nervously. "I'll get the cocaine. You want some, don't you?" He stands to leave.

"No!" Edmund lowers the gun to his lap. "Stay here. I don't want drugs. I want help. I may have done something awful."

Mal hesitates then, just long enough for Edmund to hear his grandfather's taunting. *You won't shoot him. You don't have courage enough to kill evil!* But it is Ginnie's voice that continues. *Get rid of him, Edmund. He's a monster!* In desperation, Edmund closes his eyes for a moment to ease the voices. When he opens them, Mal stands over him.

"Give me the gun. Give it to me, you fool!" Mal shouts as if he's ordering a dog to give back its bone. "You've always been such a fool."

Edmund doesn't mean to squeeze the trigger. He has not come here to shoot Mal. He has not come for the cocaine. He's come for Mal's help until—as if for the first time—he hears the voices of his grandfather and Ginnie and realizes that Mal has never once helped him. Instead, he angled for Edmund, as evil will do. He lured him through his flaws, hooked him, and then, pulled him into a boat of sorrow. He's practically been the slave of a man who'd come to know too much about him, a man who just called him a fool. Why didn't he see it coming? Why didn't he stop it? He could have stopped it. He could have listened to Ginnie and his grandfather. Now, all he hears is another loud, vulgar sound, and then its violent vibration ringing in his ears. *You have become worse than a fool. You have become the worst of all men, a monster.* Then, the words of the priest long ago at his First Communion. *God loves you, Eddie. He will love you despite what you do because God's love never relents.*

He wishes—no he prays—the words are true.

His thoughts return to the house in Montgomery, to the grave-yard with its sons and daughters of the American Revolution and their many children who fought over hundreds of years to build the new nation of America. He remembers his mother's words as she spoke of those who rebelled in the Civil War and those who struggled in its aftermath, and *her people who survived long enough to build this house, our home.* If only he still lived there. If only his family hadn't been wiped away. If only he'd been a stronger child, or a different type of child, then he might be a better man. How could God love him? How could Ginnie love him? If only he could start over. Start over. Start over. Start over!

His head slumps to his chest, and his thoughts become images of himself. He is running, jumping over fence after fence after tiring fence, and he feels Ginnie watching him. He is perspiring and can barely breathe. His entire body is in pain, but he keeps going, hardly able to lift his legs. And yet, he sees himself coming closer and closer to a finish line. Then a red-shirted official snaps down a flag. The race is over. Voices are shouting. Shouting his name. "Edmund K. Gillan! Edmund K. Gillan!" He hears Ginnie's voice. "Edmund! Edmund! You've won!" He opens his eyes and sees the gun still in his hand.

He does not know how long he's been sitting in the chair by the fireplace, the chair that belongs to Mal. His hands move up and down the chair's arms, over the soiled upholstered pattern of apples and bananas while the smell of rot increases. Perhaps he's been sitting here for hours while Mal lies crumpled on the floor, not moving, a stain of red on his shirt. But Edmund can sit no longer. He must go home to Ginnie. He must face her now, without a gift of amends.

He shoves the gun into the pocket of his suitcoat.

Any man's death diminishes me, because I am involved in mankind,
and therefore never send to know for whom the bells tolls;
it tolls for thee.
—John Donne

Chapter Thirty-Eight

Alma

When she arrives home from work Friday evening, Alma is still thinking about Edmund K. Gillan and the diamond pendant he gave her, which is still in her purse. The thought of finding him to return it still lingers in her mind. Is the gift a miracle? She believes miracles are possible, the answers to hidden prayers. Her father might show up one day, might even love her one day, even if she's never seen his face. And Angelina might be cured of the leukemia. But a diamond pendant? She has never prayed for that. She's done nothing to deserve Edmund K. Gillan's gift. And now, the seeing-eye within her soul, the nudging that—for as long as she can remember—has mysteriously directed her thoughts, is framing the gift as important, something she must act upon, one way or another.

She opens the kitchen door and is welcomed by the smell of spaghetti sauce cooking and the sound of conversation. "Tomorrow is movie day," Pauline is saying to her mother, "and I believe I'll choose *Planet of the Apes*."

"*Planet of the Apes* again?" Moline groans. "We've seen it five times already." She's standing at the stove, stirring the sauce, when Alma comes over to hug her. "Hi, sweetie." Moline hugs her back with one arm and continues to stir with the other. "Your aunt has an infatuation with *Planet of the Apes*."

Pauline crosses the room to hug Alma too. "I have no infatuation, but I'm worried about the destiny of mankind. It's where the world is headed, Sister, certain self-destruction. We can never be too prepared for the end of man as we know him."

"I declare, Pauline, you talk about *my* standards, but you surely have a distorted view of the future. Anyway, *Planet of the Apes* is science fiction. It didn't happen and won't!"

"Not yet." Pauline sits at the kitchen table and puts her napkin in her lap as if she's in a restaurant waiting to be served.

"Not ever." Moline pours the boiled noodles into a colander then fans away the hot air.

"Well then, what's your pick? No, don't tell me—I know. It's always *Silence of the Lambs*."

"What if it is?" Moline puts the sauce on the noodles and sets a plate in front of her sister.

Pauline gives a giddy laugh. "Ha! It proves my point—intelligent people taking instruction from an evil man who will obviously end up in hell."

"How do you know where he'll end up? He solved the case, didn't he?"

"Yes, he solved it because evil can always sniff out evil. The man ate people, Sister!"

Alma decides she's had enough of their bickering and goes upstairs to change into her now-much-too-small red flannel Christmas pajamas, the ones printed with snowmen. As soon as she puts them on, she notices the hole has expanded. She's grown taller, so now her entire knee is poking out, but she will not depend on Pauline to fix it. Aunt Pauline is too busy with the chicken farm, and she never likes to miss the psychology classes she sits in on at the university. The pajamas should probably be thrown away, but Alma can't do that. They hold too many memories. If she wants to keep them, she will have to sew up the holes. "All by myself," she whispers on her way down again.

Pauline smiles at Alma as she enters the kitchen, and her mother sets another plate of spaghetti on the table. "Here's your dinner, Sugar. Eat up—you're too thin. That can make you weak."

Alma pulls out a chair, then twists toward Pauline, who has finished her dinner and left the table to fiddle with the new remote Moline bought. "Did Jose say when Angelina would be home from the hospital?"

"She was supposed to be released sometime today, but I've checked, and they're not home yet. Maybe later tonight. At least, the treatments are over and she's in remission again. Oh, what that poor girl has gone through for years. I'd love to take her in my arms, give her a hug, and tell her everything is going to be all right."

"I hope she'll be in remission for a while." Alma picks up a forkful of spaghetti. "She's been so depressed lately and hasn't wanted me to come over much. I miss her."

Moline comes to the table with her own plate of spaghetti. "Trials come to all of us, Sugar. Life is risky." She turns to Pauline, who is still trying to figure out how to turn on the television. Her round, doll-like eyes glisten impishly as she asks her twin, "By the way, Sister, is life a risk worth taking?"

"Oh, be quiet. Would you just turn on the TV for me? I can't work this remote you bought."

Instead, Moline gets up to retrieve a magazine. "If you don't mind, I'd like to glance at *Rock Star Favorites*. Chancee's been on tour, you know."

Pauline rolls her eyes. "Who would care about that, Sister?"

"A lot of people care about Chancee."

"I'd rather see the news on TV. They're building a new Walmart. To tell you the truth, Jose and I can't wait to go there. There's going to be a wonderful animal feed section. Everything in one place, and cheaper too."

Moline pays no attention to her sister. She's flipping through her magazine. "If Chancee's touring anywhere within a hundred miles of here, I'm going! I'd like to see her in person just once before I die."

"Don't be so dramatic, Moline! You'll have years and years to see the crazy woman, though God only knows why you'd want to."

"Lots of years," Alma agrees. Her mother was joking, of course, but her statement startled Alma. Before now, she hasn't considered her mother's death, though she's had to consider the possibility of Angelina's. But her own mother? What would her life be without Moline? "Please don't talk about dying, Mama. There's so much more you have to do here."

Moline gives her a playful smile. "Well, Sugar, we all live here at Heaven's Gate, you know. And we won't go through it alive. But don't worry, I plan to be around a long time. Time enough to see Chancee—the real Chancee—before I go. And I will take you with me."

"Moline, the only person in this house who cares to see the real Chancee is you. You know why? Because she *isn't* real. She's made up, messed up, and mindless. Alma's not worried about that. It's your talk about dying that's upsetting her."

But Alma isn't listening to Aunt Pauline. Her thoughts turn

from her mother to Angelina, and she feels an unusual ache near her heart, the same sort of desperate ache she had once before when Angelina awakened in her hospital room without Jose, who'd gone out for a few minutes. Only Alma sat beside her. Suddenly, Angelina woke crying, "I don't want this, I don't want this!" Then she called out loudly, "Papa!"

Alma panicked. Was Angelina dying? Did she need more blood? Well, she was there, right then, to give it to her. She reached over Angelina to press the button for a nurse. Immediately, Angelina grabbed her hand. "No, I'm alright now. I'm fine. I just had a strange dream." She looked around the room. "Where's Papa?"

"Don't worry. He'll be back before you know it."

Angelina wiped her eyes. "Good." She smiled up at Alma.

"What was your dream?" Alma asked.

"I saw a staircase that stretched up to heaven. And I saw the angels of God going up and down the staircase. One of the ascending angels, a beautiful lady, reached for my hand to take me with her, but I pulled away from her because Papa wasn't there. I wanted to wait for Papa. I did not want to go without him. And the sweet lady touched my face and called us by name. 'You will not go without Jose, Angelina,' she said. 'Your father will be with you.'"

Alma's memory of that day is interrupted by her mother. Moline says, "Don't be upset, Sugar. There's nobody dying today."

But the same frantic ache Alma felt those months before, when she thought Angelina might be dying, reappears, stops her breath, tightens her heart, and will not let go.

"'Villains!' I shrieked. 'Dissemble no more! I admit the deed!
Tear up the planks! Here, here! It is the beating of his hideous heart!'"
—Edgar Allan Poe, "The Telltale Heart"

CHAPTER THIRTY-NINE

Edmund

Lying on his side, his body curved like a question mark, Mal's eyes are tightly shut as if he'd seen the bullet coming and panicked. There is only a small, red bloodstain on his shirt. Maybe he isn't dead. Edmund taps Mal's leg once with the toe of his shoe, expecting him to move or even rise up. He does neither.

"Well, that's what you get," Edmund says, mimicking the words of the bully from his childhood. "I'm tired of carrying your sins." And yet, Edmund experiences a strange feeling of desolation, even abandonment.

He steps out the front door and remembers he has no car; it is still somewhere at the mall, so he begins walking home to Ginnie. His wife. The woman he loves. The woman who loves him. She will be waiting there for him to say he's sorry. But when he tells her that he shot Mal—though he did not mean to shoot him—and that he is now out of their lives, Ginnie will smile. He's sure of it.

In that instant, he hears a voice—Ginnie's voice, not the old preacher's—pulsing in his head with every footstep, every heartbeat, quoting *Macbeth*. *Something wicked this way comes.*

He shakes his head. No! Those words signaled the approach of the monster Macbeth had become. Edmund is not a monster.

The closer he gets to home, the stronger Ginnie's voice becomes. *Something wicked this way comes.* Does she mean Mal? Always, Ginnie thought him wicked, a bully, and a monster. Always she worried that he might make Edmund a monster, too.

Something wicked this way comes.

Halfway to his house, he feels hot, blistering hot. *Something wicked this way comes.* He feels as if pieces of his flesh are dissolving and falling off as he moves, dropping behind him to be pulverized by some automobile or pecked by carnivorous birds. Fine! He deserves it. He isn't a real person anyway. He's some kind of ghost who can't even feel his feet on the pavement, on the grass, on the road.

He nears the house just down the road. He picks up his pace and begins to run toward it, while Ginnie's voice repeats, *Something wicked this way comes.*

He imagines he is still a boy in Montgomery living in the grand old house, running down the dirt roads through fields that—over a hundred and fifty years ago—used to grow acres of cotton tended by slaves. He was told the slaves who once lived there were happy, but even as a child, he never thought that was true.

His grandfather preached loudly about a different sort of slave—a slave to addictions, a slave to wickedness, a slave to sin. *The only way to be free is to atone. Give up your sinful will and make amends!* And now, after all that has happened, all the chaos, Edmund wants to atone. He wants to enter an ordered house, not a house of chaos. He wants to fall into the arms of a woman who will love him despite his disordered ways. But will that happen?

Seeing the house ahead of him, once again he recalls that he has no gift of atonement to offer Ginnie. No way to show her how sorry he is. He can give her words, but will she listen now? Is it too late?

He decides he will drop to his knees before her, tell her she was right about Mal, right about the drugs too. Tell her he only wanted relief, to forget his problems, or even to get a little courage. She knows he's never been a confident man, but neither Mal nor the drugs gave him the courage he sought. Oh, the obscenities he's chosen instead of choosing her!

Something wicked this way comes.

The house ahead grows larger in his sight. Their home, a place that holds loving memories. Has he ruined them?

He warms at the memory of Ginnie in the morning, before dawn, walking unhurriedly into their living room, slow light from a diminishing moon falling over her through slatted plantation blinds and stretching out across the blood-red carpet like fence posts to corral all things present and past, all things learned and retained. He pictures her entering, yawning, holding a mug of coffee, placing it on the mahogany drum table, then sitting on her grandmother's silk-covered sofa that has begun to split at the seams. She covers herself with a purple crocheted afghan made by her great aunt, the aunt he once met, with sea-green eyes and long, slim fingers like Ginnie's. She has many afghans made by her aunt who has now left this world. From the pocket of her red velour robe, when she doesn't know he is watching, she pulls a pack of cigarettes and lights one. He notices its orange tip and tiny stream of smoke that hovers momentarily over the coffee table and then descends, touching the shoulders of the Virgin Mary statue, an angel beside her and a tiny lamb at her feet. "Ave Maria," he hears himself say. "Ave Maria."

He can see the airport near the house now. Already, he hears planes taking off. He imagines them on a plane. Ginnie and Edmund, up in the clouds, going on a trip somewhere, laughing and looking down at the specks of earth below, looking down at those tiny pieces of life itself, pieces of a painting, a masterpiece he's never been able to master.

In front of the house, he steps up on the curb then onto the sidewalk and stops, waiting for Ginnie's voice in his head. But it is silent now.

Perspiration trickles down his forehead, into his eyes, and his heart is pounding. He pulls a handkerchief from his pocket and wipes his face, straightens his rumpled coat and tie. The first thing he'll tell Ginnie is that he loves her more than anything. "You don't have to worry about Mal or the drugs. They're gone now. I've been cured of them," he will say. And she will open her arms and gather him in, all the wayward pieces of him, until he is whole again. He takes a deep breath then a few more steps toward the house.

Close to the porch, a dragonfly with beautiful wings hovers over the mass of white flowering gladioli towering like swords. He recalls Ginnie in April, kneeling in the dirt, digging a permanent home for each bulb. As soon as they began to bloom, they bothered him. "Why gladioli?" he asked. His mother had called them funeral flowers. She said they symbolized strength and purity in the deceased and were not appropriate for just any departed person.

Ginnie looked up at him and shrugged her shoulders. "I just like them, Edmund. Why does there have to be a reason?"

The dragonfly clasps one of the gladiolus blooms with all six legs. Odd, Edmund thinks—six legs, and yet the dragonfly cannot walk. He reaches out to touch it, to commiserate with its inability, but it flies away fast to some hiding place. Like Edmund, it knows how to escape.

The idea of escaping enters his mind. He notices the air is cooler now, and that the grass looks blue. He raises his eyes to the high hill, almost a mountain, beyond the town of Bethel. He recalls his grandfather telling him that in the Old Testament, Bethel was one of the first places where the Hebrew people met with God, where Jacob dreamed of a stairway to heaven with angels ascending and descending on it and God standing above it. Then Bethel became corrupt by the worship of idols and false gods and sealed its fate, never to be mentioned in the New Testament.

His thinks he should enter his house. But he does not. Instead, he lifts his eyes to the hill as if it will tell him where to go, what to do next. The white sun and moon face each other from either side of it like twin Eucharistic hosts. Halfway up each side, there is a bluff with twin overhangs. There, the wind moves shadows of tender green pines as if caressing two separate altars, but down below the wind grows stronger, growling into Edmund's ears, asking questions for which he has no answers. Behind its snarl, a church chime beckons, obligated to ring at designated times, though Edmund is not obligated to hear it. In his self-imposed deafness, is he missing something grand?

Again, he sees himself as a child in his Montgomery home, standing in his hiding place, shaded from the early summer sun by delicate new green boughs that arch out over the lawn of the big white house, making jigsaw puzzle patterns on the grass. He sees himself standing against the trunk of a thin tree, his back pressed solidly into the rough bark. His small hands are tucked safely between the speckled gray trunk and the seat of his denim cutoffs, as if he is handcuffed to the spot. Now and then, splotches of sparse sunlight escape through the thick needles of the pine to dapple his plump arms and his smoothly rounded belly until it appears speckled with soft warm spots like the skin of a newborn pup. His head, covered with ash-colored curls, bends rigidly toward some waiting space in the puzzled grass. A space of importance. The blades of the grass move softly with the wind, beckoning like a thousand green fingers for him to come. Yet he remains securely flattened against the tree. Afraid to see, to hear, to feel, to taste, even to smell the air, and overwhelmingly afraid of stepping away.

Finally, he grips the banister and takes the few steps onto the porch of his house. In the corner is a pile of dead love bugs neither he nor Ginnie swept away. The season of those swarms is over, but the bodies are left to decay, which makes him think of Mal, left dead and alone. And of Ginnie, probably still angry, still lying on the sofa where he left her this morning.

And of himself, left unloved.

He stares at the door a moment before reaching for the knob. His hand closes around it, but he cannot make himself turn it. Not now. Here, as he once did in his childhood home, he burrows into the corner of his mind, blocking the sound of all voices that will blame him or condemn him. He disrobes his mind until it is bare. Let the sound within him snarl out questions. He will choose not to hear.

Edmund turns the doorknob and enters. "Ginnie!"

But we have this treasure in jars of clay,
to show that the surpassing power belongs to God and not to us.
—2 Corinthians 4:7

CHAPTER FORTY

Alma

Moline found nothing about a Chancee Wile tour in *Rock Star Favorites* magazine the previous night, so now, sitting between Alma and Aunt Pauline at the breakfast table, Alma's mother immediately dives into the entertainment section of the Saturday morning paper and scans through it. "Well, again, there's nothing about a Chancee tour!" She snaps the paper closed, folds it to the front page, and shoves it toward Alma, toppling the salt and pepper shakers on the table.

Alma is still thinking about the diamond pendant upstairs in her purse until she gives a preoccupied glance to the headline on the front page: MURDER IN BETHEL.

"Mama, look!" She pushes the paper back to Moline.

"What in the world?" Moline exclaims. "A doctor, a nurse, and two patients were murdered yesterday. Shot to death right here in Bethel!"

Pauline grabs the newspaper. "Not here in Bethel."

"Yes, in Bethel, Sister." Moline snatches the paper back. "I'll read you what it says: 'A lone gunman in a ski mask entered the Burke Dermatology Clinic yesterday afternoon and shot four innocent people.'"

"Who was he, the man in the ski mask? Let me see the paper!"

Moline trembles and stares at the wall, so Pauline takes the paper from her. Alma moves next to Pauline, and then all three read the front-page story in silence.

Alma looks up, bewildered. "Why? Our town is a…nice town. Why would a neighbor—?"

"We don't know if he was a neighbor or not," Moline says with uncharacteristic caution. "He might have been some crazy itinerant off the interstate." She turns quickly to her twin. "Sister, you may have been right after all about the strange footprints around our gate!"

"That happens, you know, more and more every day. Sick people wandering from place to place without a sane thought in their heads."

"That's awful," Alma replies.

Moline gives Alma's hand a quick, protective pat. "Aw, don't you worry, Sugar. There may be a few crazies out there, but most people could never kill."

"I beg to differ, Sister. Does the Bible call Cain crazy? No. It says he killed his own brother because he was resentful of him. He wanted what his brother had. Jealousy is a human flaw. We're all capable of it—just as we all have the capability to kill."

"Capability, yes. But…not everyone does."

Alma notices a sudden helplessness take over her mother's expression, as if there's something she can't figure out. "Do you think the murderer was *born* evil?" Moline asks, almost a whisper and with none of her former certitude.

Pauline looks questioningly at her twin. "No one is born to be evil, Sister. People are born to be good. It's sin that gets in their way."

Whatever mellowed her a few seconds before, Moline shakes it off quickly, returning to her usual rashness. "I don't think sin really exists. Intolerant people made it up."

Alma knows that her mother makes a lot of inflammatory statements that aren't necessarily what she believes. But Pauline's face reddens. "Oh, for heaven's sake, Moline. Then why do you—and I mean *you*—feel human shame? I know you feel it. I've seen it in your face. I've seen your tears, and I've heard you cry because of it. You *are* a sinner. We all are. We're just too obstinate to admit it. Haven't you heard of the Fall of Man? If we're human, we're sinners."

"Well, you're not a sinner." Moline defends her sister with a look of admiration.

"But I am."

"Pauline, nobody goes to Mass, or prays, or helps out at church as much as you do!"

Alma hears a bit of envy in her mother's words.

"Sinners go to Mass. Sinners pray, and sometimes sinners do a lot of good. But that doesn't mean we aren't sinners. All people have a flawed side to their nature." Pauline grabs the paper and shakes it in Moline's face. "Sin exists!" Her voice rasps as if she's spent her last breath. "Read this again and see that it does. It's a sickness of human nature." She looks to Alma as if for support. "Surely you know that sin exists."

Alma shrugs. How would she know? She can't imagine how someone could murder another human being and take them from the people who need them. She thinks of her father, who might be dead for all she knows, and of Angelina. The awful, unthinkable day may come when Alma won't see Angelina again. Then she thinks of Edmund K. Gillan, the seemingly unwell man who gave her the diamond pendant.

"Whether it exists or not, I'm ready to change the subject," Moline says. "Hand me the remote, Pauline. It's time for my choice of a Saturday movie." They move to the living room sofa and the credits roll to *Silence of the Lambs*, flashing on the television across the room.

It's quiet except for the voices as the movie plays. And then, after a while, Pauline throws up her hands with a dissonant laugh. "Did you hear that, Sister? Did you hear what that monster said about the nature of a murderer? First, a murderer covets! That's what I'm talking about, Sister. That's what sin is. Constantly coveting something you want but don't have and then doing whatever it takes to get it."

Moline seems frustrated, as if she has never heard the words before, or else hasn't paid attention. She clicks off the TV. "After what we read in the paper, I've had enough of this Movie Day. Haven't you, Pauline?"

"Yes, Sister. Yes, I have. Let's go clean up the kitchen and afterwards make some brownies to cheer us both up." The twins get up to leave.

For a while, Alma remains on the sofa, still stunned by the shooting, incomprehensible violence right in their hometown of Bethel, the house of God, the gate of heaven. She worries about the expensive pendant the man in Dillard's gave her. With the restless thoughts pricking her nerves, she springs up and dashes through the kitchen. "I'm going to get dressed," she says to her mother and aunt as she passes through.

In her room, Alma dresses in shorts and a tank top then pulls out the diamond pendant and gazes at its beauty.

The sparkling diamond reminds her of the odd snowfall they

once had in Bethel. For a while, everything was covered in white, glistening clarity, as if nothing impure or diseased had ever existed in the town. She and Angelina made a small snowman with a smiling face of raisins placed just so. Then, after the snow started to melt, Angelina had the idea of saving what was left of the snowman in a mason jar. The jar of water, still amazingly clear, is on the dresser in Alma's room beside a statue of the Sacred Heart of Jesus that Pauline gave her.

She thinks again of Edmund K. Gillan standing in Dillard's, shaking like he had an illness. She wonders if maybe he is sick with something even worse than Angelina's leukemia, though she realizes it's hard to recognize disease just by looking at a person. Edmund K. Gillan dressed well. He was a nice-looking man, surely sweet to her, and probably kind to his own family.

She sighs. As much as she wants to keep the gift, she can't. It wouldn't be right. She'll have to find him as soon as she can and give it back.

The first thing Alma tries is the phone book in Aunt Pauline's room, near her old push-button telephone. She opens it to last names that begin with "G," and there he is: Edmund K. Gillan. His address is 104 Raven Lane, and there's a phone number. She dials it, but no one answers, and for some reason, she doesn't think she ought to leave a message. She thinks, instead, that she ought to go there.

She returns to her room for her purse and puts the box with the pendant back inside, then proceeds downstairs. "I'm going to check on Angelina, see if she's home now. Then I'm going into town," she tells her mother and aunt. "Do you need anything?"

Aunt Pauline turns toward her. "No, Sugar. Just be careful out there. They haven't caught the shooter."

She drives the short distance to Angelina's and knocks lightly on the door, but no one answers. Jose's truck is not parked beside the house. She's not worried. Sometimes there's a delay in checking Angelina out of the hospital on a weekend. So, she heads into Bethel to find Mr. Gillan.

She mulls over Pauline's claim that a loving God does not inflict pain, yet Angelina suffers it. Once, after many years of fighting the disease, Angelina became angry, so angry she tore up her room, ripping down curtains, breaking lamps. *Why? Why? Why?* Then cursing God in words Alma never thought would pass her lips. Alma was with her every day then, listening to her, stroking her shoulders, and making her favorite drink, milk with Ovaltine. But nothing seemed to help until Jose came in.

He bent to kiss her forehead. "Talk to me, mi niña. What is your greatest worry?" Already, Alma knew. Angelina was afraid of dying, and why wouldn't she be?

"Tell me, mi niña," Jose urged.

Angelina paused, then said, "I wonder sometimes if when you die...is it just blackness?"

Jose drew his trembling lips into a smile. "Mi niña, if you mean nothingness, then think about this. The fact that you, as a human being, can wonder at all, shows that you were created for more than nothingness. We have something within us that allows us to wonder and to imagine, just like you and Alma imagine. It allows us to strive, to make decisions, and to love or not to love. These gifts come from our soul and are what make us human beings and not animals. On earth, our soul lives within our physical body. We can't see it, but it's there. It's part of us. After death, our soul no longer has a physical body in which to live. Yet it lives because it has never been physical, but spiritual, always the source of our ability to do spiritual things. Our soul survives earth with those gifts intact. We are not made for nothingness but for immortality."

"Was I created to have leukemia?"

"No, mi niña. Leukemia or not, you were created to love and be loved by me."

That afternoon, things changed. The signs of stress left Angelina's face. She put her arms around Jose's neck. "I love you, Papa." Then she turned to Alma. "And you, too, blood sister."

The moment struck Alma so profoundly that she wanted to tell her mother and Aunt Pauline about it. Her aunt was in the kitchen stirring a big pot of homemade vegetable soup, but her mother was not at home.

"Gone to the beauty parlor, of course," Pauline said when Alma asked. Then she stopped stirring and eyed her niece. "My goodness, you look happy."

"I am, Aunt Pauline." Alma told her about Angelina's breakdown and how Jose had given her just the right answer. "How did he know just what to say?"

Aunt Pauline turned down the heat on the stove. "Come sit with me on the sofa. I want to tell you something it took me a long time to learn."

They went into the living room. Alma sat beside her on the sofa, and Aunt Pauline put an arm around her shoulders, pulling her close. "Jose knows that somewhere there is an answer to everything. It may come later on, but it will come. He sees that answers are all around us, if only we seek them with our hearts. Answers in the rings of an old tree trunk, in the birth and death of a seed, in the momentary whiteness of a honeysuckle blossom. Answers in the changing faces of children, in the dying faces of grandparents, in the love between husband and wife. The answers don't elude us; we elude the answers. They almost scream at us, but we don't hear. All because we human beings haven't yet learned the language of our own spirit, of God's thought connecting our thoughts. Our lack of learning makes us deaf to truth, so spiritually blind to real beauty that, even if we see it with our eyes, we are incapable of replicating the totality of it in our souls. We have become like paper cups instead of treasured earthen vessels, not recognizing that our short, fleeting lifetime is barely a speck in eternity, and only a part of the whole." Then Aunt Pauline kissed her cheek and got up to go back to her soup on the stove.

Alma did not grasp the meaning of all Aunt Pauline said that day, but she never loved her aunt nor admired Jose more than she did at that moment.

We are each our own devil, and we make this world our hell.
—Oscar Wilde

Chapter Forty-One

Moline

Moline sits in a chair at the kitchen table, waiting for the timer to signal that the brownies are done. "Waiting for the brownies is your job," Pauline said on her way to check on the chickens, "since I did most of the work."

The Bethel Eagle is still on the table in front of Moline. She looks down and sees evil staring her in the face, right there, in black and white. Nothing but evil. She knows all about that. Her heart catches as she considers the things she's done. Of course she's a sinner; she covets lots of things for herself, just like Pauline said. It's hard living in the same house with Pauline who, despite the nasty things Moline often says to her, is a good and charitable woman. Has anyone ever called her, Moline, a good woman, or charitable? Well, Alma *almost* said so that day in the car after she first gave blood to Angelina. At least, she said her mother wasn't worthless, and that was something to Moline. But she still feels she is.

Moline first began to feel worthless when Alma was just a baby, when she left her with her grandparents almost every night to go to any bar that was open. Eventually, Moline realized she was leaving her child for what she thought was a good time. One night, years ago, with pulsing music in her ears, a drink in her hand, and loud voices all around, she thought about Alma and wanted only her. So she stopped going out at night, and it made her feel better.

But feeling better isn't what she needs now. Talking about sin has assured her that she wants a full confession with Fr. O'Hara, because as he said last time they talked, she needs absolution. She looks at the kitchen clock. Confessions at Sacred Heart are almost over, but she could telephone Fr. O'Hara to see if he would stay a little later.

The timer rings just as Pauline returns. Moline pulls out the brownies and turns to her. "I've got to make a phone call."

"To whom?"

Moline doesn't answer. She's searching for her cell phone, the second cell phone she's had. She lost the first one a long time ago.

Pauline turns off the oven. "It's right here, on the shelf above the stove."

Why is Pauline always right? She takes the phone outside, away from Pauline's ears, to call Fr. O'Hara. At her mention of the confessional, the priest says he will see her in fifteen minutes.

Moline is there in ten.

She is perspiring a bit, but the screen between them helps. She couldn't do it face-to-face. So, she closes her eyes, intending to let everything out this time, all that is bothering her. She doesn't just confess her drinking. She closes her eyes even tighter and confesses what happens after her drinking—the many men she's gone to bed with, so many she could not determine which one was Alma's father. Then she pauses.

Fr. O'Hara says, "It's good you're getting it all off your chest, Moline."

"But that isn't all."

"Then go on."

"Once I stole from the dentist I work for. Not a lot. He never missed it, but…" Tears roll down her cheeks as she confesses that she had two abortions before Alma was born. "And I almost aborted Alma, too."

She didn't know why, during her third pregnancy, she felt pushed to call Pauline—who had no idea Moline had ever had one abortion—and tell her how badly her life was going. To tell her why she needed to end her pregnancy, as if Pauline would make her feel better about it. Instead, Pauline kept her from doing it. Pauline promised to return home and help her raise Alma. Pauline pleaded with her twin, "You will never be sane again, Moline, if you kill your baby. Because that's what you'll be doing. That's what abortion is."

After that flash of memory, Moline stops confessing even though she isn't finished. Her sins appall her. Of course, she is worthless.

"Take your time, Moline," Fr. O'Hara says. "God is always patient, and he greatly loves those who confess their sins and return to him."

Is that what she is doing now, returning to God? Well, she is frightened of him. Does he really love sinners? She thinks she better quit while she has the chance, so she jumps ahead fast. "I am sorry for my sins and the sins of my past life. Amen." She only wants to get out of there.

After his blessing, Fr. O'Hara whispers to her, "Moline you've said you feel worthless, and I've told you that you are not. You are just like the rest of us. We are all sinners. Every sin, no matter how great or small, nailed Jesus to the cross, so we're all a bunch of bums, unworthy of God's forgiveness and mercy, yet he bestows it upon us.

Now, go in peace. Your sins are forgiven. You have the opportunity of a fresh start."

As she leaves the church to go to her car, she feels lighter, and yes, on her way to a fresh start, sort of like a beauty makeover—until her conscience seems to check up on her. "Did you confess *all* of your sins? Haven't you buried one? The worst one?"

Yes, she has buried it. For years, she's packed it far down inside herself, unable to face the vileness of it. At first, it was hard; it kept creeping up again. But then, it became easier. When it came to mind, she simply denied it, told herself she only imagined it while she was drunk. After all, there were lots of things she conjured up when she was under the influence of alcohol. So, she's gone on with her life, almost successful in ignoring what she did. Successful enough that now the circumstances of her sin are hazy, except she thinks she has been in bed with the devil. No. That wasn't right. She was not in bed with anyone. That time, sex was not her sin. "Don't go there," she whispers to herself. Again, she obstructs the path to the memory, and she drives home.

Late afternoon, the twins sit again in front of the TV to watch the news about the shooting in Bethel. Alma is out somewhere—did she have a shift at Dillard's today? Moline isn't sure, and it makes her nervous, seeing the news of evil while not knowing where her daughter is.

After Bethel's Chief of Police promises to capture the person who murdered so many of God's people, Pauline turns off the television. "I've seen enough, Sister. I'm just glad he attacked the dermatology clinic instead of the dental office where you work."

Her sister's warmth, and the warmth of the sun coming through the living room window, ought to be a comfort to Moline, but instead she feels as if she's drowning in the overflow of that long ago event about which she remembers only pieces. Has she willed herself to forget because it is as unsettling as yesterday's shooting? Should she get in the car right now and go back to church to tell Fr. O'Hara that she forgot something that occurred so long ago? Not that she has forgotten the person involved. That person who wouldn't allow himself to be ignored. No matter how long ago it was, she will never forget someone as sinister as the skulking, squatty man she met just once at a county road bar, yet the tiniest recollection of him makes her literally ill.

Pauline pats her twin's hand and rises from the sofa. "I'm going to walk over to Jose's. Surely he's home by now."

Moline nods and gives Pauline a slight smile.

A few minutes later, Pauline returns, her face flushed and her eyes narrowed. "Jose and Angelina must still be at the hospital because his truck is not there. Tomorrow, whether he likes it or not, I'm going to buy him a cell phone." She turns to go upstairs. "Lock the doors after Alma gets home, Moline."

"Don't I always, Sister?"

"No, you do not. Sometimes you conveniently forget, especially if you don't agree with the 'why' of it. When I found those footprints on the red dirt road and started locking the gate, you didn't agree that they were a sign of possible danger. But then, risks are part of your life. You've never been able to see their danger."

Moline could protest. She could say she understands the reason now for locking the gate, but at the mention of the red dirt road, the memory she's packed away rolls in like a wave of foul-smelling water as if from an overflowing sewer, sickening her, turning her stomach until she thinks she might throw up. *How could she? How could she have done such a thing!* She tries to push it back again, but the pieces are liquid now. They cannot be controlled. They keep washing and washing over her until the memory becomes whole. And then, she sees herself.

She remembers coming out of a bar on a county road at sunset. *A red dirt road.* She saw a sign: Off the Road Whiskey and Stuff, a long, one-story wooden building with colored lights blinking like devilish eyes from one end of the lengthy roof to the other. She'd been to the bar several times before, but that time, she saw a child-like young man with crippled legs—only a boy really, and probably mentally challenged too—sitting on a wide board with wheels. She saw his cheerful grin as he propelled the board with his hands on the red dirt road. She went into the bar alone. She can't remember everything that happened inside, but coming out, she felt a weighty arm around her shoulder, the arm of a squatty man she'd met inside, a man she thought was halfway decent—until she heard his disturbing laughter when he noticed the afflicted boy on the board, as if the boy was the one toy he always wanted and never had.

The squatty man pulled her along with him until they were behind the boy's wheeled board, just as the smiling kid reached the top of the hill to a ravine. And then the awful man shoved the back of the board with his shoe, and it began rolling faster. The crippled boy laughed as if the man's pushing was a game, a game of kindness. The squatty man laughed too. Again and again, he ran behind the boy and shoved the board with his shoe until the innocent, laughing boy on the board was right on the edge of the deep, vine-covered ravine. That's when she realized the man was not decent in any way! With one last kick, the boy's laughter became a shriek of terror as his board plummeted down, down, down!

Moline was horrified. She slapped the man's face. "What kind of devil are you?" She scrambled down the overgrown hill, tangled with scrubs and underbrush, tripped and fell to the bottom of the ravine. She felt the pain in her soul when, in the last rays of sunset, she saw the board turned over in a patch of blackberry bushes. The young man was nearby, twisted and mangled like roadkill, bleeding from his mouth, his nose. His unblinking eyes stared up at the fading rust-colored sky, and around his neck hung a silver chain with the medal of a saint, tinged in red.

She pulled out her cell phone to call 911, but the hideous man came at her from behind, pushed her hard, snatched the phone from her hands, and stuffed it into his pocket. When she turned, she saw the shovel raised in his hands. Was he going to kill her? A slow, callous smile spread across his face as if he knew what she was thinking and enjoyed the control he held over her. Then he chuckled, stuck the point of the shovel into the dirt beside him, and said, "I keep this in my truck. Never know when I'll have to bury something."

"Call 911!" she cried, but he only stood there, staring at her as if he were amused. "Give me back my phone!"

He growled then like the animal he was. "We don't tell anybody about this! You hear me? Nobody! Not ever! That boy was a worthless human being, and you can see he's dead as a doornail. No one will miss him or care that he's gone." He looked around and pointed to a space of red dirt. "We'll bury him over there."

"We will not!" She scrambled to her feet.

He yanked her back. "I wouldn't do that if I were you. We are accomplices now."

"I will not be your accomplice. I did not do this. I did not do this," she sobbed. "Leave me alone!"

"Listen, you found *me*, honey, in that bar up there. You put your arm around *me* and asked me to buy you a drink. I wasn't looking for you. I'm not fond of arrogant women. But you couldn't leave *me* alone, could you? I know your type well, and turnabout's fair play." He glared at her with cold, dark eyes. Glared as Satan might.

Before that dreadful day, she discounted Satan's existence; but she remembers what that man said—*You'll help me dig that grave and bury him, or I'll bury you both!* Since then, she has understood that Satan is real.

Now, here in the living room, the memory is whole and clear. She helped him! And worse, she never told anyone about it. Nothing appeared in the paper or on the television news concerning a missing crippled boy or a body found in the ravine. Just as the disgusting man had said, no one cared. Yet for months—years—Moline felt the weight of dragging the innocent boy's broken body to his grave, felt the dirt on her hands and his blood on her fingers. Always, she tried to bury the memory just as she helped to bury the young man. Finally, she was able to ram it down so far in her mind that it became clumped into the one word she used to describe herself, the same word the squatty man had used to describe the boy on the rolling board: worthless.

She is sure what she did is unforgiveable. How can she ever confess such a thing to Fr. O'Hara? How can she tell him she partnered with a man as evil as the unknown killer who shot all those people at the dermatology clinic?

The clock in the living room strikes three times, reminding Moline how the clock in the bar had struck three times too, before it all happened—just as the squatty man stuck out his hand and said to the bartender, "I'm Malcolm J. Hawkins the Third," as if the bartender ought to be impressed.

The shape of true love isn't a diamond. It's a cross.
—Alicia Bruxvoort

CHAPTER FORTY-TWO

Edmund

Ginnie won't look at him. She stares across the room to the window with its closed curtains, where shadows move like faceless actors on a fabric screen. The actors' arms are raised, their fingers stiff, their bodies stretched upward as if every part of them is reaching for something untouchable. Below them is the blood-red carpet.

Has she pushed him again into the role of Macbeth?

The words he shouted in the play are now in his head: *I am in blood. Stepped in so far, that, should I wade no more, returning were as tedious as go o'er.*

He looks again at Ginnie, her eyes still fixed on the shadowy actors. "But this is not our play, Ginnie. Not our performance." And yet, the thought comes to him that it might be. Even in his present state of chaotic consciousness, he identifies with the part he played: A man with an affliction from his youth and a cowardice he could not handle on his own.

He feels her eyes on him, sees her lips move.

Her words rush into his soul. *A little water will not wash away your sins, Edmund.*

At once, he hears his grandfather preaching in the pulpit before his devoted congregation. He recalls the old man's peculiar power over them, and himself too. He sees his grandfather raise his right hand to the wood-beamed ceiling of his church, sees it cast a hook-like shadow over the believers as if he were Peter fishing the seas. "Praise the Lord God Almighty for all those who suffer!" the old man shouts. "Suffering plus faith equals salvation!"

"Hallelujah!" the believers answer.

"Praise the Lord for giving us troubles so we can rise above them! Praise Him for making us all imperfect creatures who seek his perfection. Cut from us, O Lord, all our unholy parts!"

"Amen! Amen!" Edmund hears the congregation shout.

He sees his grandfather breathe out relief and turn his ice-blue eyes from face to face, pulling them together like fish on a line. He sees his grandfather turn to him. His once-fierce eyes are now gentle: *There is no sin that cannot be forgiven. Ask now, Edmund. Beg for forgiveness before it's too late.*

Tears flow from his grandfather, and from Edmund as he drops to his knees.

Many that live deserve death. And some that die deserve life.
Can you give it to them?
Then do not be too eager to deal out death in judgment.
For even the very wise cannot see all ends.
—J.R.R. Tolkien, *The Fellowship of the Ring*

CHAPTER FORTY-THREE

Alma

No driveway leads up to 104 Raven Lane, so Alma parks in front of the house. A ray of sunlight glints off the roof, and on its dark peak she notices a bird. At first she can't tell what kind, but on second glance, in the sunlight, it looks like a dove.

She takes a concrete walkway to the house. On either side of it, there is barely any grass, as if the lawn has never been watered. She steps onto the porch and stares at a mass of wilting gladioli struggling to survive.

What should she say to Edmund K. Gillan?

Taking a deep breath, she rings the doorbell and knocks on the door. Seconds tick by. Her heart pounds so loudly, she can't think of the right words.

She decides she's made a mistake. He's not home anyway.

As she turns to leave, the door opens.

A whiff of something rotten coming from inside the house causes her to step back a little. The man in the threshold is Edmund K. Gillan to be sure, but not the neatly dressed man she met at the mall, not the man she'd imagined her father might resemble. He's wearing pajamas, his hair is uncombed, and he's sweating profusely as if there's no air-conditioning inside. His skin, sallow as peanut butter, seems to hang on the bones of his face, and he stares at her with blank eyes, glazed over.

"I'm so sorry to have disturbed you, Mr. Gillan." She tries not to inhale the revolting odor. "Do you remember me? You gave me the pendant you bought for your wife. I'd like to return it. I mean I can't keep it—"

"The gift of amends?" His voice is excited but hoarse, as if he's been shouting or crying.

She decides that he must be awfully sick like Angelina, maybe even terminally sick. He hadn't known what he was doing when he gave her the diamond. Now, she only wants to give it back to him and leave. But he looks so ill. Is he being taken care of? Should she call 911? He's trembling just the way he did in the mall, and the smell coming from the house is growing stronger, a sort of festering decay. It can't be a good place for a man as sick as Edmund K. Gillan.

"You have the gift?"

"Yes, I have the gift. I want to return it." She reaches into her purse and takes out the box with the pendant inside. Impolitely, he snatches it from her and goes back into the house to what looks like a small, dark library off the living room.

"Ginnie!" he calls to someone lying on a sofa. A woman, Alma thinks, but the room is shadowed. "Ginnie, I'm sorry, so sorry." He's crying now, his head bent over the woman lying stiffly on the sofa, one arm extended, hand open as if in expectation. She doesn't say a word, though Alma thinks her eyes are open. Maybe she's sick, too; both sick with some awful disease.

"Can I help, Mr. Gillan?"

There is no answer except his sobbing, and even from the porch, she can no longer stand the putrid smell. Gently, she pulls the door closed and goes to her car. Once inside, she takes her cell phone from her purse and calls 911. "There's something wrong at 104 Raven Lane," she tells the operator. "A man and his wife are very sick. I think someone should come quickly."

Alma waits in the car, peering through the windshield at the sky, her thoughts on Edmund K. Gillan. What happened to him? What sort of sickness did he have? Then her thoughts move to Angelina and the disease she lives with every day, all the pain and suffering it causes. She does not really know Mr. Gillan, though he'd given her an astonishing gift, meant for his wife of course. Mr. Gillan must love his wife very much to buy her such an extravagant gift. She would love to give such a gift to Angelina.

Through the windshield, she notices two elongated contrails of airplanes, and when she squints her eyes, they seem to converge into the shape of a pale yellow cross. She wishes Angelina were here to see it; it would be a perfect addition to her painting of Heaven's Gate. Then, just as the cross fades, an ambulance from Bethel Hospital, a fire truck, and a police car all spin around the corner, sirens raging. A police officer and the paramedics rush up to the house. One of them knocks on the door. Edmund K. Gillan stumbles onto the porch as if he's barely alive. Alma says a silent prayer for him.

The police officer goes into the house but comes out quickly. He takes a pad from his pocket and strides across the brown grass to Alma's car. "Are you the person who called?"

"Yes, I thought I'd better. Mr. Edmund K. Gillan and his wife are very sick." She glances toward the porch. The paramedics are ushering Mr. Gillan into the ambulance just as a dove on the roof flies down to the parched yard. "Is Mrs. Gillan all right? She's inside the house too."

The officer responds curtly. "Yes, she's inside." He writes down Alma's name, address, and phone number, and thanks her for looking out for a neighbor. "You can go now," he says. She turns on the car's ignition and watches the officer go back into the foul-smelling house.

Driving home, she thinks of yesterday's shooting, wondering if her mother and aunt have gotten over the shock that it happened in their beloved Bethel, at Heaven's Gate. Then she thinks of Angelina again, and of Edmund K. Gillan and his wife—poor people. She will buy Angelina a special gift from Dillard's when she goes back to work. And tomorrow, she'll call Bethel Hospital to see how the Gillans are getting along. Maybe she'll even go visit them; and then, afterward, she'll drive to their house and see if she can save the gladioli and what's left of their dying grass.

Some places in this world are sacred.
Upon entering, one bows with respect
because the hallowed lie here,
one day, to be made whole.

HEAVEN'S GATE GRAVEYARD

The Heaven's Gate Graveyard is much older than the town—some say as old as the Chattahoochee River that runs beside it. Others say its very earth was set here by God, after Noah and the flood, as if to place heaven's portal on earth. It is a beautiful place traced by tall trees—pine, soapberry, chinaberry, and magnolias. During summer, liriope with spiked purple blooms edge the borders, with camellias and gardenias taking their places as the seasons turn. But despite its beauty, heaven's portal brings few people joy.

Dozens of Confederates from all around Bethel, and some Federals from who knows where, are buried here. The graves all look alike. There are no flags waving above them now; no one can tell the difference between friend and enemy. Near the end of the war, there was a battle near Bethel between invading Union soldiers and Confederates, old men and boys by then, holding on to their homes. All are buried side by side. No disagreements now.

Sightings of phantom soldiers are not uncommon in Heaven's Gate Graveyard. Neither is the smell of gunpowder and awful shrieks from the pain of death. People often report apparitions of dirty, disheveled children, or hearing children giggle when there are none about. The most famous reported sightings are of four children, two from the South and two from the North.

The first is a boy of twelve from Georgia who served the Southern army because he was found alone in the woods and taken by the dreaded Confederate Guard; a boy with a limp from birth who'd held the Confederate flag; a courageous boy with a mother and brothers who loved him; a boy who died in a battle that was not his.

The second is a girl of ten from Alabama, who came with her father to war because her home had been set on fire, her mother burned to death, and there was no one else to watch over her; a girl who tended the dying; a tender-hearted girl who was loved by the soldiers; a girl who died in a battle that was not hers.

The third is a boy from Ohio who enlisted as a drummer and died at the age of eleven when a fragment from a shrapnel shell crashed through his drum as he played it; a boy whose father deserted him before he was born; a boy who loved his big brother enough to follow him into war; a boy who died in a battle that was not his.

The fourth is a motherless teenage girl from Pennsylvania who, while she was helping to load a cannon, saw her father lying wounded on a battlefield; a girl who ran through a hail of bullets to get to him; a girl who was shot three times as she threw her arms around her father; a girl who died in a battle that was not hers.

Those children and others have been seen often playing around the high statue dedicated to them—a statue of two children standing side by side and entitled, *The Children of Battles*. No one knows why the children are smiling and holding hands after going through such labors. And no one knows who sculpted the statue. Neither is it known when the statue was erected. It just appeared one day. The words on its pedestal read:

All the children could remember beyond the wooden bars of their cribs was betrayal.

All the children could see in every direction was the bright blue sky turning drab.

All the children could feel were rough roots waiting beneath the grass to scrape into their skin.

All the children could hear was the song they tried to sing and the slap of hands that ended it.

All the children could taste was a bitter broth of falsity from foul mouths.

All the children could smell was the stench of putrid flesh decomposing in an unkempt orchard.

All the children could imagine was a splendid gift as a reward for their struggle.

All the children hoped for was a faithful embrace, to be pressed to a breast and suckled in love.

But that's not the way it happened.

Only a year ago, eight new graves were dug here on the same day after a different sort of war: the graves of a doctor, a nurse, two patients, a psychology professor from the university, a English professor from the university, and a father and his daughter from a nearby farm—all but one, victims of a battle that was not theirs.

Soon, another burial will take place here. A burial no one expected.

A soul no one thought was ready to find its way toward Heaven's Gate.

Murderers are not monsters, they're men.
And that's the most frightening thing about them.
—Alice Sebold, *The Lovely Bones*

CHAPTER FORTY-FOUR

Moline
One Year Later

Alma is leaving for classes at Bethel University where she's now a student in the nursing program. Moline follows her slow-moving car on foot to the mailbox at the gate, unlocked earlier by Pauline and left open for Alma. Moline waves goodbye to Alma, then pulls the *Bethel Eagle* from the mailbox and takes it back to the house to read. She sits on the sofa next to Pauline and turns to the obituaries first, because nowadays that's what she does. At once, she straightens her back. "What? Edmund K. Gillan has died in prison! He was a young man, wasn't he? I wonder what killed him."

"My goodness!" Pauline reads the other side of the paper, opened in her direction. "Take a look at the front page, Sister, and you'll see."

Moline closes the paper to the front page: *Bethel's Mass-Murderer Dies from Brain Tumor.* She lets out a huff of disdain. "Well, I'd like to say it serves him right, but…"

"I know what you mean, Sister. We should pray for his soul."

"If he has one," Moline says. "Anybody that could do what he did? You wonder."

"Of course he has a soul, Sister. Every human being has a soul, saints and sinners alike."

Moline thinks about that awhile because she's come to see herself as a sinner, and Fr. O'Hara told her in confession that every sin, no matter how great or small, nailed Jesus to the cross. His words struck hard. Not hard enough though. After a whole year, she still hasn't confessed the sin that torments her, the sin that involved Malcolm J. Hawkins III, who right here on earth got what he deserved—justice. But what did she, Moline Broussard, deserve for what she did that night as his accomplice? What would be justice for her?

She knows she must confess. But what will she tell Fr. O'Hara? She could say she was in the wrong place at the wrong time. She could say Malcolm J. Hawkins made her do it and made her keep quiet about it. But is that true? She could have turned him into the police after it happened, and herself as well. But she did not because she feared for herself. Then she has an overwhelming thought. It is not about herself, or what might happen to her if she tells the truth, but rather about justice for the poor young boy on the rolling board. During all the years gone by, has anyone missed him? Or is he still buried where she and Hawkins laid him?

She never meant to be a bad person. She did not act from greed or hatred, and she was brought up decently enough, with a sense of right and wrong. Well…at least, she has a conscience that bothers her. She just doesn't pay enough attention to what the "bothering" is telling her. *Moline, change your ways.* She hid her "bother," tucked it away like she did the pointy metal bustier from her old Chancee costume, pushed it far away from any silk or lace it might rip to the back of her bureau drawer where she could—not that she would—forget it.

Today, she will start paying attention. Today, she will go to Fr. O'Hara and get the sin off her chest once and for all!

Moline rises abruptly from the sofa. "Pauline, I'm going to church."

"To pray for Edmund Gillan's soul?"

"No, to pray for my own."

Pauline stands. "I'm going with you."

"No, Sister. I want to talk to Fr. O'Hara. Alone."

Pauline puts her hands on her hips. "You can talk to him alone in the confessional. But I am going with you!"

"Why?"

"Because I know you, and you're acting odd. I think you have something besides church in mind. So, tell me what it is."

"Okay! After church, I'm going to look for…a grave."

"I knew it! You can't fool me, Sister." Pauline lifts her chin. "Whose grave?"

Moline sighs. Sooner or later, she'll have to tell her twin what happened and the part she played in it, and who knows who else she'll have to tell, if she can even find the body of the crippled boy on the rolling board after all this time.

"Whose grave, Moline?" Pauline repeats.

"I'll tell you everything after I talk to Father. So, if you're coming, come on."

God cannot forgive a sinner who does not acknowledge his sin.
—Mother Angelica

Chapter Forty-Five

Pauline

Pauline sits in the front of the church, praying first for Moline, then for the soul of Edmund Gillan because it's the right thing to do, while her twin goes into the confessional with Fr. O'Hara. After a while, Pauline thinks of Dr. Hawkins and prays for him too, even though she'd hardly been able to stand the man. A professor with authority teaching falsities! She should know; she sat in on his class numerous times. An education of lies is what's wrong with the world today, she thinks.

Moline has been in the confessional a long time. What in the world has she done? But when she comes out, Moline looks happy, almost brand new, as if she's just gotten a new makeover and her hair highlighted again. On the way to the car, Moline is quiet, so Pauline is quiet too, not wanting to spoil her sister's new disposition. But once inside the car, Moline turns to her. "Sister, I have something upsetting to tell you. Promise me you won't say a word until I have finished and that you won't despise me when I'm done."

Good grief! Pauline will never despise Moline—she might get angry with her sometimes, but she'll never, ever despise her. "I promise."

Moline begins by saying the name of Malcolm J. Hawkins III, and Pauline can't hold back. "I knew it! I knew he was somebody's devil, but I never thought he was yours!"

"Pauline, you've broken your promise. You said you'd be quiet until I was finished... Wait, what do you mean, you knew he was somebody's devil? I didn't know you'd even met that awful man."

"Well, I did meet him. I sat in on his classes for an entire semester. Somebody has to take up for the Lord. After all, we cannot allow our common destiny as a whole people to just *happen* without our input. We have to get in the fight. We have to engage the enemy."

"Okay, go ahead, Pauline—engage the enemy. But this is my story, and it's hard enough to tell without your comments."

"I'm sorry, Sister." Pauline draws a finger across her lips. "No more comments."

Pauline struggles to stay silent, but she is truly speechless while Moline reveals the dark happenings on that night with Malcolm J. Hawkins and the poor, innocent boy on the wheeled board. How has her sister lived with herself? But then, Hawkins might have killed her too. Thank God he did not.

When Moline finishes telling the awful events, there are tears running down both their faces. "Oh, Sister, what you went through!" Pauline pats Moline's hand. "You must talk to the priest."

"I've done that, Pauline. I've just confessed and been forgiven, but Fr. O'Hara said I must try to find his grave, tell the police, and right the wrong I did."

"Oh, Sister, do you have to? Hawkins is long dead and can't be questioned or prosecuted. You may be the one who gets the blame. It might be in the paper, and Alma could read it, and..."

"I *am* to be blamed for some of it, Pauline. No one except myself took me to the bar in the first place, and no one except myself told me to cotton up to a devil. When we find the boy's grave, I will go to the police, tell the truth, and hope they believe me."

"Well, I don't want to visit you in prison if they don't believe you. You won't be able to dress like Chancee ever again, you know, and I don't think you'll like their jumpsuits." Pauline sees a sudden crease form between Moline's eyes and thinks her twin might be close to changing her mind. Or else, she is getting ready to cry again. Neither of those is good. So, Pauline says, "Okay, Sister, you're right. If we have to find the poor boy's grave to let out the truth, then let's go find it."

Pauline drives, with Moline giving directions. "It's on the red dirt county road, just after Highway 32. It's called the Off the Road Whiskey and Stuff Bar. I suppose it's still there. I never went back after that night. I tried to forget the place and every awful thing that happened there. And I did forget it for a long while."

Pauline could have said that an awful act, an evil act, never truly leaves the mind of a wrongdoer. It hangs around waiting for another opportunity unless it is atoned for. But she doesn't say it. It would be anticlimactic now. Moline is finally doing the right thing.

The rest of the way is quiet for both. Pauline keeps her eyes on the road, her hands on the wheel, occasionally glancing at Moline, who stares into her lap at her tightened fists.

The dirt road curves, and the bar is there, but years of apparent neglect have taken a toll. "This is it?" Pauline asks as if she expected more from a structure of vice, now in complete decay with a crumbling foundation and half a roof.

Moline takes a breath. "Yes. This is it." She points to the left of the bar. "The ravine is just over there." So, Pauline continues on slowly until she gets to the edge of the ravine and stops.

Pauline gets out of the car first and walks a few yards to the edge of a gully so deep that from her view, the tops of tall trees appear as only bushes. "It's nothing but a wasteland," Pauline says, then turns to see Moline hesitantly approach the edge and peer downhill. "How in the world did you ever get down there?"

"I climbed down. I had to," Moline murmurs sadly. Then the sound of her voice fractures. "I couldn't let the boy stay down there. I knew he had to be hurt, but I didn't know he'd be dead." She touches her twin's shoulder. "I realize I've been forgiven, Sister, but I'll never get over my part in burying that poor innocent creature."

"Well, you'll have to get over it! At least for now, if we're going to find his grave and make it right, like Fr. O'Hara said. So quit crying." Then Pauline takes the first step down. "Just follow me."

They descend the steep hill of scrubs entangled with vines. They snatch the trailing plants and bristles from their clothes. They trip over roots and fallen dead branches. Still, they go on. The trees grow taller and taller until, at the bottom of the ravine, the treetops tower over the two women. Moline gives a hopeless look around. "This place is much more overgrown than it was when I was here those years ago. I don't know where to start."

"Try to remember, Sister." Pauline is red-faced and out of breath. "Was there something special about the spot, some sort of landmark?"

"We went through some blackberry bushes—" Moline's lips begin to quiver—"before we found a place to bury him."

Pauline looks to the right then to the left. "There are some blackberry bushes over there, Sister. Let's go see." Again, she takes the lead.

On the other side of the bushes, Pauline uncovers a small, open area of red dirt covered by leaves. Moline finds a rusted wheel nearby. Her hands shaking, she shows it to Pauline. "This is from the boy's board. I'm sure of it."

"We'll take that with us to show the police chief." Then Pauline spies something metallic. "Look at this, Sister." She crouches down to pick up a crusty medal on a chain and rubs it with her fingers. "*Saint Christopher Protect Us,*" Pauline reads.

Sorrowfully, they look at each other, as if thinking the same thing. "Yes, there it is," Moline says. "That's what I did not do. I did not protect an innocent one from evil. Instead, I was so afraid for my own well-being, I buried him." She falls to her knees then and wildly begins brushing away leaves to get to the red dirt beneath.

Pauline, afraid she might unearth the poor boy's bones, pulls at her sister's arm. "No, Moline, you can't dig deep enough without a shovel. Anyway, that's the job of the police. We've done our job. We found the spot. When we get home, we'll notify the police department, and they'll do the rest." Moline gets up slowly. Her face is the color of rust, streaked with dirt and the tracks of tears. For a moment, she slumps into Pauline's arms, just as she did on the night, long ago, when Alma was born. Then they climb back up the ravine to the car.

At home, Pauline says, "Let's get cleaned up, Sister, then we'll call whomever we need to call." She watches Moline practically drag herself into the bathroom. Pauline wishes she could take this from her. Of course, it isn't possible. Moline will have to go through it again, but Pauline will stay by her side.

Pauline washes up too, then she calls Fr. O'Hara. He comes at once to escort them to the police department—because she asked him to, and because the police chief is a friend, one of his longtime parishioners.

Fr. O'Hara waits outside while Pauline, with an arm around her twin's shoulder, goes into the interrogation room so Moline will have support as she tells her story again.

When Moline shows the police chief the rusted wheel and the medal, he says, "I knew that boy on the wheeled board. He was the only person I've ever known not to tell a lie or take what wasn't his. Plain honest in his soul. Over the years, I've wondered where he was. I'm truly grieved to hear what happened to him."

Moline bows her head and tears up. "I'm so sorry I had anything to do with Malcolm Hawkins. I took a great risk. I ought to have known he wasn't a good man."

Pauline sniffs. "Well, that is surely my opinion of him too."

The police chief draws down one side of his mouth. "Yeah, I knew Malcolm. The only good I can say about him is he's dead."

When the interview is over, Moline tells Fr. O'Hara, "I don't know what will happen, if I'll be arrested, or what."

Pauline puts a hand on Moline's shoulder. "Let's not say anything to Alma about it. Not yet."

"Not ever." Moline wipes her eyes with a tissue. "Unless they send me to jail. I'll have to tell her then."

Fr. O'Hara pats Moline's shoulder and agrees.

The weak can never forgive. Forgiveness is the attribute of the strong.
—Mahatma Gandhi

CHAPTER FORTY-SIX

Alma

On Monday, Alma drives to Heaven's Gate Graveyard for the burial of Edmund K. Gillan. No one else is there except Fr. O'Hara and two altar boys. The only flowers are the ones Alma brought to lay on the casket—a sword-like spray of snow white gladioli. A feeling of genuine sadness strikes her as she sets them on the closed lid.

Mr. Gillan will not be buried next to his wife or any of his victims in the shootings. Mrs. Gillan's cousin, the lawyer from Huntsville, would not allow it. Mr. Gillan will be buried on the opposite side of the cemetery. Mrs. Gillan's cousin even tried to block Mr. Gillan's burial anywhere in Heaven's Gate Graveyard, threatening a lawsuit. But he was unsuccessful. Alma was told that Fr. O'Hara had a heart-to-heart talk with the cousin about leaving vengeance to the Lord. So, the bodies of Mr. Gillan and all his victims inhabit the same place. But are their souls in the same place? Alma wonders how God works all that out.

She tries to picture Mr. Gillan's face the first time she saw him in Dillard's, when she imagined her father might be as handsome as he was. The last time she saw him, about a month ago, when she visited him in prison, he had not looked well. Her mother and Aunt Pauline were against her monthly prison visits, and neither wanted her to go to the cemetery today. "He murdered so many people, Alma," Aunt Pauline said, trying to reason with her.

But Alma said she thought she was doing the right thing, and that if Angelina and Jose were still alive, they'd say so too. "It's not that I think what Mr. Gillan did wasn't terribly evil. I know it was. But he was ill and was not thinking right, and I know he was sorry for what he did. Jose said God loves and forgives all repentant human beings even if they're sick or not thinking right. If God can forgive Mr. Gillan, shouldn't I?"

The faces of Aunt Pauline and Moline blushed bright red. Then both of them hugged Alma.

Fr. O'Hara prays over the casket: "Into your hands, O Lord, we humbly entrust our brother, Edmund. In this life, you embraced him with your tender love; deliver him now from every evil and bid him enter eternal rest."

At first, Alma had a hard time entertaining the idea that Mr. Gillan could be forgiven because the police said he'd been ultimately responsible for the deaths of Jose and Angelina as well as all the others. Mr. Gillan rushed in front of their truck, causing Jose to swerve and then run off the four-lane road where the truck flipped over. Both Jose and Angelina died immediately. Oh, how she misses them! But she takes comfort in the picture Angelina drew of their mountain, now framed and hanging on the wall of her room. Every night of a full moon, the light and shadow move on it, one step at a time, all the way up to the tenth commandment, *You Shall Not Covet*, until Angelina's drawing comes alive at Heaven's Gate and Alma sees her walking through it with Jose.

The first time she visited Mr. Gillan in prison, she was surprised that he recognized her. "The girl from Dillard's?" he asked softly. His blue eyes brightened as if he'd hoped she might come.

"Yes. The girl from Dillard's."

But then the brightness vanished, and he seemed to wonder who she was. Was it a mistake to come? She thought again of Angelina and Jose. Was she right in thinking they would want her to visit him?

"I was once an innocent boy."

Mr. Gillan was not speaking to Alma or looking at her; he seemed to be reassuring himself, which made her sad. She believed that every child was born innocent.

She decided to see him that way and talk to him as if he were a blameless child. "Yes, you were." He looked at her then and smiled as if he knew her again. And so, during her visits they talked only about his childhood, before his family was killed, a sad fact that had been printed in *The Bethel Eagle*.

Alma doubts many people know all the things she knows about Mr. Gillan. They only know what was printed in the newspaper article on the day he was sentenced to prison.

The article did not say that he loved his family, his mother especially, and that he thought they loved him. He told her about one of his sisters and how her kitten was killed because he left the door open, and the kitten got out. He seemed especially upset about that. Mr. Gillan also told her that his grandfather still talked to him, even though his grandfather died a long time ago. She didn't know what to think about that, and honestly didn't believe it, but she went along with him. She told him about her own grandfather singing to her as a child on their side porch. She told him he sang "Froggy Went a Courting," and Mr. Gillan got all excited and said his mother used to sing that too. She didn't know if that was true, either, or if any of Mr. Gillan's accounts of his boyhood were true, but she listened to his stories, some of them several times. They were always about his family when they were alive, only about his life as a little boy in a big and beautiful house. His eyes brightened then. He never talked about his job as a sociology professor or about his wife, except to say he loved her best in all the world. Her heart sank when she heard that, and she wanted to ask him, "How could you destroy what you loved best in all the world?" But she did not.

Alma was sad to hear of his death, no matter what he did. She knows his innocence as a child, and that is how she chooses to remember him.

Fr. O'Hara continues with the Rite of Committal, sprinkling holy water as he says, "The old order has passed away: welcome him then into paradise, where there will be no sorrow, no weeping nor pain, but the fullness of peace and joy with your Son and the Holy Spirit for ever and ever. Amen."

After he finishes the prayers, he approaches Alma. "Tell your mother I need to speak with her, please."

"I'll tell her, Father." She wonders why her mother is now communicating with the priest when she ignored him for years.

Fr. O'Hara and the two altar boys drive away, and Alma sits on the concrete bench beside the gravesite. In the distance, she sees three gravediggers coming across the cemetery. One is an older man who appears to be in charge; she can tell by the sound of his voice, deep and confident. The second man is younger. He appears to be listening intently to the older one. The third is a boy. She can see that he's filled with exuberance, maybe like Mr. Gillan used to be when he was an innocent child.

Soon, Mr. Gillan's body will be underground. She imagines his hands folded in the casket as if he's praying. A crucifix hangs on a curtain of purple velvet above Mr. Gillan's closed casket. Fr. O'Hara said that Mr. Gillan's death set him free. But it did not set free the others affected by his murders. The pain he left behind wasn't erased. Much was still left of him that was not buried, would never be buried, but only passed down in memories by those who suffered from it. She thought it was a good thing that Mr. Gillan and his wife had never had a child, a child who'd be so sad and angry over all he had done. Still, the child would have cried over his death, cried over his absence, and loved him anyway, just as Alma loves the father she's never known. And as long as she lives, she always will.

She decides to drive to the other side of the cemetery and say a prayer at the graves of Jose and Angelina. When she arrives, a short, heavy woman with dark hair is standing at the next grave over. Alma notices the name on the tombstone: Malcolm J. Hawkins III. The woman obviously cared about him because she is dabbing her eyes with a tissue. She glances at Alma and gives her a kind smile. Alma smiles back then recalls that Malcolm J. Hawkins was another of Mr. Gillan's victims. For some inexplicable reason, as if Mr. Gillan was a member of her family, she feels she should apologize to the tearful woman for his awful deeds, since Mr. Gillan can no longer do it himself. So, she approaches her. "I'm Alma Broussard," she says then indicates the resting places of Jose and Angelina. "These were my dearest friends."

The woman holds out a hand. "I'm Charity Hawkins, Malcolm Hawkins's sister. I'm happy to meet you, Alma. Do you live here in Bethel?"

"Yes, I'm a nursing student at the university."

"Oh, Malcolm was a professor there. Did you know him?"

"No, he was...gone before I became a student, but I'm sure your brother must have been a wonderful teacher. I'm sorry he was killed." She touches Charity's arm. "Mr. Gillan was a very ill man."

Charity tilts her head and stares at Alma as if she's puzzled, as if she wants to ask, who is Mr. Gillan? "I didn't know my brother had died until I arrived in Bethel yesterday. I went to his house and was told of his death by the present owner."

"That must have been shocking."

"Yes. I came, after all this time, because I wanted to mend things between us." The tissue reappears. "He'd cut himself off entirely from our family, and...I believe he may have hated me. I wanted to change that."

"Oh, how could he hate you?" Alma puts an arm around the woman's shoulder. "You seem so loving and kind." She recalls Aunt Pauline's words: *A nurse has to be kind and loving. So, you'll have to seek out and study kind and loving people.* In fact, Charity reminds her of Aunt Pauline—plump and about the same height, though she has brown eyes and Aunt Pauline's are crystal blue.

Charity is still dabbing the tissue around her cheeks, but her face has changed; as introspective now as Mr. Gillan's face when he talked about his innocent childhood. "You seem to be a lovely young lady, Alma. If I'd had children, I would love to have had a daughter like you."

"See? Your kind words once again. Absolutely no one could hate you, surely not your brother. He must have loved you."

"No. Even when he was a boy, Malcolm seemed unable to love anyone. He had a hateful streak. Maybe he was born with it, but he did not change as a man. I can't explain why, but he had no regard at all for other human beings. Everything was about him and no one else. I tried to help, to show him differently, but he would have none of it. I don't know, maybe he just had a selfish gene that couldn't be prayed away, though I did try." Looking down again at the tombstone of her brother, she says, "Still, it's hard to believe he's dead. I wonder where he…"

She notices a small, green-leaved branch with orange berries lying on the slab and bends over to pick it up. "Oh, this is from a chinaberry tree!" She looks around to see where the branch came from. "There it is, just over there. Do you see it?" She points a few yards from the gravesite to a tall, umbrella-shaped tree with orange berries.

"Yes, I see it. It's a wonderful shade tree, isn't it?"

"Yes. It has developing berries now, but it's lovely in the spring, with purple clusters of fragrant flowers—and yet its leaves and berries are extremely poisonous. They can kill animals, or even people, if swallowed." She returns her eyes to her brother's gravestone, and her tone of voice changes to sullen. "I think of it as a deceiver. That's why it reminds me of Malcolm. He was always a liar. Always using people for…well, awful things."

Alma is stunned. Here is a sister who must have been injured in some way by her brother, and yet despite that, she appears to love him.

"Once, I could have almost killed him."

"Oh, you seem so kind, too kind to do something like that!"

Charity's brown eyes grow darker, as if a lot is going on behind them. "Alma, I've just met you. You don't know me, and I don't know you, but let me warn you, evil exists in all of us. We all have a bad side. Some control it. Others, like Malcolm, do not."

"My Aunt Pauline says the same thing. You're a lot like her. She's even fond of chinaberry trees, too."

Charity smiles. "There seem to be quite a few of them in Bethel."

"Oh yes—but I didn't know they were poisonous."

"Well, be careful! Legend says that the chinaberry is symbolic of the Tree of Knowledge of Good and Evil in the Garden of Eden and represents both the good and evil in people."

"Are you a teacher? You sound as if you are."

Charity gives a gentle laugh. "I'm a botanist. I've studied lots of trees." She looks again at the tree twig in her hand and continues as if thinking out loud. "A good many years ago, I worked hard to get my degree. Malcolm, of course, thought I was too stupid to learn anything except prayers and often told me so. This chinaberry branch is appropriate for his grave. I loved him and took care of him for a time, but quite frankly, he was as poisonous as its berries."

Alma doesn't know whether she should say what she needs to say to Charity, but she is Dr. Hawkins's sister, and if his sister doesn't know how he died, she ought to. So, she takes in a breath and says, "Your brother was murdered. I'm not sure if you're aware of that. He was shot by Mr. Gillan." She indicates Mr. Gillan's grave, the workers laying him to rest just visible across the cemetery. "He's dead now too. He died in prison."

Charity looks away, slowly shaking her head back and forth. "Malcolm must have done something awful to have gotten shot. But it doesn't surprise me. Most people get out of life whatever they put into it. In Malcolm's case, evil was finally returned for evil."

"I suppose they do." Alma thinks about Angelina, her disease, and how much suffering she had to do because of it. "What about people sick with a disease they didn't cause? What they put into life is mostly their suffering, isn't it?"

Charity takes Alma's hand and squeezes it as if she thinks Alma might be talking about herself. "It may be hard to believe, but suffering people can greatly bless others, even change hearts for the better."

Of course, Alma agrees. Angelina was a huge blessing for Jose, and also for Alma, her mother, and Aunt Pauline, as well as her doctors, nurses, and everyone else she encountered. She is glad Charity reminded her of that, glad she's met Charity too, so different from the brother she described. She wonders what it is about people that so often causes them to choose the opposite of being kind and loving.

She and Charity talk a bit more then give each other small hugs, and Charity leaves the cemetery. Alma stays behind for a while, as if pasted into the space around her. One tiny piece of an intricate, infinite collage.

The armour of falsehood is subtly wrought out of darkness,
and hides a man not only from others, but from his own soul.
—E.M. Forster

Chapter Forty-Seven

Moline

I n the past, Moline swallowed many dangerous lies; and of course, she told some herself. But her lies aren't the worst sin she committed. The worst thing she ever did was to be aware of the truth and then hide it for years. Now that she knows she might be arrested for it, she's promised herself to stay loyal to the truth, not to lie, and to stay clear of people who do.

This afternoon, Chancee is going to be on a television talk show—*The Unveiling of Chancee Wile*—to promote a book she's written. Moline thinks it must be about new makeovers, or enhancing fashions, or other beauty transformations, which is what Chancee usually talks about on TV.

So, Moline takes off early from the dental office and hurries home. When she enters the house, she calls for Pauline to watch with her, but Pauline doesn't answer. She must be tending the chickens. Without Jose, she has to do that all by herself now, poor thing. But just as well—Moline won't have to hear her opinions about Chancee. She sits on the sofa and clicks on the television just in time.

"How did you come to believe in reincarnation?" the TV host asks, holding up a book entitled *Chancee Wile's Reincarnation*.

What? No makeover? Moline is at once disappointed. Here she is, trying to turn over a new leaf, wanting to hear what Chancee says about how to do it, and instead, Chancee is going to talk about reincarnation! Then Moline has to think a minute—what does reincarnation even mean? Is it religious, like resurrection? No, not like resurrection. She thinks it's a Hindu belief where people are reborn in a different body on earth. "Well, Moline," she says to herself, "that would be the ultimate makeover, wouldn't it?"

Chancee answers the TV host. "I didn't believe in reincarnation until a memory came back to me. One day, after my last show of the night, when the people were applauding me, blowing me kisses as if I were beloved royalty and begging for another set, it simply came to me that in another life I had been Marie Antoinette."

Moline does a double take, but the TV host looks as if she expected this answer and she's trying hard to keep from laughing.

"It's true!" Chancee says, pointing a finger at the impolite host. "I remember it all. I was standing in front of lots of people who were bowing down to me because I was the Queen of France. I remember how beautiful I was, the jewels in my crown, the gorgeous dresses I wore, and the enormous castle of Versailles. Just lovely!" Chancee giggles in her characteristic way. "I also recall that I was a vivacious social butterfly who loved to party and eat cake. But mostly I remember that all the people loved me."

The TV host grins again. "As they do now?"

"Yes, the people loved me then, and they love me now." Chancee smiles sweetly, lowering her forehead and her long, false eyelashes as if to be humble. But Moline realizes she isn't humble at all.

"But Miss Wile," the TV show host says with a tight-lipped smile, "Marie Antoinette was beheaded by the people during the French Revolution. They couldn't have loved her. Don't you remember your beheading?"

Chancee raises a hand to each ear as if to hold her head on her shoulders. "That is just legend. It did not happen! If it had happened, I would tell you. The truth is, I was loved by the people. They would never have killed me. And they didn't. I *was* resurrected." Chancee pauses then and looks a bit lost. "I mean...I lived a past life. Marie Antoinette's life. I was her, and then I was...reincarnated. Yes, that's it. I misspoke. I was reincarnated to be Chancee Wile."

Moline has a substantial suspicion that Chancee might be losing her marbles. She moves up close to the television screen to look into Chancee's eyes to see if she is telling the truth. Then she feels sorry for the star she esteemed for so long. Up close, the sad truth shows. It isn't so much that Chancee has aged and looks way too stretched in her newest facelift, but even Moline, her biggest fan, knows she could never have been Marie Antoinette. She probably isn't even Chancee Wile. Moline always thought "Chancee Wile" had to be a made up name. She nearly turns off the TV, but then, the TV show host encourages Chancee as if someone behind the set, someone who wants ratings, has ordered it.

"That's amazing. But you first said you were resurrected. Right?"

"Right, but—" Chancee looks befuddled.

"So, do you believe in resurrection?"

Chancee gives a pompous groan. "I just said so, didn't I?"

"Then can you tell our audience the difference between the two?"

Chancee grits her teeth. "No. Can you?"

Pauline comes into the room in time to see Chancee prance off the set. The station goes to commercial.

"Good grief! That woman has always been out of her frame," Pauline says. "Like a screen door hung wrong."

Moline is still hunched in front of the television, her mouth open, staring at the screen as if the woman in the commercial talking about how to get bright, white teeth, is more authentic than Chancee. "Well, Sister, Chancee does have a bestseller." It's all she can think of to say.

"Yes, that's impressive, I suppose. But a lot of people impressed by her are misled by her as well."

"But, Sister, think about this." Moline touches an index finger to her twin's forehead. "If you can get someone else to swallow your lie, even one person, then no matter how crazy it is, belief in the lie has begun. Do that thousands and thousands of times, through TV, books, and social media, and you have a brand new, off-the-wall lie that lots of people will accept as truth."

Pauline gives her twin a playful shove. "Moline, are you actually agreeing with me about Chancee?"

"Believe me, Pauline, I don't want to, but I just saw Chancee tell us who she really is, which is a phony. I know about phonies, having recently learned that I've been one myself."

"Sister, don't beat yourself up. I've been a phony too. Most of us have. When we see ourselves mirrored as phonies, of course, we don't like how we look. But we don't expect reincarnation to change us into somebody else. We try to fix the self we're born with. And when we do it, that's the true makeover."

On movie day that Saturday, Pauline chooses what Moline thinks is a boring documentary about the American Civil War. "All the things a flood covers over," Moline says. "Old and broken things you'll never see until a drought comes along to dry up all the water and expose the fragments, like raising secrets out of the muck." She does nothing but file her nails while it plays.

Pauline is engrossed. "You should pay attention to this, Moline. The Civil War is a lesson for all of us, like the parable about two brothers, born of the same God but each with his own free will, one jealous and despising the other, so he kills him for his own sovereignty. Of course, both lose everything in the end. That's the lesson in all wars, especially the ones that go on in our own heads, where good and evil get all mixed up just because they can. We struggle to be born, battle to live and love, and finally grapple with death. Our entire existence on earth is one fight or another in a lifelong war."

The kitchen telephone rings, but Pauline acts like she hasn't heard it. She doesn't budge. Well, Moline thinks, an agreement is an agreement. Tonight is Pauline's turn to choose a movie. If it had been Moline's turn, she wouldn't have budged either. So, she goes to the kitchen to answer the phone.

When she picks up, Fr. O'Hara starts talking right off. "My parishioner, the police chief, said he isn't going to arrest you, Moline. He said he would arrest Mal Hawkins in a split second if he were still alive, but he isn't, and you were not responsible for his wickedness."

"Oh, Father, thank you!"

"Moline, I'm proud of you. God knows, you did the right thing."

She hangs up the phone. "Pauline!" She rushes back into the living room. "I'm free! I'm free of it all! No more worry! No more sleepless nights! Praise be to God!"

Still captivated by the documentary, Pauline raises a hand for her to be quiet. "Wait just a minute, Sister. The South is about to win the second Battle of Bull Run. General Longstreet—he was related to us on Mama's side, but nobody liked him much. Now, he's launched a counterattack, one last battle and…"

Pauline stops suddenly and looks up at Moline with her crystal blue eyes, as if she hasn't seen Moline's excitement or heard anything she said. "Sister, if only I didn't know the rest of the story, I'd be happy as a lark. One last battle won't end the war. There will always be more to come. Evil never gives up."

Moline gives a triumphant smile, as if she just had the world's best makeover. "The beauty of it is," she says to Pauline, "neither does goodness."

SHOOTING AT HEAVEN'S GATE
Reader's Guide

THEMES: The complexities of family relations, destructive secrets, suffering, brutality, and forgiveness.

BOOK DISCUSSION QUESTIONS

1. There is no denying that we have the ability to influence the people in our lives. This is especially true in families, where we actually show our loved ones what is important and true by our own everyday actions. Spouses influence each other. Mothers and fathers teach and influence their children. And older children influence younger ones, many times pulling the younger ones along with them. Think about the families of Edmund, Alma, Mal, Angelina, and Jose. What is similar about these families? What is different about each of their responses to the influences in their lives?

2. Moral theology addresses the different methods of moral discernment, the definitions of right and wrong, good and evil, sin and virtue. It deals with the goal of life and how it is achieved. Due to our free will, each of us has the capability to act in immoral ways. We may be sorry and ask God for forgiveness. Amorality, as it pertains to humans, usually refers to words, actions, or attitudes. Choices usually have moral judgments applied to them in some way, and a person who

shows blatant disregard for any morality associated with his or her choices is said to be amoral. An amoral person seems to have no conscience, no concern about whether an action is right or wrong. An amoral person will do whatever it takes to retain his/her power—lie, steal votes, pay hush money, murder, etc.—with no compunction about his actions. Discuss Mal, the narcissistic manipulator, and Edmund, the mass-murderer—how are they different from each other? Both do awful things, but are both amoral?

3. Suffering in all its forms is almost inseparable from man's earthly existence. Since suffering is, has been, or will be a challenge we each face, this novel looks at suffering from the standpoint of redemption and examines reasons for understanding and accepting suffering's redemptive value. Discuss Angelina's acceptance, or not, of her long-term disease. Discuss Jose's reaction to it and how it transforms him. Discuss how Angelina's suffering affects Alma.

4. Would you classify *Shooting at Heaven's Gate* as a Theology of the Cross novel? (Suffering plus Faith equals Salvation.) Why or why not?

5. We all hold secrets. Every main character in the novel has secrets to be exposed. Choose one character at a time (Moline, Mal, Edmund, Jose) and reveal her/his secret. How do their individual secrets affect the lives of the other characters? Which do you think is the worst secret?

6. Discuss theater symbolism in the novel. Edmund acts in two plays; the gravedigger in *Our Town* and as the lead in *Macbeth*. How is he like each of them in real life?

7. Discuss Alma's goodness. Why would she visit Edmund in prison? How can she choose to remember only his innocence as a child after he has murdered so many people? Which do you most identify with: Pauline, Alma, or someone else in the novel?

8. Why are the scenes at Heaven's Gate Graveyard important? Discuss the symbolism, as it applies to the novel, of the Civil War, the lost children buried there, and the chinaberry trees.

9. Discuss Pauline's statement in light of God's gift to us of free will. "That's the lesson in all wars, especially the ones that go on in our own heads, where good and evil get all mixed up just because they can."

10. Despite the tough issues in this novel, does it leave you with hope and a chance to heal? Why or why not?

SHOOTING AT HEAVEN'S GATE
Quotes for Discussion

The world is full of suffering, boy. Overcome it or live under Satan's foot!
—The Old Preacher, Edmund's grandfather

The whole is not always equal to the sum of its parts. —Alma

I am a noble man, Edmund. I said I would help you with your problems, and I will. But on my terms. —Mal

What good was he to Angelina? He could clear a field in a day, put up a fence in a week. In even a few seconds, he could play yet unheard music on his guitar and sing words that simply came to him as if from God. But he was not God. He could not cure his daughter and could not fathom a reason for his beautiful child's affliction by such a dire disease. —Jose

The house is important, not because it is the building in which she lives, but because it is, itself, an idea. It is home. —Angelina

Shakespeare keeps before his audience the consciousness of choice between good and evil, which is at war in the soul of every human being. Each of us is both a child of God and a sinner, Edmund. —Ginnie

The god of most people is their own pleasure. —Mal

Good and evil do not exist when human nature wants the best way to

*scratch an itch. The only pertinent question then is, Can I get away with it? —*Mal

*A tiny ray of sunlight puddles on the pew just in front of her. She reaches for it as if to grab her place in something bigger—just in case the something bigger turned out to be more important than she was. Immediately, her hand and arm are immersed in the glow. She feels as if the regular Moline has absconded, leaving behind only the part of her the sun has lit. —*Moline

*Why do you say you're worthless? You're not! I love you, Mama, and I wouldn't love someone worthless. —*Alma

*This is life, after all, and it is a risk. Sometimes it will hurt and won't go the way we want it to. But you and I? We won't quit living because of it. —*Moline

*Today, she said there was foulness inside him. She said she wouldn't make love to him anymore until what he loved most was her. —*Edmund

*I'll tell you one thing for certain, Alma. That boy knew what he was going to do when he walked up to your counter, and he used your inexperience to do it. So, next time, don't be so naïve. Never let down your guard. —*Moline

*Yet there were moments during his childhood when Edmund was certain he felt God's desire for him. God's longing to covet him. And he would shout back, "Thou shalt not covet!" Immediately, he would be sorry he said such a thing to the God to whom his grandfather said Edmund belonged. —*Edmund

Do you think you're at Heaven's Gate? Do you think God wants you enough to allow you to climb the ladder? Well, you'll never climb it

unless you're pure as fallen snow. Unless you leave room for God's wrath, not your own. Repent! –The Old Preacher

Pauline felt as if she was holding something of God in her arms. And then, it was so obvious! This time, the person who would save Moline from herself wouldn't be Pauline but this God-given child, Alma. Pure and simple. –Pauline

It's not God who sends us to heaven or hell. We determine where we end up by what we do here on earth. It's why we pray for each other. –Edmund's mother

Some people forget that the price of restoration sometimes takes the pain of a crucifixion. –Ginnie

A confusing light from the ceiling falls on the flawless glass of the counter, and within it is the girl's reflection, all crystal clean and golden. He sees goodness in it. He sees innocence. He thinks he sees what he once was, and what he is meant to be. And it scares him. "You keep the gift," he says to her, and quickly walks away. –Edmund

He rubs his perspiring forehead, driving his thoughts back to the old pictures on the end table beside the sofa. In his mind, the picture glass lights up like diamonds, and the tarnished brass frames turn to gold. He lowers his head in memory of his parents, the priest, and the missal he gave him. If only he could be like he was back then. An innocent child with none of time's fractures. –Edmund

He'd seen the kid before, paddling around downtown Bethel, grinning at anyone who would grin back at him. Funny thing, the kid seemed happy and even had a following. People actually liked him. But Mal couldn't stand him. The creep was always in his way, grinning and looking at Mal as if he would grin back. Of course, Mal never did. He usually put a shoe to the back of the wheeled board and shoved, sailing him down the street. –Mal

He sees Mal staring at the gun, the color draining from his face, and the man he has come to for help, suddenly looks shriveled and small. Is Mal afraid of the gun in his hand? Does Edmund hold the power now? He smiles; that would be something grand. –Edmund

The first thing he'll tell Ginnie is that he loves her more than anything. "You don't have to worry about Mal or the drugs. They're gone now. I've been cured of them," he will say. And she will open her arms and gather him in, all the wayward pieces of him, until he is whole again. –Edmund

You are just like the rest of us. We are all sinners. Every sin, no matter how great or small, nailed Jesus to the Cross, so we're all a bunch of bums, unworthy of God's forgiveness and mercy, yet he bestows it upon us. –Fr. O'Hara

We have become like paper cups instead of treasured earthen vessels, not recognizing that our short, fleeting lifetime is barely a speck in eternity, and only a part of the whole. –Pauline

When we see ourselves mirrored as phonies, of course, we don't like how we look. But we don't expect reincarnation to change us into somebody else. We try to fix the self we're born with. And when we do it, that's the true makeover. –Pauline

One battle won't end the war. There will always be more to come. Evil never gives up. –Pauline